Impending Love and Promise

by

Laura Freeman

Impending Love Series

Impending Love and Promise

COPYRIGHT © 2018 by Laura E. Freeman

Cover Art by *Debbie Taylor*

The Wild Rose Press, Inc.
PO Box 708
Adams Basin, NY 14410-0708
Visit us at www.thewildrosepress.com

Publishing History
First American Rose Edition, 2018
Print ISBN 978-1-5092-2372-5
Digital ISBN 978-1-5092-2373-2

Impending Love Series
Published in the United States of America

Dedication

To my brothers, Bill, Dave, Eric, and Steve,
who helped define who I am.

Chapter One

Jules Beecher had borrowed her father's buggy on the promise she would return to the home of Dr. Sterling Beecher's patient by eight p.m. and take him home, but she was late. The guests at the fall harvest party had asked her to sing another song, and even though Lara Herbruck hit several wrong chords while accompanying her on the piano, she had managed to stay on key.

She worked her way through the crowd, acknowledging their compliments and returning as many as she received. The Civil War had been over for more than a year, and most communities had resumed their seasonal routines. The fall parties would continue into the winter holidays before the bitter cold and heavy snows of Ohio forced the residents of Darrow Falls to seek shelter inside, huddling by fires and yearning for spring.

Jules wore a pink silk gown that shimmered in the candlelight. She had saved money from midwife duties and helping her father on medical calls to purchase the expensive material. She labored for weeks cutting out the pattern, sewing the slippery material on the family sewing machine, and painstakingly finishing the hem by hand. Her mother had tatted intricate silk lace to edge the bodice and puffy hint of sleeves that was in style. Crinolines were smaller beneath narrower skirts that gathered in the back to create a slimmer silhouette. The bodice fit snugly over a longer corset that pressed her breast to the edge of her low-cut décolletage. She had been flat chested last year but had filled out beyond her expectations.

Jules rushed to the hallway beside the staircase where coats and hats were hanging on wall pegs. She located her wool cloak and arranged it over her shoulders. She retrieved her straw bonnet from a small table nestled beneath the stairs and tucked her curls inside the cap. She paused when she heard her name spoken by Lara Herbruck.

Lara and others were descending from the second floor, their shoes pounding overhead on the steps. It couldn't be praise. Old Sourpuss never had a kind word to say about anyone. Jules had been the target of her criticism since she was a little girl. As the youngest of the Beecher sisters, she was the easiest target.

"Juliet has been begging Matt Wheeler to be her Romeo since he began working for her father," Lara said in a judgmental tone.

Begging? Matt helped around the Beecher farm with the heavier chores like chopping wood, plowing fields, and cutting hay. The Romeo reference was on purpose. Lara never missed an opportunity to taunt her about her given name, linking it to a boy and a fake romance. That was why she preferred to be called Jules. She had burst into tears in the past at the unrelenting teasing, but she was too old to allow Lara's stings to make her cry.

She gathered the ribbons of her bonnet with her fingertips. Before she left, she would muster the courage to confront Lara. The next words stopped her hands from tying a bow beneath her chin.

"After Matt cleans out the stalls, he fills them with fresh straw, and they roll around like animals in heat," Lara said.

The others gasped. One of the women giggled.

"She seems so sweet," one of them said in her defense.

"Pretty flowers can attract plenty of bees," Lara said. "But they don't stay after taking the honey."

Lara's vicious accusations were unforgiveable. A lady had to vigilantly protect her reputation from any hint of impropriety, but Lara's lies, if believed, could leave her a social pariah. Jules had done nothing to warrant the unprovoked verbal assault.

Jules clenched her fists, breathing slowly in and out to control any outburst. She wouldn't cry and make Lara the winner. She thought about the sharp retorts her sisters had suggested in the past, but her mind was blank. She abhorred violence and was a helpless creature when it came to fighting in a battle. How did she remain a lady and defend her honor against slanderous falsehoods?

When the three women reached the main floor, Jules stepped forward, directly in their path. Her knees trembled beneath her skirt, and she fought to steady her voice. "How dare you speak such horrible lies, Lara Herbruck!"

"Lies?" Lara put her hands on her thick waist. She resembled her older brothers with a high forehead and deep-set eyes. Her thin lips were set in a perpetual frown, earning her nickname. "Then how does Matt know you have pink ribbons on your bloomers, Juliet Beecher?"

Jules bunched the fabric of her gown in her fists, searching for an answer. How had Matt seen her bloomers?

"Matt said it's embarrassing the way you throw yourself at him," Lara taunted. "A child desperate for attention."

Lara was three years her senior and teetering on spinsterhood. She wore her mousy brown hair slicked on each side and bundled in a chignon at the base of her neck, a style favored during the war. Like Jules, most of the young women preferred using decorative combs to arrange their hair off the face and piled on the crown or cascading down the back in a wave of curls or intricate braids. An insult entered her mind. "Even an old woman would appear young next to you."

Jules regretted the harsh words as soon as they left her lips, and she saw the painful expression on Lara's plain features. Her mother constantly stressed beauty was inside as much as outside. "I'm sorry. Your bad manners don't excuse mine. I shouldn't have insulted you."

"I don't need your pity!" Lara slapped her across the face. The sharp sound echoed in the hallway. The other young women shrieked and backed away.

Jules touched her bruised cheek as the sting subsided. No one had ever struck her, male or female. Shocked, she wasn't sure what to do. Did she hit Lara back? Violence was against her nature. She squared her shoulders and confronted the older woman. "Your actions betray your true nature."

The noise had attracted the other guests from the parlor and dining room, and they crowded into the narrow hallway. Beyond Lara was the front door. Her escape. The clock in the hallway tolled the hour. Nine? She had promised her father she would be prompt, and she was an hour late. All thoughts of Lara disappeared. She dashed for the front door.

Matt Wheeler stepped into her path. His father owned the dry goods store in town, making him a good catch as a husband. He was big, strong, and handsome by most standards, but Jules considered him no more than a friend in spite of Lara's speculation.

Although numerous young men called on her Sunday afternoons, none had captured her heart, and she was content to remain at home in the role of beloved daughter. She had shared the attention of her parents with her older sisters until they married and savored being an only child.

"Some of the guests would like you to sing again," Matt said.

Jules turned to Lara. "And some of them would like me muted." She faced Matt. "I have no respect for cads, Matt Wheeler. The only person you dishonor with your lies is yourself."

He looked surprised by her words, but she didn't have time to explain. "I'm late." She bolted through the door. Her father's buggy and the horse, Black Knight, were among the others tied to a line in the yard. She released the rope, boarded, and slapped the reins on the gelding's rump. She headed across the yard toward the road.

She was too angry to cry. How did she fight lies? She had no champion, and Lara was a formidable foe in spreading gossip. What tale would she share with the other guests in her absence? She considered firing Matt so she wouldn't have to face him in the morning, but then she would have to do all the chores at the farm. With all her older sisters married, she was the only one helping her mother and father. Matt had been a welcome addition. She hated to lose his strong back.

In addition to her numerous chores, last week she had helped her mother can the fall harvest. A burn on her palm was slowly healing, but the bite of the rein reminded her of the injury. She retrieved her father's gloves from the box on the front of the buggy and covered her bare hands.

Jules kept her leather gloves in the other family buggy. A wheelwright was repairing the wheel she had broken racing against her cousin, Paddy Donovan. Her reckless behavior had resulted in a few bruises on her body, but Paddy had sprained his ankle jumping from his buggy to rescue her. Without an escort, she had to beg and then promise to follow her father's rules in order to attend tonight's party.

Dr. Sterling Beecher had agreed she could take his buggy to the party if she promised to pick him up promptly from the Kramer house at eight p.m. He would scold her for her forgetfulness. Lately, she had been the target of his reprimands for too many things. She couldn't do anything right.

Jules shivered, and goosebumps rose on her bare forearms exposed by the opening in the front of the cloak. The air temperature had dropped suddenly. Fall weather in Ohio was ushered in with brisk winds, cold nights, and early darkness. Jules strained to see the road as clouds gathered and blocked any moonlight. She trusted Black Knight to stay on course.

A flash of lightning zig-zagged across the sky. A storm was blowing in. She urged Black Knight forward toward town. A gust of wind rattled the canvas on the buggy and sent her untied bonnet flying into the blackness. The bonnet was new, and she pulled back on the reins to stop Black Knight and look for it. Heavy droplets of rain suddenly fell from the sky, bouncing on the hard dirt road.

She abandoned any search and urged Black Knight forward. The awning of the buggy offered little protection as wind blew in her face, washing it with the cold moisture. Lightning flashed again, followed by a roar of thunder. Black Knight fought the reins. The oversized gloves made it difficult to grip the leather strips and control the anxious horse.

The torrential downpour showed no signs of abating, but with the lightning, she didn't dare seek refuge beneath a tree. Thunder bellowed nearby. Black Knight cried out in fear, and the reins slipped through the wet leather. Lightning struck a tree ahead and severed a tree branch, blocking the road.

Black Knight bolted into the neighboring fallowed field. The rough terrain jarred Jules from her seat, and she tumbled to the ground. She gasped to capture the air knocked from her lungs, but the tight corset hindered any deep breaths. Jules struggled to her feet, mud clumps clinging to the pink silk. The empty field had been harvested of any cornstalks, and her dainty party shoes stuck in the furrows of mud. She stepped on her hem, and the fabric ripped before she could shift her weight. A curse word came to mind, but she didn't speak it. She looked around, and shouted, "Black Knight!"

A shadow moved against a lighter background, and she headed toward the shape. The heavy downpour drenched her as the wind billowed her cloak and stole any warmth from her body. Her slippers stuck in the mud as rain gathered in low pockets. She pulled the mud-coated shoes free and trudged onward in her ruined stockings.

A split rail fence had stopped Black Knight's escape. The whites of his eyes showed his fear, and she hummed a soothing tune as she approached him.

"*Beautiful dreamer, wake unto me, starlight and dewdrops are waiting for thee.*"

The Stephen Foster tune calmed the gelding, and she grabbed the harness. She tossed her ruined shoes and muddy gloves into the buggy. She stroked the horse's wet black coat and cooed calming words. "That's a good boy. No need to be frightened. I'm right here."

Jules kept her hand in contact with the frightened gelding as she made her way to the buggy seat. Her muddy stockings slipped on the metal step, but she hauled herself onto the bench seat, pulled on her gloves, and gathered the reins. She directed Black Knight to the road. Downtown Darrow Falls was deserted. No one in his right mind would be outside in a storm like this. She continued on Main Street across the covered bridge and stopped at the Kramer house where she had dropped her father off earlier in the evening.

She pulled on her muddy shoes and jumped to the ground. The slate pathway had collected water and was slippery. She lost her footing and fell on her butt. Her crinoline frame crumbled beneath her. Her undergarments absorbed the water pooled on the smooth stone. She screamed her frustration, struggled to her feet, and knocked on the door. Mrs. Kramer answered. She was warm, dry, and stared at her in surprise and horror.

"Is Dr. Beecher here?"

"He left twenty minutes ago," Mrs. Kramer said. "You're soaked."

How kind of her to point out the obvious. "Do you know where he went?"

"He said he was walking home." She called after her. "He was quite upset you didn't show."

He'd given up waiting for her. Jules sloshed to the buggy, boarded, and turned it toward town. She turned at River Road and headed toward the Beecher farm. The storm continued its onslaught. The sculptured coiffure she had spent hours creating was plastered to her head. Her gown was soaked, trimmed with mud stains. Her shoes were boats filled with water. The wool cloak was a heavy weight on her shivering shoulders. Jules urged Black Knight onward. Home would provide a much-needed shelter for her body and soul.

She recognized the familiar form of Dr. Sterling Beecher in the road ahead of her. Her father had a hat and coat to protect him, but the wind was battering him with the needle-sharp rain.

She pulled beside him. The wind tore the apology from her lips.

He tossed his medical bag on the floor, and she moved aside to make room. He snatched the reins from her hands. "You promised to come for me at eight o'clock."

"I'm sorry. The time slipped away."

"Juliet Donovan Beecher, if you don't intend to keep a promise, don't make it." He sneezed, followed by a raspy cough. Sterling had been ill, but as the only doctor in Darrow Falls, he had gone out to make a medical call. His work was a priority, but she had cajoled him into using the buggy so she wouldn't miss the party.

She removed his gloves. He put them on and slapped the reins, urging Black Knight forward through the storm. "Look at your dress. I agreed to loan you the buggy so you would keep your gown clean."

"I was caught in the storm."

"If you had been on time, it wouldn't have been ruined."

She shrank against the seat, bruised by his harsh reprimands. She rarely had to defend herself in the past. As the youngest, Jules and her mistakes were normally overlooked. Her older sisters claimed she was spoiled, but they no longer shared in the labor of maintaining a farm. Initially, she had savored the special position that allowed her parents to focus only on her, but when approval turned to criticism, she had to bear it alone.

"Why can't you be more responsible like your sisters? I would think after wrecking the family buggy, the one your mother depends on to run her errands, and causing your cousin to sprain his ankle, you would have learned to be more careful. It was a mistake to trust you so soon. How difficult was it for you to remember to return to the Kramers? I planned to leave for Kentucky tomorrow. Or have you forgotten about your orphaned cousins? Or do you think their welfare isn't as important as a party?"

Her lips trembled, and the hot tears she had restrained earlier, slid down her wet cheeks. Eager to please her parents, each reprimand was a dagger to her heart.

Her father drove the buggy into the barn. The rain pounded in rapid fire on the tin roof making conversation impossible. She unhitched Black Knight on her side while her father did the same.

"I'll put him in the stall," Sterling said.

"Let me do it, Papa."

"Go!" His voice echoed the thunder outside. "And take my bag."

Jules grabbed the medical valise and dashed across the yard to the back door of her home.

Her mother, Maureen, was in the kitchen in her robe. She had the same cold as her father but was recovering while he was getting worse. "What happened to your dress? It took weeks to make. How could you ruin it in one night?"

Her teeth chattered. "I was caught in the storm. Black Knight was frightened by the thunder and…"

"Go into the pantry and remove it." She pointed to the narrow room in the corner of the kitchen. "If you soak it overnight, you might be able to save it."

Jules hung her cloak on the hook by the door and turned her back to her mother. She couldn't unhook the gown without help. "Can you undo it?"

Her mother unhooked the fasteners, and Jules disappeared into the storage room, her clothes dripping on the floor. Her body shook as she kicked off her shoes and removed the wet garments. The bodice was followed by the skirt and petticoat. She untied the strings of the crinoline and sat on the floor to strip off her wet stockings. She grabbed a dish cloth from the shelf to wipe the moisture from her body. She stared at the pink ribbon edging her bloomers. How did Matt know about that? She looked at the pile of wet clothing

11

to be added to Monday's laundry and hung on the line. *The line.* Matt had seen her undergarments hanging on the clothes line. But why mention it to Lara, who used it as fuel against her?

Her father entered the kitchen and continued his tirade against her. Hidden in the pantry from his view, she cringed with each harsh word. "I can't understand why Juliet couldn't wait until your buggy was fixed to attend another party? It was her fault it was broken. Her life is a series of social events. The people of Darrow Falls count on me to attend to their medical needs. I can't do that when I have to walk through a downpour."

"Take off your wet clothes," Maureen told her husband in a soothing tone.

He coughed for several minutes. "That child knows nothing about hard work or responsibilities. I needed to visit my patients before I leave for Laurel Holler on the morning train. It'll be at least a week before I return home." Another coughing fit ended his speech.

"I think you should postpone the trip. You're not sounding any better."

"That's your daughter's fault."

"Someone else could go."

"No one is available. The only one in this family who has time to fritter away is Juliet." He sneezed. "She's the last person who would volunteer to travel to Kentucky and return home with three orphaned cousins. She might miss a *precious* party."

"You need to go to bed," Maureen said. "You're grumpy when you don't feel well."

"I am not grumpy."

"I'll heat a brick for the bed and make some tea with honey," Maureen said.

"I need a mustard plaster."

"I can make you one."

"That child will be the death of me."

Jules waited until they had disappeared into the master bedroom next to the kitchen. She gathered her clothing and tiptoed to the family room and upstairs to her bedroom.

She dumped the muddy skirt and stockings into a washtub she used for baths and poured the water from her washstand pitcher onto the fabric. The bodice was untouched and her undergarments were wet but clean of mud. She stripped off her corset cover, struggled out of the corset, and draped her camisole and bloomers on a chair to dry.

She pulled on her cotton nightgown and sat on the edge of her bed as she combed the tangles from her wet hair. According to her father, she had time to fritter away. Who did he think milked the cows, hoed the garden, or helped Mama with the cleaning, washing, and ironing? Parties were a reward for her hard labor.

Sobs shook her body. She'd nearly been killed in the storm, Lara Herbruck had ruined her good name, and Papa thought her incompetent.

She pulled on a pair of thick knitted socks and huddled beneath a quilt her grandmother CJ Donovan had made. Warmth returned to her body, and a plan developed in her mind. She would go to Laurel Holler. She would prove to Papa and Mama she was a mature, responsible adult.

Chapter Two

In the morning Jules put her plan into action. She dressed in a faded work dress and crept down the stairs. She paused at the newel post and looked down the hallway toward the kitchen. Her mother was stoking a fire in the stove. Her father coughed in a long, painful fit in the bedroom. His worsened condition stiffened her resolve. To her left was the parlor where she had entertained beaus and friends, seeking praise and admiration. Vain pursuits on her part. She crossed the rug-covered floor and entered her father's office.

Morning sunlight streamed across the wide desk where several books were stacked to record births, deaths, and ailments of his patients. She sat in the wooden chair and surveyed the familiar surroundings. Bottles of blue, green, and brown were neatly arranged behind a glass cabinet. Bandages, towels, and other items were stored below. She had stocked supplies and cleaned his instruments two days ago before asking to use his buggy. All his harsh accusations returned with remorse. She loved her father and would do anything to restore the harmony in their fractured relationship.

Inside the top drawer was the letter informing Grandma Donovan that her nephew George Bauer and his wife Maria had died suddenly from an unknown illness. Their three children, Caroline, George, and William, were staying with a neighbor, but they would be sent to an orphanage if a family member didn't claim them. It was signed Sheriff Marvin Peel, Laurel Holler, Kentucky.

Grandma Donovan owned an inn in Peninsula. She had her hands full taking care of lodgers while Grandpa Donovan finished the shipping season on his canal boat, the *Irish Rose*. Captain Michael Donovan traveled the route from Akron to Cleveland and back. It was a family tradition for the older grandchildren to teach the younger ones how to work the locks and tie the ropes. Jules and her cousin Paddy were the youngest of the cousins, the last to share the experience.

They had worked as crew during the summer, but Grandpa had replaced them with strangers after Paddy sprained his ankle and Maureen enlisted Jules to help with the canning. Everything was changing, and she wanted desperately to keep the familiar, comforting surroundings the same.

Another letter in the desk was addressed to Dr. Sterling Beecher. Her father had written Sheriff Peel about his planned visit, and he had replied. She read the short missive. Her father had placed a train schedule and money inside for the trip. The next train would depart at eight-fifteen this morning. She tucked the envelope in her skirt pocket.

Jules had never traveled alone farther than the neighboring county, and she lacked the courage and ingenuity her older sisters possessed in a crisis. On her first trip as crew on the *Irish Rose*, Blake Ellsworth had been a passenger. He had sold his inn, The Lucky Gambler, in Memphis in 1862 for gold that had been stolen from the Confederacy. Clyde and Buck Cassell were big brutes armed with guns and knives who had decided to recover the gold for themselves. They had shot Blake on the deck of the *Irish Rose.* Her sister Cole, short for Collen, had to yell at her to grab the deck and stay down. The image of Blake's pale body in a pool of blood haunted her nightmares for months. Afterwards, Blake had given her a five-dollar gold coin for helping to save his life. She had fetched a few towels to stop the bleeding. Hardly praiseworthy, but Blake had survived the vicious attack and bestowed the lucky coin to her.

She removed the stopper on the ink well on the desk and removed a page of stationery from the desk drawer. She dipped the pen nib into the ink and wrote a note.

Dear Mama and Papa,

I am sorry for my irresponsible behavior last night. I am heading to Laurel Holler and promise to return with the Bauer children. It is the least I can do after all the trouble I have caused.

Your devoted daughter,

Juliet

Jules tiptoed upstairs. She placed the note on her dresser. If her parents missed her, they would search her room and find it. Her mother would worry, but the harsh words of her father made her doubt any remorse on his part. Six daughters was one too many.

Jules braided her hair and pinned it in a place at the base of her neck. She would do her normal routine. She didn't want her parents to stop her before she started. They might find someone else to go. She had male cousins, and her sisters had husbands, but she had to redeem herself. All her sisters had gone on adventures and proven they were independent young women. She needed to do the same.

She packed two day dresses and a plain work dress in a small wooden travel chest. She added undergarments and a nightgown. She placed her personal items in a smaller bag and tucked it next to her lace-trimmed bloomers. The ones Matt must have seen on the clothesline.

Her parents would need Matt to do the chores around the farm while she was gone, but once she returned, she would confront him about his lies. Would her father feel compelled to fire Matt or dismiss her indignation about her honor being besmirched as childish? How did someone prove they were grown up?

Jules examined her gown soaking in the tub. She didn't have time to salvage it. She dropped the wet fabric. She placed a plain brown skirt, white blouse, and a short tan jacket on the bed. Once she convinced her mother she needed to go to town, she would change.

She grabbed her travel bag and tiptoed down the stairs. She opened the front door and placed the chest outside on the slate path where she would retrieve it later.

Her mother was cooking oatmeal on the stove when she entered the kitchen. "Was that the door I heard?"

"I wanted to see how much rain we had," Jules lied. "How is Papa?"

"He's worse," Maureen said. "And doctors make terrible patients."

"Is he going to die?"

"Of course not, silly. You make ordinary experiences into a life and death drama, Juliet. Life is not a theater play." She poured the oatmeal into a bowl and added honey. "Papa has a bad chest cold. In a few days, he'll be as good as new." She placed the bowl and a cup of coffee on a tray and carried it to the bedroom.

If Papa was getting better, why was he eating in bed? "Has he canceled his trip?"

"We decided he should wait a few days."

She would go instead. "I'll fetch the eggs and milk." Jules grabbed a shallow basket for gathering the eggs and an empty milk bucket. Her wool cloak had dried during the night, but mud stained the hem. She looked around as she approached the barn. It was too early for Matt Wheeler. She found a stiff brush and cleaned her cloak. Then she milked the two cows and gathered a dozen eggs before returning to the kitchen.

Jules fixed a hearty breakfast. Papa had said the trip would take about a week. It might be the last good meal before she returned home. "I noticed Black Knight's shoe is loose. I could take him into town." Did her voice sound too eager?

"How are you going to return home?"

"I can wait for Noah to finish." He was the town blacksmith. They wouldn't miss her until the afternoon, if that.

"If you're going to be in town, you can run some errands."

"I'd love to." Jules wiped her mouth and rose. "Why don't you make a list of what you need, and I'll dress."

The excuse had worked, so why was her heart racing? Jules removed her work dress and hung it on a wall peg. She counted the money her father had put aside and added her own to the total, dividing the bills and coins. She shoved the larger portion inside a pocket hidden inside her corset cover and added the remaining money and sheriff's letter to her reticule. It should be enough for her ticket and any expenses on the initial trip. The amount in her corset was for the return trip.

She dressed and glanced around her room. It appeared the same as always, but a sense of dread gripped her. She picked up her note left on the dresser. She shouldn't go. Her father would be well in a few days and able to travel.

She saw her reflection in the mirror above the dresser. She had the features of a child, big blue eyes, fat cheeks, and a full mouth. No wonder nobody took her seriously. "Coward. You're acting like a baby." She returned the folded paper and searched her top drawer. She found Blake's gold coin and added it to her reticule. A little luck wouldn't hurt.

When she entered the kitchen, her mother was mixing mustard and flour with warm water to make a mustard poultice. The pungent odor filled the room. Her father began to cough in the adjoining room. The barking sound was worse. "The list is on the table."

Jules glanced at her mother's neat handwriting and shoved the note into her skirt pocket. Her mother cut a length of cheesecloth. "You better take a basket."

Jules searched the pantry. On the top shelf was a basket with two pink-dyed slats woven into the pattern. Her sister, Jennifer, known as Jem, had dubbed it the *magic basket*. It had gone on all her sisters' adventures. "One more," she whispered. She packed a jar of peaches, cheese, bread, a pie wedge, and a couple of apples.

"If you see Matt before you leave, tell him we need wood chopped today," her mother called from the bedroom where her father's coughing drowned out her reply. It was now or never. She needed a bonnet to replace the one lost in the storm. She lifted the lid to a wooden bench by the door and searched the contents of a box built beneath the seat. Her sister, Jessica, had discarded an old slouch hat she had used when hunting. The brim sagged, but beggars couldn't be choosy. She pulled the man's hat on. At least she wouldn't have to worry about attracting unwanted advances from any men on her journey.

She fastened her cloak and headed for the barn. Jules hitched Black Knight to the buggy and drove to the front of the house where she retrieved her bag. She glanced at the windows, expecting someone to spy her furtive behavior. Why did she feel like a runaway?

Black Knight moved briskly. It would be difficult to convince Noah the horse needed a new shoe, but what was one more lie? Matt Wheeler rode toward her. She slowed the buggy. She needed to behave normally. "The wood needs chopped."

He reined his horse. "I still have a job?"

Did he feel guilty about the lies he had shared with Lara? "Don't you want one?"

"More than ever." He looked tired. "You didn't tell your father about last night?"

"No, he wasn't feeling well. I hope you don't upset him."

"I don't know why Lara had to blurt everything out."

"She's never been known for tact," Jules said. "I expect you to make amends, Matt. Have you forgotten my oldest sister, Courtney, is married to a lawyer? Tyler Montgomery likes challenging cases."

"What case?"

She raised her chin. "You slandered my good name."

"I didn't say anything," Matt defended. "It was Lara. Everyone warned me she was trouble." He shook his head and turned his horse away.

Jules wanted to believe him. Lara possessed a viperous tongue. Perhaps, they were both victims.

She stopped at the depot and dropped her bag on the platform. "I need a ticket to Cincinnati," Jules said to the man behind the window. He was a railroad employee and didn't know her. He collected her money and gave her the ticket and a tag to attach to her bag.

"What are you going to do with your horse and buggy?"

"I'm leaving them at the blacksmith shop." She smiled. "Do you mind watching my bag?"

He squared his shoulders and stammered an answer. "Not at all, miss."

Not everyone had heard about her scandalous behavior with Matt, but it wouldn't take long for it to spread farther than the party guests. How many would believe the lies?

The Wheeler Store was on the corner of River and Main streets. Marcus Wheeler turned when the bell rang as Jules entered. He was behind the counter placing wooden spools of thread on the shelf behind him and turned. "Miss Beecher."

"Good day, Mr. Wheeler. She handed him her mother's list. "My mother needs these items."

He studied the paper. "How soon does she need them?"

"Matt could deliver them tomorrow." She'd be

safely gone.

Marcus shook his head and made a tsk noise. "That boy never does anything right."

The words echoed her father's harsh condemnation. "Everyone makes mistakes, Mr. Wheeler."

"You're kinder than most folks," Marcus said. "There are always consequences. Some are greater than others."

His words troubled her as she drove Black Knight to the blacksmith shop across the street. Was it too late to change her mind? Whether she was running from Lara's tall tales or seeking redemption from her father, circumstances had set her feet on this path. She'd had her fair share of trouble already. What more could go wrong?

Noah St. Paul was in his blacksmith shop. He was a big man and had served in the army with other black men toward the end of the war. He had been shot several times and had a limp. He wore a heavy apron and gloves to protect his clothing from the hot embers used to forge metal. She waited for a pause in his pounding to ring the bell by the door. He turned, smiled, and stepped forward before remembering the red hot axle in his hand. He dropped the rod into a bucket of water. Steam rose and hissed. He removed his heavy gloves and rubbed Black Knight's nose.

"What can I do for you, Miss Jules?"

"I think one of Black Knight's shoes is loose. Do you mind looking?"

He positioned himself near the horse's leg, lifted it, and examined the shoe. "I can't believe you're all grown up, Miss Jules. You were a little girl when Tess and I first passed through Darrow Falls."

Tess had been a slave of Edward Vandal and had run away from Vandalia, Virginia, in 1860. Noah had followed to find his wife and infant son before Edward and his chasers, Clyde and Buck Cassell, found them. It was the first encounter between the Cassell brothers and Beecher sisters, but wouldn't be the last. Tyler Montgomery and Cory helped Noah, Tess, and Adam escape. Once the war began, Noah and his family returned from Canada and settled in Darrow Falls.

The door opened to the small white house next door. Tess stood on the porch with a baby in her arms. Seven-year-old Adam and five-year-old Addy ran down the steps. "Miss Jules, Miss Jules," they chimed as they circled around her.

"Go play," Tess said. The children ran across the street to the square where sheep were grazing. "Do you have time to visit?"

"I can't stay long," Jules said. "I have to board the train."

"You'll hear the whistle." Tess patted the seat and invited her to sit. "You look tired, Miss Jules."

"The storm kept me awake last night."

"It was a nasty one. A couple of trees fell on the road." She placed the baby in a wicker basket.

Jules peeked at the month-old baby wrapped in a blanket. "He's grown since Jennifer and I helped bring him into the world."

Jem was a midwife and married to Logan Pierce. Logan had worked in Washington City during the war, but they had moved to nearby Akron last year. Jem had dubbed the basket she had packed as magical after taking it to Washington City and Richmond in 1861.

Logan and Jem had encountered Edward Vandal and the Cassell brothers at Manassas. They had named their daughter Chauncy Theodora after two Confederates who had helped them escape from Clyde and Buck. Last year they had added a boy named Derek to their family, which included Logan's eleven-year-old niece, Deidre.

"You and Miss Jenny have helped deliver a fair number of babies this year."

"Papa calls them post-war babies."

"I like to think of this one as a free baby. We named him Abraham after the late president."

Jules looked at the little girl on the square. "But wasn't Addy born free?"

"She was born in Ohio, but not free. I was a runaway. Don't you remember how Edward Vandal and his chasers searched for me? Adam was a baby then."

"I remember the Cassell brothers," Jules said. "They scared me."

"They scared plenty of people," Tess sighed. "Buck is dead, but nobody knows what happened to Clyde."

"Isn't he the one with the scar?"

"A long scar on the side of his face." Tess ran her finger down her cheek. "It turned the hair in his beard white."

Jules shuddered. "I saw the Cassell brothers two years later when I was working on the *Irish Rose*. I could never forget them."

The Cassell brothers had graduated from chasers to mercenaries in 1862 after deserting the Confederate army. Clyde and Buck had tracked Blake from Tennessee to Ohio, where he boarded the *Irish Rose*, and the would-be thieves shot him. Her fingers traced the gold coin inside her reticule. Not ones to give up, Buck had been killed in a shoot-out at Blake's hotel, the Mermaid's Mirth, and Clyde had escaped. Blake had married Cole, and they named their son, Jake, after their cousin. A daughter had been born in the spring, and they had named her Lauren.

Jules shook. "Those two gave me nightmares for months."

"They were vicious brutes without any restraint," Tess said. "The slaves at the Silver Pheasant were terrified of them." Tess huddled in the shawl she wore, her face pained by the recollection.

"How did you find the courage to walk all the way from Vandalia to Darrow Falls?"

"Once I left Virginia, I couldn't go back," Tess said. "I had to keep going forward toward freedom. When those chasers caught me, I wanted to give up. I was so sure I was going to die, I gave Adam to Miss Cory. I didn't know she had a plan to rescue me."

"My cousin Jake was one of the rescuers." Jules looked at the cemetery across the square on the far side of the Community Congregational Church. "He was killed at Antietam."

"I won't forget what Jake and the other soldiers did to give me a better life." Tess swiped at a tear. "They promised us freedom from slavery. They kept their word."

The whistle of the train sounded in the distance. Jules jumped to her feet. "I have to go."

"Are you visiting Miss Cassie at Ravenswood? Your sister made a beautiful bride. It won't be long before your father escorts you down the church aisle."

Cassandra had married Zach Ravenswood last year. They lived on a horse farm in the next county. Cass had shared the news last month she was expecting a baby. All her sisters were married, but Jules had vowed never to wed. She was going to remain at home and never leave. A storm and her father's anger had changed her plans.

"I'm going to visit my cousins." It was the truth. She said good-bye and headed for the buggy to retrieve her basket.

"I don't see anything wrong with the horseshoes, Miss Jules," Noah said. "When will you be back?"

"Not for at least a week," Jules said. "Matt Wheeler can take the buggy to the farm tomorrow. He's delivering some items for Mama."

"Then I'll clean Black Knight," Noah said. "He has mud on his legs and hindquarters."

"We were caught in last night's storm," Jules said. "Thank you for taking care of him."

"My pleasure, Miss Jules. You have a nice trip."

Jules climbed the incline toward the train depot. The steam locomotive blew its whistle as the big iron horse slowed to a stop. The engine exhaled white smoke around its wheels and puffed clouds from the smokestack. The trainman placed a step for her to board, and the porter loaded her bag. Jules stood at the door of the passenger car and looked around at her hometown. It had been a friendly place until Lara's lies. Hopefully, her life would feel normal by the time she returned. She sat by a window, arranging her basket beside her to dissuade anyone from sitting beside her.

Jules retrieved her handkerchief from her reticule and dabbed at tears on her cheek as her hometown disappeared from view.

Chapter Three

Roe Greystone examined his shirt. A button was missing. He searched his drawer for a housewife sewing kit. None. He knew where he could find a needle and thread, but his medical bag was under his bed gathering dust.

He knelt and reached beneath the ropes supporting the mattress and pulled the leather valise toward him. He sat on the bed and stared at the symbol of his occupation. The war had interrupted his life. The son of a professor, Roe had finished college at the age of nineteen but had been drafted in 1862 before pursuing his dream of becoming a doctor. He'd spent the past year attending classes in the Medical Department at the University of Virginia in Charlottesville, but no classroom compared to the hands-on experience of the battlefields and army hospitals.

During the war, his orderly duties had evolved from retrieving broken bodies from the battlefield to stitching wounds and ultimately to the brutal task of amputations long before the South surrendered. Returning to school had been a reprieve from the horrors he had witnessed during the war. Although certified to practice medicine, Roe wasn't ready to take up a scalpel and begin the gruesome occupation of physician.

He opened the double locks, and the hinges

expanded to reveal the tools of his trade. His hand shook as he examined a scalpel. He had boiled and cleaned the blades and saws that had severed limbs, but he couldn't look at the sharp edges without seeing them stained with blood.

Roe had served in General Robert E. Lee's Third Corps and had been at Appomattox Courthouse when Lee had surrendered. His pardon was tucked in a pocket of the medical bag.

Roe had fared better than most Confederate veterans. After the loss at Gettysburg, he had written his parents and warned them that victory was unlikely for the South. They had heeded his warning and traveled to Europe where his father secured a position as a tutor for a wealthy family.

After the war, he had written his parents. They had no wish to return to war-torn Virginia but sent money for him to complete his education and to build a life. He was certified to practice medicine, but Roe had spent too many nights reliving horrific nightmares. The war was over, but the memories lived on.

Roe abandoned the task of sewing on a button and replaced his shirt with another. He slid the bag back to its former location in the shadows of his bed. After dressing, he grabbed a wide-brimmed hat and exited the cabin on the top deck of the *Jenny Lee* sternwheeler.

When Roe's former commanding officer, Colonel Chauncy LaDonte, wrote him about raising money to purchase a steamboat, Roe had volunteered his funds and services. Chauncy was the boat's pilot and had made Roe his partner.

The deck of the *Jenny Lee* was a refuge from death and the pain of the past. She had three decks with a

stern wheel and four boilers for power. The twin pipe
stacks for venting the steam framed the bell on the main
deck used to communicate with the engine room on the
lowest deck. The passenger accommodations were on
the second deck, immediately below him. The pilot
house where Chauncy guided the boat was located
behind him on the hurricane deck above his room and
the adjacent captain's cabin. A thirty-six-star flag was
attached to the Jack Staff in the center of the bow to
help navigate the boat. A mast with a boom was located
to the starboard side.

The freshly painted *Jenny Lee* had a full cargo hold
waiting to be unloaded tomorrow. Cincinnati sat high
on the bank, safe from flood waters. Theo Jameson,
another veteran of the war, stood on the bow, tossing
lines to men on the shore to tie the boat along with the
others that traveled the Ohio and Mississippi rivers. It
was getting late in the day, but a few wagons were
winding their way up the trails from other ships to the
warehouses lining the banks.

Tonight, they would open the dining hall for
guests. Tomorrow they would unload cargo from
Louisville and then fill the hold with goods from
Cincinnati. The short day trips transporting goods and
passengers between the northern and southern cities on
the Ohio River were easy to navigate and beginning to
show a small profit. The layovers made the boat
available to men and women who enjoyed games of
chance in the large inner room. The war was over, and
people wanted to celebrate and have fun. The loose
money also attracted the thieves, pickpockets, and
swindlers who had not fared so well in the war and
were willing to recoup their losses any way they could.

Roe had never fired a shot during the war, but he carried a revolver on his hip to deter any trouble.

Chauncy joined him. His dark hair had streaks of gray, and his beard and mustache were clipped short and neat. He chewed on a cigar but didn't dare light it. He'd been shot early in the war by the Cassell brothers when they deserted with the regiment's payroll. It had taken a year for Chauncy to recover from the near-fatal wound, and his breathing had a rasping sound like the wind in a tunnel.

Chauncy had returned to command in time to lead the regiment at Gettysburg, but a chance to end the war slipped through their grasps in the three days of fighting. Roe had traveled with the wagon train transporting the wounded to Virginia. Major Morgan Mackinnon had joined the rain-soaked refugees with his wife, Miss Jessie.

"Now there's a rare sight," Chauncy said.

Roe looked around. "What?"

"You were smiling."

Roe rubbed the stubble on his jaw. "I was thinking of Miss Jessie."

"That would bring a smile to any man's face. You never met her sister, Miss Jenny. Voice like an angel."

Roe fought a grin. "I think you've mentioned her once or twice. Is that the woman you named the boat after?"

Chauncy searched his coat pocket. "Miss Jenny sent me a photograph. He showed him the picture of a little girl with curls and dimples. "Chauncy Theodora Pierce. It only seemed fair to name my boat the *Jenny Lee* after she named her daughter for Theo and me."

"She's a beauty."

31

He returned the photograph to his coat. "Speaking of beauties, we need to hire a few waitresses after tonight. They have all informed me they are remaining in Cincinnati and won't be heading south on this trip."

Roe raised his hands. "I am no judge of women."

"But your medical expertise will eliminate the sickly. Too many women seeking employment are drunkards or addicts."

"Former prostitutes," Roe said. Brothels flourished during the war, but afterwards the women were kicked to the streets with the clothes on their backs and diseases that robbed them of their health. There was no cure for syphilis, and its victims drifted like phantoms, waiting for death.

Chauncy slapped him on the back. "I'll count on you to sift the wheat from the chaff."

"Why did the waitresses leave?"

"They found better jobs. Until I can pay them more than free passage and meals, we'll have to keep hiring women for the short term," Chauncy said.

"When do you think we'll start making a noticeable profit?"

"It takes time." Chauncy frowned. "You worried about your investment?"

"What do I need money for? I have everything I need aboard the *Jenny Lee*."

"You're destined to be more, Roe. Someday you'll return to doctoring."

"I can't cut into a man's flesh without my hand shaking." Roe leaned against the rail. "All my life I wanted to be a doctor and save lives. Now when I hear the thud of a peg leg or see a hook in place of a hand, I become sick. How can I heal others when I need a physician?"

"You have to stop dwelling on the past." He surveyed the town. "We survived the war and have an opportunity for a better future."

"I'm not as optimistic as you, Colonel."

He removed the unlit cigar. "It's captain now."

"Captain," he corrected. "I've seen what's left of the South. Vultures are picking its carcass clean. The slaves are free, but dark forces are determined to keep them enslaved in other ways. The war didn't resolve anything. It only created a target for hate."

"Men will come to their senses with time."

"I've heard men talk." Roe scratched at the stubble on his face. "It's easier to blame others for life's misfortunes, especially when those you thought inferior have success."

You're too young to be a cynic."

"I've seen too much not to be one."

Chauncy pointed toward Theo talking to the crew. "Tomorrow, I'll send Theo to post notices around town for new waitresses."

"Let's hope Theo finds a few roses among the thorns."

****

Jules searched for any crumbs left in her basket while Edna Stall continued with her endless prattling about her travels. The plump woman in a patched coat had taken the seat next to her a couple hours ago, and Jules had politely offered to share the food she had packed. The woman had devoured everything inside. They were approaching the depot in Cincinnati, and Jules was hungry. She put on her floppy hat and buttoned the top of her cloak, preparing to disembark.

"Do you have anything more to eat?" Edna lifted the basket lid. "You should have packed more, Miss Beecher."

A man stopped in the aisle and turned. "Beecher?"

Harriet Beecher Stowe had lived in Cincinnati before writing *Uncle Tom's Cabin* and was well known in the area. Her relationship would make her a minor celebrity. "I'm a distant cousin." Jules closed the basket's lid and looked up, the man coming into view as the brim of her hat revealed him.

The stocky man's worn coat was open to reveal a revolver hanging in a holster and a sheath for his Bowie knife strapped to a belt. His beard was dark except for a long white stripe that ended in a nasty scar on his cheek, barely missing his eye. The face had haunted her nightmares. She recoiled, hugging the basket to her chest to protect herself. "Clyde Cassell!"

He stared long and hard. "You." His lips parted in a frightening smile that revealed tobacco-stained teeth. "You ain't no man."

"Anyone can see that." Edna gathered her meager belongings tied in a faded towel.

Clyde's hate-filled eyes made Jules tremble. He was forced to move forward as the train slowed to stop at the depot and others gathered in the aisle to exit. But he paused at the front of the car and turned, touching the brim of his hat with his forefinger as if to salute her.

Jules knuckles were white from clutching the basket. She watched his bulky figure until the departing passengers blocked him from view. She peered out the window, searching the crowd for his phantom image, but he had disappeared.

"Who was that man?" Edna asked.

Jules trembled. "A ghost from the past," she whispered. All the horrible memories of that day on the canal rushed back. Clyde and Buck had emerged from the woods, ordering Grandpa Donovan to steer the *Irish Rose* toward their shore of the canal. After they shot Blake, Grandpa and Jess fired back, wounding the younger Cassell brother. Jules had cowered on the deck, too frightened to move. Cole had said she was in shock then. She was again. Age hadn't changed her reaction. She remained in her seat as Edna stood.

"Are you staying on the train?" Edna asked.

Jules looked around. Most of the people had exited the passenger car. She stood on wobbly legs and used the seat backs for support as she walked to the doorway.

She looked around the depot, searching for Clyde, but he was hopefully gone. She concentrated on her task. She needed to reach her cousins. She searched for her baggage ticket in her reticule, and the trainman retrieved her bag.

She turned and bumped into Edna. "Do you have family meeting you?"

"No, I have to find a boat to Louisville." Jules searched for signs of the river.

"You won't find a boat tonight," Edna said. "I know a place where we can stay."

We? It was better she didn't travel alone. It was dusk, and large cities weren't safe for women at night. Besides, Edna owed her for eating all her food, and sharing the cost of a room would be cheaper. She nodded. "Where's your bag?"

"Oh, I have everything I need in here." Edna lifted her bundle which was knotted to form a handle. "Easier to travel this way."

Jules carried her travel bag in one hand and her empty basket in the other. The railroad ran parallel with the two main streets in Cincinnati. Edna led the way across the main thoroughfare and rows of reputable hotels. Buildings four and five-stories high created a maze that Edna navigated with twists and turns that left Jules confused and lost.

"I would prefer a hotel close to the river."

Edna urged her forward. "I know just the place."

They reached a rundown part of town. Women waited in doorways, dressed in gowns that barely contained their breasts as they shivered in the cool air of the autumn evening. Jules pulled her cloak around her and gripped her belongings. Why had she trusted Edna? Her sisters had warned her she was naïve, treating everyone as a friend. Lara's hateful behavior should have been a lesson in betrayal.

She looked back over her shoulder. Could she retrace her steps to the main streets?

"Here it is." Edna waved at a sign that identified the inn and tavern as the Smuggler's Cave. It was small and neglected, but Edna ushered her inside. A fire blazed in the main room, and the smell of fresh-baked pies filled the air. Her hunger pangs returned with renewed vigor, and her mouth watered for a hot meal. A woman served a shepherd's pie to a man seated at a nearby table. He broke the crust, and steam escaped. He dug a spoonful of meat and vegetables from inside.

Jules drooled and opened her reticule.

"You pay for the meal, and I'll pay for a room," Edna volunteered.

Maybe Edna wasn't a total leech.

Chapter Four

Jules fought for a share of the blanket with Edna all night in the lumpy bed and finally won. She huddled beneath the solitary cover and fell asleep from exhaustion. When she woke, Edna was gone. How long had she been alone in bed? She threw the cover off. She had worn her nightgown over her camisole, bloomers, and her corset. She wasn't taking any chances with her money. She reached inside the opening in the corset cover lining and found the hidden bills. Everything had cost more than anticipated. Would she have enough for the return trip, especially with three children along?

The floor was cold. Jules had worn wool stockings to bed. Where were they? She searched the bed. Nothing. Her travel chest was open, and her clothes tossed on the floor and chair. A dread spread from the core of her stomach, growing into panic. She gathered her belongings, taking inventory of what was missing as she packed.

Edna was twice, no three times her size, and had left her dresses and undergarments. But her wool cloak, hat, and gloves were gone. Edna had removed the stockings from her feet and taken her second pair. She stared at the empty space on top of the dresser. She had placed her brush and combs on top before going to bed. Also missing from the dresser was her reticule.

Her purse was considerably lighter after Edna had

ordered a second pie at dinner, and few coins remained. The biggest loss was Blake's gold piece. Five dollars in gold. Why hadn't she thought to hide it? It wasn't as lucky as she had thought. She searched the dresser drawers, but they were empty. Anything of value had been claimed by Edna.

Jules stared at her reflection in the small mirror hanging on the wall. "You thought you were so mature and clever? Stupid child. You should go home where you belong. Everyone was right about you."

She slumped on the bed and debated her course of action. Either way, she needed to dress. She put on her wrinkled travel clothes. Without a brush and combs, how was she going to arrange her hair? She ran her fingers through the tangles and braided from the front to the back, tying it off at her neck with a ribbon she found in the pocket of her jacket. She left the remaining length in a curly mass down her back. She packed her remaining belongings, grabbed her empty basket, and headed downstairs.

"Where do you think you're going?" demanded the innkeeper she had met last night. He blocked her exit.

"I'm leaving. I need to board my boat."

He stood his ground, wiping his hands on the apron knotted around his bulky waist. "Not until you pay your bill."

"But don't you remember? I paid for dinner."

"You owe for the room."

"No, Mrs. Stall agreed to pay for the lodgings." Jules looked into the main room. "Is she having breakfast?"

"No, your companion left an hour ago and said you would pay the bill."

What? "There must be some mistake. We agreed to split the costs, and I've paid my portion."

"I made no such agreement. I only know she's gone, and you owe me for a room." He jabbed a thick finger in her face. "And don't look at me with those big blue eyes brimming with tears. Stop bawling," he ordered. "I'm calling the police." He signaled to a boy standing by the door. "Fetch an officer."

"You do that." Jules searched for her handkerchief before she remembered Edna had stolen it. "Edna is a thief."

"She entered with you."

Jules squared her shoulders. "I met her on the train. I thought she was an honest woman. We don't have crooks in the town where I come from."

He offered her a towel draped over his shoulder. "You must come from a small town."

"Small enough to know everyone by name."

A policeman entered. He was young and stood tall like so many of the men who had returned from the war, proud of their service and sacrifice. "What do you want? I have a detective down the street who needs my help."

"This woman refuses to pay her bill."

"That's not true," Jules said. "I arrived with Edna Stall last night. We agreed to split the cost. I paid for dinner, and Edna agreed to pay for the room we shared."

The policeman pointed at Jules. "Did this woman pay for the meals?"

"Yes, but the other woman left this morning without paying the rent."

Jules stomped her foot. "You should have made her

pay last night."

"She said your name was Beecher, and it would be an insult to ask you to pay in advance."

The policeman studied her. "Is your name Beecher?"

"Yes, but I'm a distant cousin to Harriet Beecher Stowe. I don't know anyone in Cincinnati." Jules shook her trunk. "I trusted Edna, but she stole my hat, cloak, and personal items."

"What color was the cloak?"

What difference did the color make? He waited. "Blue with white clasps at the throat."

"Is Edna a plump woman with gray hair?"

She nodded. "Have you found her? Has she stolen from others?"

He didn't answer. "Do you know a Dr. Sterling Beecher?"

"Yes, that's my father." Had he followed her? She looked around. "Is he here?"

The officer's face remained stoic. "No, we found a letter addressed to him."

She had placed the correspondence in her purse. "Edna stole my reticule. It had the letter and a five-dollar gold piece in it."

"Gold?" the innkeeper interrupted.

"We didn't recover the purse. The letter was discarded in a puddle," the policeman said. "There was no gold piece."

The innkeeper stepped forward. "What about the money she owes me?"

"Edna can pay it." Jules turned to the police officer. "You found her with my things, didn't you?"

"You'll have to identify them." He reached out his

hand. "You need to come with me."

The innkeeper blocked her exit. "Not until she pays her bill."

"Do you have half?" the policeman asked.

The innkeeper crossed his arms. "She's owes all of it."

"Edna can pay her half," Jules argued.

The innkeeper turned to the policeman. "You have her in custody?"

"Yes, the detective is with her now."

Jules turned her back and reached into her blouse, searching her corset cover for her hidden bills.

"I knew you had the money."

"It isn't a matter of the money." Jules handed him a bill. "It's a matter of principle. Edna agreed to pay the rent. I believe a promise is sacred."

The policeman pointed at the innkeeper. "You owe her some change."

Jules sniffed the air. "I'll take it in biscuits and bacon." She raised her basket. "I have no food, and I'm hungry for breakfast."

The innkeeper called over a waitress holding a tray with plates of biscuits, scrambled eggs, and crisp bacon strips.

"You better take it with you," the policeman said.

Jules tore two biscuits in half and stacked the eggs and bacon inside. She tucked one in her basket inside a napkin Edna had left behind and raised the other to her lips.

"You better wait to eat," the policeman said.

"But I'm hungry."

"Trust me."

Something in his tone made her heed his words.

She added the biscuit to the other, taking a long inhale of the mixture of hunger-inducing odors and followed the policeman to the door.

"Don't come back," the innkeeper said. "Next time I won't be so understanding."

The policeman held the door. "You could improve your clientele by telling folks a relative of Harriet Beecher Stowe slept here."

A queer smile creased his face. "Hey, that's right. And I'll expect the other half of my rent from your friend."

"She's not my friend." Jules berated herself. "I was foolish to trust her."

The policeman led the way. "It was smart of you to hide your money in your corset."

She shrugged. "I wish I had hid my gold piece."

"Why didn't you?"

"I didn't think of it as money. I carried it for luck." She shivered from the cold morning air. "I'll be glad to have my belongings returned."

"You may change your mind when you see them."

What was wrong with her things?

A crowd was gathered in the street at the entrance to a narrow alley. He pushed the gawkers aside and made a path. What was so interesting? She recognized her cloak and froze. It covered a body lying on the cobblestones. "That's mine."

A detective stood. "What do you mean it's yours?"

"This is Miss Beecher," the police officer said.

The detective showed her a wrinkled envelope. Her father's name was written on the outside with their address in Darrow Falls beneath. Some of the ink had smeared. "Yours?"

She examined the enclosed letter, nodded, and shoved it into her skirt pocket.

"Miss Beecher shared a room at the Smuggler's Cave with an Edna Stall, who stole her belongings, including that cloak," the policeman related.

The detective stepped aside. "Is this Edna Stall?"

Jules had seen the dead and dying before, but the sight never got easier. She studied the body. The hair was the right color, but her face was turned away. She took a deep breath to calm her nerves and stepped over a stream of red liquid winding its way through the cracks of the cobblestones for a closer look. Edna's bundle of meager possessions was gone and her feet bare. "They stole her stockings and shoes?"

"Scavengers," the detective said. "They don't waste any time claiming anything they can sell or trade. They only left behind items stained with blood."

Jules had been furious with Edna for her betrayal, but her anger was replaced with pity as she circled to the front of the body. Edna's eyes were open but vacant, blankly staring down the dirty alley. Her skin was pale, and a bloody puddle in a hole among the cobblestones reflected the dead woman's image. The murderer had slashed Edna's throat, leaving a savage wound. She bunched her hands into fists. "Why would someone kill her for a few trinkets?"

"You said you had a gold coin in your reticule," the policeman said.

"How would a thief know that?" Edna was hardly dressed in the finery that attracted pickpockets and thieves. It didn't make sense.

The detective knelt by the body. "The thieves may have expected more and were angry. It's a nice cloak.

43

Do you want it?"

No amount of washing would remove the stains. She shuddered. "No." Scavengers had taken the rest of her possessions. Even her floppy hat was gone. She wanted to go home where the worst thing she had to worry about was someone slandering her good name. But others were counting on her. Jules squared her shoulders and looked around. "I need to board a steamboat. Which way to the river?"

The police officer pointed toward the smoke stacks sticking above the skyline. "Take this street to the main intersection and turn left, Miss Beecher. The dock master's office is at the end of the road. You can find a boat there."

Jules gathered her bag and basket. When she entered the main road, the crowd swallowed her up. Bodies pressed around her, forcing her to flow toward the singular destination of the river. The towering buildings ended at the crest of a hill that sloped to the water's edge. The only structure continuing across the Ohio River was the tall stone supports for the railroad bridge.

Lined along the shore were numerous boats bathed in bright sunshine that sparkled on the water. A row of wagons waited to claim unloaded cargo. Other wagons carried barrels and crates or cords of wood to be loaded on the main decks of the boats before they departed on their journeys. Trails crisscrossed the open shoreline somehow avoiding collisions in the confusion of import and export transportation.

Jules followed the crowd to the dock master's office. A schedule of the boats and their fares was posted on the bulletin board beside the door. A bed in a cabin costs twenty-five dollars. That was all the money she had hid in her corset. Even if she shared the room, she wouldn't have enough for the return trip. It was five dollars to sleep on the deck, but for a woman, that was too dangerous to consider. What was she going to do? Going home without the children wasn't an option. She wasn't going to fail her father.

A flyer was pinned to the corner of the public board. It was a notice for waitresses for the *Jenny Lee*. One of her sisters was named Jennifer. That had to be a good omen. She adjusted her basket on her arm and lifted the bottom of the flyer where it was creased. Payment was *free* passage and meals to Louisville. "Where is the *Jenny Lee* docked?" she asked the man standing in the doorway.

"I can take you." A man who had been standing nearby stepped forward. He had been staring at her, but she had politely ignored him. He removed his cap. "I'm first mate on the *Jenny Lee*."

Her experience with Edna made her wary. The man was short and rail thin. His mud-colored hair was shaped like a bowl. He smiled. He was missing a few teeth.

"I'm sure I can find it." Jules looked at the man in the doorway. He pointed north. She walked along a packed trail in the dirt leading to the waterway. The strange man tagged along. "May I carry your bag?"

She gripped the handle tighter. "It only has clothes in it. I can manage."

"What's your name?"

It was the one thing that might protect her. "Miss Beecher."

His smile faded, and his shoulders slumped. Why

had her name disappointed him? It impressed others.

The Ohio River was crowded with a wide-range of boats, from large sidewheelers with four smoke stacks and long layered decks to simple rowboats. The *Jenny Lee* was a sternwheeler, smaller than the big boats but larger than her grandfather's canal boat.

A group of women gathered on the shore waiting for the stage to be lowered so they could board. Her uninvited escort shouted to a crew member who lowered the walkway to the side. At least he hadn't lied about being a crew member. "Come aboard." He led the way to the bow and told them to wait outside on the foredeck in front of the staircase.

Along the shoreline beside a wagon, the crew were placing barrels and crates on top of a wooden platform. With a shout, a net beneath the platform was raised by a boom, and the load of cargo was lifted into the air, swung up over the railing, and deposited on the deck nearby.

"When does the ship sail?" one of the women asked.

A crew member laughed. "This boat don't sail. It's powered by steam, lady."

"When does the *Jenny Lee* cast off?" Jules asked.

The crew member studied her. "Tomorrow morning. The captain don't like navigating the river in the dark."

It would take most of Wednesday to reach Louisville. Everything was taking longer and more expensive than she had calculated. She needed free passage. She needed this job.

Jules studied the other women. All of them were older, seasoned veterans of labor. But the lives of three children depended upon her reaching Laurel Holler. She couldn't fail. Her father's description gnawed at her like the gangrene that took so many limbs during the war. She enjoyed singing, dancing, and attending parties. What seventeen-year-old woman didn't? In addition to her chores and helping her mother, she had assisted her father on his medical trips. She could stitch a wound, apply chloroform, and deliver a baby, but all her skills had been forgotten in an angry outburst. She had to prove to her father she wasn't a silly, frivolous girl.

"If they don't rescue us from this sun soon, I'm going to melt," the woman next to her said. She had a battered parasol that provided a small circle of shade. Jules inched closer, trying to share the reprieve from the hot sun. She could have used the shade from the wide brim of the old hunting hat Edna had stolen. Who was wearing it now?

Her neighbor had attempted to create a sophisticated look with a matching jacket and skirt and a small cap trimmed with feathers, but like her parasol, the once expensive outfit showed signs of wear and mending.

"I'm Jules Beecher. Have you done this work before?"

"It's the same whether in a saloon or private parlor. I'm Rita." She moved her parasol, leaving Jules in the sun. "Where's your bonnet?"

"Stolen."

"You can't trust nobody," Rita said. "Did they steal your money, too?"

Jules hesitated to share too much information. "They left me paying the bill."

"Sounds like a man," Rita said. "You make them pay first, Julie."

"Jules."

"I'm Lizzy," an older woman next to Rita introduced herself. Lizzy wore a faded gown with a newer panel of fabric along the bottom hem. It was the easiest way to replace a damaged skirt without throwing out yards of material.

Lizzy wore a straw bonnet with faded silk flowers tucked into a ribbon decorating the cap. Her hair was brown and was beginning to gray near her temples. Her eyes had small squint lines on the outside corners, but the lines around her mouth showed she smiled. A lot. "You want to know about working the tables, ask me." Lizzy raised one plump arm with her palm up. "I never spill a drink even when they're pinching my hide."

"Pinching?"

"Pinching, slapping, grabbing," Lizzy rattled off. "Drunk men are the worst, slobbering all over you like mad dogs. These boats attract the scum of the earth, gamblers, and con men. I hope you're not looking for a husband."

"No," Jules said. "I'm traveling to Laurel Holler to find my cousins."

Rita twirled her parasol with her lace covered palm. The mitt had been darned. "Then you're not a professional?"

"I worked at my grandmother's inn. I know how to wait on tables and clean after meals."

"She doesn't mean that sort of profession," Lizzy said with a wink.

Jules gasped. "Prostitution?"

"I don't believe in free love," Rita said. "I look for

men with fat pockets."

Jules processed the news that Rita worked between the sheets and brazenly bragged about it. "Fat pockets?"

"Filled with gold and silver." She rubbed her fingers together with her thumb. "Then I cast a line and wait for a nibble."

Lizzy laughed. "On your maggot eaten carcass?"

"Look who's talking," Rita challenged. "You're so old, the only men who look at you are undertakers."

The women were older but not ancient. The insults were said with a smile and a challenge. "Are you friends or enemies?"

"We've traveled a few miles together," Lizzy said.

"Bumpy miles," Rita added.

"Sometimes we're friendly, and sometimes we bare our claws. It's survival of the most desperate when the pickings are slim," Lizzy said.

Rita walked around Jules. "Why don't you have a man taking care of you?"

"I don't want a husband."

"I wasn't talking about a husband," Rita said. "A woman with your youthful beauty could demand a house and carriage." She stepped back and sighed. "With that face and figure, you could have anything you desired and more."

Jules had a roof over her head, meals to eat, and plenty of friends, if they didn't turn against her because of Lara's gossip. She worked on the farm and helped her parents because she loved them. She had never considered being taken care of by a man. Besides, she understood what he would demand for his generosity. She shuddered. "I'm content with what I have."

Chapter Five

A man stepped out from the shadows created by the upper deck and made his way through the maze of crates and barrels readied for transport. Cargo was stored around the boiler room on the main deck. Each space was filled from floor to ceiling with precious goods that would be sold between the Northern and Southern cities. He joined them in the bright sunlight, silencing the chatter from the women. He was tall and lean. His white shirt was broad across his shoulders and the sleeves were rolled to his elbows as if he had been working, but his hands and nails were clean. He removed a wide-brimmed hat. His long dark brown hair curled above his shoulders, and a shadow of beard outlined a strong jaw and face carved by a Renaissance sculptor.

Jules searched for a flaw and found none. Was it the heat that made her lightheaded? Her heart raced, and her breathing was rapid. Too bad Edna had stolen her fan. She stepped beneath Rita's parasol and took a deep breath to calm her odd reaction.

"Welcome ladies." A dark eyebrow rose as if he questioned the title. "I'm Roe Greystone. Normally we would hire men to do this task but so many lost limbs and lives in the war, we have lowered our standards."

He had boldly insulted them and hadn't apologized. Women were second-class citizens. The war had given black men freedom and the right to vote, own land, and serve in the army. Women had gained nothing from the war. The right to vote had been denied them, and only a few states allowed a woman to own property, usually if she had no husband. Jules had been raised on the writings of Elizabeth Cady Stanton and other suffragettes. She didn't like Roe Greystone's archaic beliefs.

"We plan to hire four women for the journey. The *Jenny Lee* travels back and forth between Cincinnati and Louisville during the day. We dock two nights at each port to first unload and then load cargo. Besides serving food and drinks, you will clear tables and wash dishes."

Jules had acquired all those skills working at her grandma's inn.

"In the evening, we entertain guests with games of chance in the dining hall," Roe said. "In exchange for your work, you will be provided with a room and meals. No pay."

A few of the women departed. Hadn't they read the notice? Or perhaps they couldn't read. Education wasn't seen as a necessity for the female gender. Maureen Beecher had thought otherwise. Jules, like her sisters, had finished eighth grade. Cory and Cole had teaching certificates.

"Each woman hired will be required to work tonight and tomorrow evening after we arrive in Louisville," Roe said. "You can return to Cincinnati by working the same schedule or take your leave in Louisville once your duties are completed."

Some of the women murmured about the terms, but no one left. Jules would have free passage to Louisville.

Could she return the same way? They would expect payment for the children. She felt the thickness in her corset. Somehow, she would find a way to return home with her cousins without compromising her honor or safety.

****

Roe surveyed the line of desperate women searching for a job. Too many of them had suffered abuse or starvation during the war and wore padding or makeup to disguise their wasted bodies. Theo had found more than enough candidates, and he would have to send the majority away.

"Form a line!" Roe Greystone walked to the starboard side and examined each woman with a physician's eye per Chauncy's orders, dismissing those who showed signs of illness or addiction even though they were desperate for work. The *Jenny Lee* wasn't a charity.

As expected, they cried and begged for him to reconsider. He steeled himself against the tears and begging that followed rejection. He stood firm but felt sorry for the women who left in silence, their faces drawn and downcast. They had given up. Soldiers hadn't been the only casualties of war.

He asked names, noting if they had the majority of their teeth when they spoke. He looked for sores beneath the powder and rouge. Up close he could see bloodshot eyes and smell the odor of cheap liquor on their breath when they answered his questions. He allowed those to remain who appeared healthy and had a spark of life still glimmering in their desperate eyes. The work wasn't easy, and they'd earn their passage.

He reached the end of the line and stopped in front

of a girl. He glanced at the other women who were older, dressed in garish mismatched outfits, or had lacked any signs of education, grace, or manners when they had spoken.

This one didn't belong. The young woman wore a tailored jacket and simple skirt that emphasized her trim figure. Her face startled him by the resemblance to another woman he knew. He'd been thinking of Miss Jessie yesterday. He had admired her for her beauty and courage, but she had been married, and with a husband like Major Morgan Mackinnon, entertaining thoughts of seduction would have been suicidal. He glanced at the girl's bare hand. No ring.

Her features were similar yet differences existed between the two women. They could have been sisters. This one had large blue eyes that met his gaze. She smiled, and he was captivated. "You have all your teeth."

Her eyebrows arched above a look of surprise. "Are you buying a horse or hiring a waitress?"

He fought a smile. She had a sense of humor. Her face relaxed into a pleasant expression. Most women set their lips in a grim line of survival or used a falsely seductive glance to lure a man's wallet from him. Her expression was sincere and sparked concern.

Why was this innocent traveling alone? Most of the women in line were widows from the war or members of the petticoat sorority. His curiosity was aroused. "What's your name?"

"Jules Beecher." She curtseyed, and a few women snickered.

"Jewels?" Roe asked.

"J-U-L-E-S," she spelled. "Like the author, Jules

Verne."

He chuckled. "You read Verne?"

"After it's translated from French. I only know Latin."

"*Vita numquam mirari desino me.*" Life never ceases to amaze me. He waited for her response. He doubted she would know more than the first word.

"Me, too. Each day brings new surprises."

She was telling the truth. Well educated with manners. Who was this woman? Her face was pink from sunburn. He gripped her chin and turned her face side to side. "Where's your bonnet?"

"Stolen, sir."

No one would have stolen a hat from Jessica Mackinnon. She had beat Texan Will Starr in a shooting match. Roe had met Miss Jessie after the battle of Gettysburg. She had helped with the wounded, but this woman's blond hair was tinged with red. "What color is your hair?"

"Strawberry blond." She brushed back a few strands that had fallen from her braid.

"It's hot out here," Rita said. "Could you admire her inside?"

The other women had been staring at their exchange. His face was warm, and it wasn't from the sun. Roe waved the eight women upstairs. He followed Jules. Her single braid ended in a swirl of curls that bounced as she carried her bag and basket. He clenched his fist to fight the urge to touch the fiery strands. Was she as innocent as she appeared? He had two nights to find out.

They made their way up the stairs and along the promenade to a narrow hallway that opened into a large interior room. It was dark and cool inside the dining hall. The six chandeliers hanging from the copper ceiling and a dozen sconces along the walls were unlit. A platform framed with Corinthian columns was at the stern end of the boat with a piano the only furniture on the stage. Along the side was an elaborate walnut bar with a large mirror framed by built in shelves to secure a stock of liquor bottles. A wooden barrel with a tap was at the far end. Beer was cheap and served with dinner. In the corner was a door leading to the galley.

Dark oak tables were arranged around the room with chairs overturned and stacked on top except for a pair where Chauncy waited. He stood and directed the women to sit at the two tables.

"This is the captain of the *Jenny Lee*, Captain Chauncy LaDonte."

Jules dropped her bag and stared at the captain, a soft smile playing on her lips. Did she think she could charm him into a job? Chauncy looked at Roe, a quizzical eyebrow raised as he nodded toward the girl. He had recognized the resemblance as well.

Before she could sit, Roe called her name and pointed at the bar. "Retrieve a tray and serve everyone."

Jules left her bag on the floor and placed her basket on the table. "Yes, sir."

Her skirts swayed as she made her way through the maze of tables. A wave of curls bounced along her back. The erratic rhythm made him dizzy.

She grabbed a tray loaded with empty tin mugs and plates. She lifted it to the side, balancing the tray with her hand as she made her way back. How could a woman's body maneuver in a plethora of movements and the tray remain motionless?

She served Chauncy first, placing the empty plate in front of him. "I hope you enjoy your steak and potatoes." She served the mug. "This homemade brew should quench your thirst."

Chauncy laughed and played along with her humor. "I doubt I can finish such a large serving."

Jules moved around the table, serving the others and setting the last empty plate and mug in front of Roe. "Enjoy your meal."

Roe handed her his plate. "Now gather the dishes and take everything back to the bar."

Jules accomplished the task without incident and took her seat while the next woman served. Lizzy and Rita passed the test. The tray was too heavy for one woman, and she dropped it. Jules rushed to her aid and helped gather the items from the floor. None of the other women had moved. They were survivors, willing to sacrifice others for their success. When Jules gathered her skirt to rise, she revealed bare legs. She wore no stockings. What other undergarments did she lack?

The battlefield had limited Roe's patients to men. As a doctor, he knew the anatomy of women from drawings in medical books. He'd seen a female cadaver, but Jules was a living, breathing, perfect specimen of feminine attractiveness. The full curve of her breasts and hips were balanced and emphasized by a narrow waist. Her face was symmetrical with huge blue eyes, a delicate nose, and full lips. A porcelain doll would have been jealous.

Where was her flaw? Her teeth were straight, her laughter musical, and his body was reacting like any man would to a pretty young woman. Jules returned to her chair. Chauncy was staring. "What is it?"

"We can eliminate that one from the list."

Roe dismissed the woman who had dropped the tray even though she burst into tears.

Jules, Rita, Lizzie, and a woman named Babs remained.

"Theo!" Chauncy called. He rushed from the galley and removed his cap.

Jules clapped her hands. "Theo Jameson." She rushed forward and hugged him. "I'm so sorry I was rude before. You should have told me *your* name."

Theo's cheeks pinked above a grin so wide, it should have hurt. He pointed to her basket on the table. "I recognized the two pink slats in the weaving, but your name is wrong."

"Do you know this woman?" Roe demanded.

"Look at the basket." Theo showed it to Chauncy. "You remember it, don't you, Captain?"

Chauncy examined the container and the girl. "What's your name?"

"Jules Beecher."

"Beecher?" Chauncy frowned. "That can't be. "Miss Jenny's name was Collins and Miss Jessie's name was Mackinnon."

"They were married." Jules laughed. "We were all Beechers at one time."

Roe groaned. "Good Lord, she's an abolitionist."

Jules turned toward him, her hands on her hips. "I hope you don't hold that against me. When Congress passed the thirteenth amendment, they put abolitionists out of business." She raised her chin. "Now I'm a disappointed suffragette."

"That's even worse," Roe replied. The truth

dawned. He had never met Miss Jenny, but this was Jessica Mackinnon's sister. No wonder the resemblance had tormented him. He needed to quell any romantic notions. "Miss Jessie was prettier."

"I don't know how to answer," Jules said. "I would be vain to argue and ungracious to my other sisters to agree."

Roe grunted. The chit had turned his insult back on him. He looked at Chauncy for help.

He stroked his mustache. "I knew you looked familiar. How are your sisters?"

"Well, Morgan and Jessica have a boy they named Jackson, and Chauncy Theodora has a baby brother named Derek."

"Chauncy Theodora is my namesake," Theo said, standing taller.

Jules gasped. "Did you name your boat after my sister?"

"Miss Jenny was kind enough to name her daughter after Theo and me. I figured we owed her to do the same."

"I'm sure she'll be honored," Jules said. "She always spoke fondly of you."

Rita crossed her arms and leaned back in her chair. "I guess she has the job."

"You all have jobs," Roe said. "Theo, show the ladies to their room."

"Room?" Rita stood. "We don't have private quarters?"

"Your labor isn't worth a private room. You will share quarters. Is that a problem?" Roe looked toward the door where the last woman had exited. "I can replace you with one of the other women."

Lizzy nudged her.

"No, it sounds cozy." Rita's voice was thick with sarcasm.

Babs sniffed the basket. "You got food in der?"

"My biscuits!" Jules withdrew two biscuits stacked with scrambled eggs and bacon. "Are you hungry?"

The women gathered closer. "You don't mind sharing?" Lizzy reached for one.

"We can each have a half," Jules said. "Anyone have a knife?"

"Miss Jessie carried a knife in her boot," Roe said.

"I left my knife on the dresser, and Edna Stall stole it."

Who was Edna Stall? Before Roe retrieved the knife in his pocket, Theo offered his.

She wiped the blade on her skirt and divided the food. Jules looked at the men. "I forgot my manners. I should have offered you something." She held out her half of a biscuit. "Are you hungry?"

The other women quickly devoured their portions before they might be asked to share.

"We've eaten, and you'll have a meal after dinner is served." Chauncy removed a watch from his vest pocket. "Which will be in an hour."

"Theo will show you to your room," Roe said. "Store your bags and report back here for your assignments. You'll want to wear work clothes."

Theo lifted the empty basket. "Do you want me to fill this, Miss Jules?"

"I won't need it until I reach Louisville. My little cousins were orphaned, and I'm going to take them home to Darrow Falls."

"Aren't you sweet," Rita said without masking her

ridicule.

Jules frowned. "Haven't you read Dickens? Being an orphan isn't nice."

Roe coughed to hide his smile. Nice? Was the girl putting on an act, or was she a childish simpleton?

Theo took her bag and led the women out the door.

Roe waited for them to exit and laughed. "The customers are going to eat that child alive."

Chauncy shook his head in disagreement. "I'll wager she's the same age Miss Jessie was when we met her after the battle at Gettysburg."

"She was married to Morgan Mackinnon."

"Not until a year later."

Roe disagreed, "Morgan introduced her as his wife."

"He used his name to protect her. A Union nurse in a Confederate camp?" Chauncy's eyebrow rose. "Miss Jessie was good with a gun but not against half the Southern army."

He nodded toward the door. "Do you think Jules knows how to shoot a gun?"

"I have no idea."

"How well do you know the Beecher family?"

"I only met two of the sisters, and I didn't know the family name was Beecher," Chauncy said. "Miss Jenny read us the letters she had written to her husband. She said her sister Courtney was bossy, Colleen was a troublemaker, Jessica had won a five-dollar gold piece in a shooting contest, Cassandra loved animals, and Juliet…"

"Juliet?" Roe smacked his palm against his forehead. "That's grand. Romeo and Juliet."

Chauncy patted him on the shoulder. "Shakespeare

made you star-crossed lovers."

"Have you forgotten? Romeo dies in the play."

Chauncy stroked his beard. "Then we better not tell her your name is Romeo."

Chapter Six

Theo led the four women along the open walkway on the deck that circled back toward the stairway. Sturdy trusses supported the upper deck. A railing with wide decorative balusters circled the entire outside edge to prevent anyone from falling overboard. On the inside wall passenger cabins were spaced at regular intervals with an occasional small window.

"This ain't so bad." Babs was close in age to Jules. She had light brown hair that was braided and coiled at the nape of her neck. Loose strands had come loose and framed her long narrow face. Her plain linen dress was too big for her, and she used a strip of cloth as a belt. She paused at one of the rooms. "Which one is ours?"

"Your room is up here." Theo stopped by the stairs and searched through a metal box filled with tagged keys. He located the one for the room beneath the stairs and unlocked the door.

"He offered Jules the key, but Lizzy snatched it. "I don't like being locked out."

Theo handed Jules her travel trunk, tipped his hat, and headed downstairs to the lower deck where crewmen had finished loading cargo and were securing the wares from Cincinnati to take down river.

The women crowded into the small room. Two sets of bunkbeds were separated by the underside of the single staircase to the upper deck. A washstand was placed in between. Wall pegs along the wall provided a place to hang clothing and personal items.

Rita surveyed the cramped quarters. "We're working to sleep in here? It looks like a storage room."

Jules dropped her trunk on the floor and placed her basket on top. "At least we don't have to share a bed and fight for covers like I did last night with Edna."

"Who's Edna?" Rita asked. "Your maid?"

"No, a woman I met on the train."

Footsteps echoed above them. "No wonder they gave us this here room," Babs complained. "How do they expect us to sleep?"

"You've never worked on a river boat," Lizzy said. "The hours are late. You'll be so tired, you won't hear anything once your head hits the pillow."

"Do you have anything else in your basket, Jules?" Babs stared at the container. "All that piece of biscuit did was make me more hungry."

She lifted the lid to reveal the empty hold. "No, Edna ate all my food."

"Yah shouldn't share food with strangers," Babs said.

"I shared food with you." Jules comment was greeted by an uncomprehending stare from Babs.

"Are you always so trusting?" Rita claimed the bottom bunk, tossing her bag and parasol on the blanket covered mattress.

"I never had a reason not to be trusting before," Jules said. "Edna agreed to pay for the room at the inn if I paid for the evening meal. Only she stole my belongings and left early in the morning without paying the bill."

"You were conned." Rita removed her feather-decorated hat and lace mitts and tossed them on the bed next to her parasol. "You're lucky she didn't steal the clothes off your back." She unbuttoned her jacket and skirt, carefully folding them. Rita was thin but muscular. She was no stranger to hard work. She removed a dark work dress from her bag and packed away her audition outfit.

Jules removed her jacket. "We weren't the same size, or she would have taken everything."

Lizzy examined the jacket Jules tossed on the bed above hers. "This looks new."

"I made it," Jules said. "I make all my clothes."

"You?" Lizzy ran her fingers along the intricate stitching. "If you're this clever with a needle, you should be a seamstress."

"My mother has a sewing machine."

Babs paused from washing her face. "Are you rich?"

"No, with six daughters, Mama thought it prudent to buy one."

"Prudent?" Babs repeated, a puzzled look on her face.

"It means smart," Rita said. "So why did you leave home, or do you expect us to believe that phony story about rescuing orphans?"

"It's true," Jules defended. "Caroline, George, and William Bauer live in Laurel Holler in Kentucky. I'm on a mission to find my cousins and take them home."

"Why you?" Rita tugged her work dress over her corset and crinoline. "You couldn't find a man to do the job?"

Jules removed her blouse and squared her shoulders. "I volunteered."

Rita buttoned the front of her dress. The cuffs were frayed, and a patch of new material had been used to mend a hole. "All you have to show for your kindness is a sunburn."

Lizzy had left her skirt on but exchanged her bodice for a plain white blouse. "Mr. Greystone was examining more than your flushed face. Or were you blushing because he's so handsome?"

Jules tugged on the strings holding her skirt in place and formed a knot. "Mr. Greystone was determining whether or not I could do the job."

Rita ran her combs through her hair and pinned them in place. "Waitressing wasn't the only job you were auditioning for."

"Rita," Lizzy hushed. "Jules is a lady."

"Every woman is a lady until a man seduces her. Cads choose the young naïve ones because they're the easiest prey," Rita said. "Men that handsome don't pay for a good time, and they don't stay with one woman. Not for long. Pick an older man with money. Then you won't be left penniless with a baby on the way."

Jules fought the knot. "I would never let a man compromise me."

Rita pushed her against the bed frame, her nose inches from her own. "Sometimes you don't have a choice."

Rita was strong for a small woman, but Jules remained on her feet, and Rita backed off. "Did I do something to anger you?"

Rita scanned her, a snarl on her lips. "You're a princess." She snorted. "You never wanted for anything. I don't buy your story about looking for cousins. I bet you're eloping with some man your parents don't approve of. Why else would you travel alone? You could have a dozen men begging to escort you or do your bidding. You don't know how good you have it."

"We've only met. You don't know me, and I know nothing about you."

"You haven't heard about me?" Rita laughed and twirled her skirt. "My life is an open book, and unfortunately, not unique." She leaned against the door. "My pa liked to drink, and when he was in the cups, he beat my mother. When he was done throwin' her around, he started on me and my sister." Rita slammed her palm against the wooden surface, startling everyone. "The sheriff said he couldn't do anything. It was the right of the man of the house to exercise control over his family. Even the preacher warned not to spare the rod."

"He was wrong," Jules said. "Men who resort to violence are cowards."

"If you said that to my pa, you'd be the one cowering." She shook her head. "Then the war began. When the army asked for women to volunteer their services for the troops, my pa saw an opportunity to make a few dollars." Rita's face darkened. "I never saw any money. Plenty of men. Too many to count. Any woman who thinks she's safe from rape is deceiving herself. If he doesn't overpower you, he befriends you. I don't know how many girls talked about uncles or beaus who took their innocence after a few presents or lies about love. Now if a man wants to use me, he has to pay me and me alone."

"I'm sorry." Jules finally undid the knot and let her skirt drop to the floor. "I didn't know."

Rita laughed. "You think that fairytale is true? You're gullible and stupid."

Rita had seemed sincere. "It was all a lie?"

Rita laughed. "Did I shock you, Princess?"

"No. My father is a doctor." Jules folded her clothes. "I've helped with patients who were beaten or worse."

Rita narrowed her eyes. "Now who's telling fairytales?"

"I'm not lying. Edna stole my belongings, and then someone stole from her." Jules failed to block the image. "I saw her in an alley in a pool of blood after someone slit her throat. She was a thief, but she didn't deserve to die like that. It was horrible." She stifled a sob. "Have you ever seen a woman murdered?"

Rita smacked the door. "My sister."

Jules removed her work dress from her bag and placed her travel clothes inside. "Do you think it's funny to shock people with your tragic tales?"

"Rita isn't lying," Lizzy said. "People just don't believe her when she tells the truth."

She looked at Lizzy. "All of it was the truth?"

Lizzy nodded. "Some of us don't have nice families."

"I'm sorry," Jules said. "I can't imagine one of my sisters being murdered. What happened?"

Rita turned her back. "What do you care?"

"Why wouldn't I? I may lack your worldly experience, but I've never been accused of lacking compassion. When veterans come to my father about nightmares and problems from the war, I listen," Jules said. "By sharing their stories, they shift the burden. My papa says I have wide shoulders when it comes to carrying a load."

"You think you can bear my tragedy?" Rita stepped closer but without menacing her. "You want to know about my sister? It was the second year of the war. We'd been at the brothel a few months. Someone said it becomes easier with time, but they were wrong. How can you enjoy a stranger with lust in his eyes touching you in the most intimate of places, trying to elicit a response other than disgust? They thought we shared their enjoyment. Some of the men were young, sweet, and grateful. They made the others tolerable. I learned to plaster a smile on my face and praise their efforts."

Jules gasped. "Couldn't you leave?"

"We had no place to go. At least the brothel gave us a room and food. The owner didn't beat us…much." Her voice turned hard and cold. "It was after Antietam. The returning soldiers wanted to forget what they had seen. We were busy comforting them. Some of the things they said can't be forgotten." She shuddered. "A man arrived blubbering about his poor dead brother and a fortune of gold. He had a gunshot wound in his arm and had tied a kerchief around it. My sister offered to take care of it. She would have made a good nurse, but the army didn't hire soiled doves."

Bab's eye were wide with fright as Rita told her story. Jules gripped the fabric of her work dress, too mesmerized to put it on.

"I was in the next room when I heard her scream, but I had some oaf on top of me who wouldn't get off. By the time I reached her room, he had cut her up with his knife. He stabbed at me and ran out the door." Rita fought a sob in her throat. "She died in my arms. I won't ever forget his ugly face."

Lizzy put her arm around Rita. "Why don't you stay here and take a nap? We can set up the tables."

She shrugged her off. "I pull my own weight." She pointed at Jules. "Don't feel sorry for me. My past made me who I am today. I don't deny it like some. You either accept me or despise me, but don't pity me."

Jules gathered the skirt to slip over her head. "I think you're brave."

Rita jabbed her finger in her face. "Don't you dare try conning me. I'm not fresh off the farm like Babs."

"I'm not," Jules defended. "It takes courage to be a woman in a world ruled by men. You want to know why I traveled alone? I wanted to prove I wasn't afraid. All my older sisters went on journeys. Some were nurses on the battlefield. I don't know how they did it. I couldn't even travel on the train without finding trouble. I'm terrified of failure. What if I can't find the children? What if I disappoint my father?"

"You can't please some men no matter what you do," Lizzy said. "My husband only found fault with me. I couldn't do anything right. When he left for war, he said he wasn't sending any money home, and I could beg on the street." She laughed. "I did just fine without him."

"How?" Babs said. "I struggle every day to find food or a place to sleep."

"Don't you have any family?"

"All my brothers were killed in the war. The bank took the house after my mother died this summer. I've been wandering, working when I can."

Jules stared at the girl. "You're all alone?"

"I wouldn't mind having a husband, but nobody

wants me." Babs frowned. "I'm not nearly as pretty as any of you, but I'm a hard worker." She rubbed at a stain on her dress. "Life sure would be easier if I was married."

"Not always." Lizzy raised her chin. "An overbearing lazy man is a dead weight for a woman to bear. After my husband left for war, it was easier to take care of myself. I never felt pride my entire life until I earned my own money."

"In a brothel?" Babs shook her head. "I could never do that."

"I never had to work in the brothels," Lizzy said. "I was a cook. Worked in a hotel until word came about my husband."

Babs tucked the loose strands of her hair into her bun. "What happened to him?"

"Wounded at Gettysburg. I visited the hospital in Alexandria where they had taken him. He was my husband even if I didn't love him." Lizzy smiled. "I met Rita in the market. She taught me how to stand up to him, but he still complained until the day he died."

"If he made it to heaven, he's probably complaining about the harp music," Rita said. "But I'll wager he's in a warmer climate."

"Some men never change." Lizzy smiled at Rita. "But I made a friend."

"Friend?" Rita said. "We helped each other survive. When you don't have any family, you take what support you can get."

"Thanks," Lizzy said. "I wouldn't want you to admit you liked me."

"Don't get your corset strings in a tangle," Rita said. "I was the outcast. You were the first respectable woman who would talk to me. I owe you."

"I'd say we were even by now," Lizzy said.

Babs clapped her hands. "I wish I had a friend like you two."

Rita groaned. "Next thing you know, the princess will want us to adopt Babs so she's not an orphan."

"My cousins are the orphans." Jules pulled her dress over her head, but it refused to slide down. "I'm stuck."

"Don't you know how to dress?" Rita laughed.

Jules had her arms in the sleeves, but the bodice was bunched above her chest.

"You forgot to unbutton the front." Lizzy fumbled with the buttons.

Someone knocked.

"Don't open the door," Jules said as she struggled to slip her head through the opening and pull her dress down.

Chapter Seven

Roe knocked again. What was taking the women so long to change into work clothes? Rita opened the door. She leaned against the door frame. "Welcome, handsome."

Roe stared into the crowded room. The women were dressed except for Jules. Lizzy and Babs were struggling to pull her dress over her undergarments. The bodice was open, exposing her corset cover. But it was the creamy expanse of skin above the lace trimmed camisole that took his breath away. As a gentleman, he should turn away, but he was mesmerized by soft mounds of flesh bouncing for freedom. He held his breath, waiting for their escape.

"You interrupted the ladies-in-waiting dressing Princess Alexandra," Rita said.

Jules looked up, and a warm blush crept across her pale skin. She closed the buttons, but not before he memorized every curve and swell exposed to his view. Jules raised her chin. "I think it's an honor to be likened to the Princess of Wales."

Roe bowed. "Report to the kitchen, your Royal Highness and ladies."

Rita rested her hand on Roe's forearm. "There are too many rules for a prim and proper princess. She never has any fun." She leaned toward him. "Now, I bet you're the sort of man who enjoys a good time."

"Save your charm for the customers." Roe stepped back to allow her to pass. "Set the tables, serve the guests, and then you can eat."

Babs followed Rita. "But I'm hungry now."

Lizzy waited by the door with the key in her hand.

Jules packed her clothing in the trunk on the floor and examined the latch. She removed a small bag and shoved it into her skirt pocket.

Roe chuckled, and she met his gaze. "You don't trust your ladies-in-waiting?"

She lowered her voice. "I trusted Edna Stall, and she stole everything but my clothes. She only left those because they didn't fit."

"The woman who took your knife?" And stockings, Roe added mentally.

"Yes, we met on the train. She was friendly, and I thought she'd be a safer companion than sitting next to a man." Jules sighed. "I offered to share my food, and she ate all of it."

He pointed at the basket on the floor. "Why was Theo so interested in your worn out food hamper?"

She stepped outside the room. "It's magical."

"Magical?" Lizzy closed and locked the door. "You're daft."

"That basket has been to Bull Run, Antietam, Gettysburg, and here."

Roe's voice deepened. "Your sisters carried it?"

"Yes." Her voice was like a bell, light and musical. "They said every time it was empty, a good fairy filled it."

Roe scoffed at her words. "A good fairy?"

"Theo Jameson," Jules said.

Roe followed them. He fought a smile. "I don't

think Theo is a fairy."

"Then he's an angel who came to my sisters' aid when they needed it most."

Roe opened the door to the dining hall. "I admit, you couldn't find a harder worker during the war or now."

Babs searched the room. "Did you serve with Theo?"

"Yes. We were together from Gettysburg to Appomattox Courthouse. Theo was a constant during the turmoil. He's a good friend."

"Does he have any family?" Babs asked.

"No, we're his family."

"No wife?" Her voice was hopeful.

Roe wasn't a matchmaker. If Babs wanted a husband, he wasn't going to aid her. "You'll have to talk to Theo about his matrimonial plans."

Babs blushed.

Roe handed the women aprons and pointed to the linens. "Make the tables look pretty, ladies."

Jules hesitated, chewing on her bottom lip. "What's wrong, Princess?"

She gathered a stack of tablecloths. "When I'm done, I'd like to talk to the captain."

"Better talk to him now. He'll be busy later."

"We'll save your tables for you," Rita said.

Jules dropped the linens, and Roe escorted her upstairs. He tried not to stare at her, but a glance wasn't enough. He could spend a lifetime studying her features and never be disappointed. Her lashes framed pools of blue, and her full lips beckoned with secrets he wanted to discover. What did she need to talk to Captain LaDonte about? Was she planning to return home?

The top hurricane deck had few travelers. Those seeking deck passage would wait until late at night or board early in the morning. Roe knocked on the captain's door, and they entered. Chauncy was seated at his desk reviewing a business ledger. Behind him on the wall was a sword, a symbol of his military service. General Ulysses S. Grant had allowed officers to retain their sidearms and swords during the surrender at Appomattox Courthouse. Roe had a revolver he had only fired a few times.

Chauncy closed the ledger and stood. "Miss Beecher, how may I help you?"

"I need to send a telegram to my parents." Her voice broke with emotion.

"I knew it!" Roe pointed at Chauncy. "She ran away from home."

"I'm not a child," Jules defended. "I'm going to Laurel Holler to find my orphaned cousins and take them home."

"Because being an orphan isn't nice." Roe examined her. "That doesn't sound like a task for a girl, alone."

"My father was ill, and I took his place."

Roe leaned forward, studying her face. "Is he an idiot?"

"Papa is not an idiot." She stomped her foot. "He's a respected and admired man in Darrow Falls."

Roe crossed his arms and studied her. "Don't they know you're missing?"

She examined a scab on her palm. "I left a note."

"A note?" Chauncy softened his voice. "You didn't speak with them in person about your plans?"

Jules fought tears. "No, I didn't want them to stop

me, but now I'm afraid they might worry."

Roe handed her his kerchief. There was more to the story, but Jules didn't share it. Jessica Mackinnon was a tigress who could silence a man with a steely gaze or a sharp retort, but Jules Beecher was a vulnerable kitten. How could two sisters be so different?

She wiped her cheeks. "If I could leave the boat for a little while to send a telegram, I promise to come back."

Chauncy withdrew paper from his desk and shoved an inkwell toward her. "Write your message, and I'll have Roe take it to Western Union."

Had he been reduced to an errand boy? Chauncy may have his heart strings tugged by a few tears from a helpless female, but he was made of tougher hide. "While I'm at it, why don't I run some errands for the princess?" Sarcasm dripped from every word. "I can replace the items Edna Stall stole."

"A thief is on my boat?" Chauncy demanded.

"No, Edna shared a room with me last night at the Smuggler's Cave. She took my belongings and left without paying the rent."

Chauncy unlocked a drawer. "What do you need?"

Jules reached into her skirt pocket and withdrew the bag he had seen earlier. It smelled of lavender but instead of aromatic herbs, the sachet contained coins. "She stole your purse?"

"Yes, but I hid some of my money." Jules emptied the coins into her hand. "I have money for the telegram, and I can do without the cloak and hat."

"With your skin?" Chauncy stared at her face. "You'll need something to protect you from the sun and something to keep you warm in this cold weather. What

76

else do you need?"

Jules touched her braid. "A brush and combs to style my hair."

Roe grabbed the pen from her hand and a second sheet of paper. He began to make a list. He dipped the pen in the inkwell and paused. "Anything else, Princess?"

Jules steadied her breath, clutching the kerchief in her fist. "I need stockings. One pair will do."

"Don't forget handkerchiefs." He added the item to his list, blew on the wet ink, and folded the missive. He handed her the pen. "You're going to want to keep your message home short. Western Union charges per letter."

"How much will everything cost?" She felt the bills hidden in her corset.

"Don't worry about the money." Chauncy reassured her with a warm smile. "We'll work something out."

Roe snorted. Chauncy would surrender every penny of profits to the girl, the old softy.

Jules dipped the pen and took a deep breath before penning her note.

On boat to Louisville. Chauncy LaDonte is captain. In good hands. Home soon with cousins.

Juliet.

She wrote in a delicate neat script whereas his was bold and erratic. She showed her message to Chauncy. "Do you think this will keep them from worrying?"

"They'll worry, but it will reassure them." Chauncy handed the note to Roe. "We'll guarantee you return home safely."

We'll guarantee? He hadn't agreed to the role of

nanny. Roe read the salutation. "Dr. Sterling Beecher?"

"Papa is the doctor in Darrow Falls. Everyone depends on him. I shouldn't have borrowed his buggy, but I broke the wheel in our other buggy racing Paddy, and I wanted to go to the party."

Party. He should have known she was a spoiled debutante. "Who's Paddy?"

"My cousin Padrick Donovan." Jules sighed. "He sprained his ankle, and I had to attend the party without him."

"It must have been embarrassing to arrive without an escort."

Jules smiled wide. "I like going to parties with Paddy. He knows how to have a good time. If he was well, he would have come with me." She frowned. "Nevertheless, I'm determined to find my cousins and take them home."

"Do you know where they are?"

She blew her nose with his kerchief. "Laurel Holler."

"That's about a day's travel from Louisville," Chauncy said. "I'm sure we can spare Roe for a couple of days."

Chauncy looked at him to volunteer his services. He steeled himself against any sympathy. She was a spoiled child who deserved her father's wrath. Now she had compounded a minor error in judgment by running away from home on a fool's errand. And he was being forced to play rescuing knight to her damsel in distress role.

"Oh, no," Jules said. "This is something I have to do to prove myself."

"It could be dangerous to travel alone," Chauncy

said.

"I'll trust in the kindness of strangers."

Roe waved the list at her. "How has that been working out for you so far?"

"Maybe Edna needed my things more than I did. Papa dedicated his life to helping others. I wouldn't be his daughter if I didn't follow his example."

Chauncy leaned forward. "Did Dr. Beecher teach your sisters their medical skills?"

"All of us helped Papa. I go on calls with him when I'm needed. I also help my sister Jennifer with midwife duties. Mama says you shouldn't waste your talents."

"I agree." Chauncy looked at Roe.

He wasn't wasting his talents. He was learning new ones. He waved the notes in the air. Come along, Princess. You have work to do, and I have errands to run."

Chauncy frowned. "Why are you calling her princess?"

"Oh, I don't mind," Jules said. "It's better than Juliet."

Chauncy raised a brow. "Why don't you like your name?"

"Old Sourpuss makes fun of it."

Roe snickered. "Sourpuss?"

"Lara Herbruck. She's been teasing me since I was a little girl about being named Juliet. She would say, *O Romeo, Romeo, wherefore art thou, Romeo*. Then she would name a boy as my Romeo and taunt him to kiss me." She made a face that illustrated her displeasure. Did she still hate to be kissed? "The latest one was Matt Wheeler." Jules shuddered. "She spread horrible lies about us."

"Why didn't you punch her in the nose?"

Her eyes widened. "I abhor violence."

Roe laughed. "Are you sure Jessica Mackinnon is your sister?"

Her eyes narrowed. "How do you know Jess?"

"I met her at Williamsport waiting to cross the Potomac River and escape General Meade after the battle of Gettysburg. She beat a Texan in a shooting contest."

"I remember Miss Jenny said Jessica won a five-dollar gold piece in a shooting contest," Chauncy said.

"Jess likes challenges. Old Sourpuss was afraid of her. That's why she picked on me." Jules sagged her shoulders. "I don't mind my fan and reticule being stolen by Edna, but my brother-in-law, Blake, gave me a five-dollar gold piece for saving his life."

Roe appraised her delicate figure. "You saved his life?"

"My sister Colleen did all the work." She sighed. "I fetched some towels."

"Towels?" Roe leaned against Chauncy's desk. "How did you save his life with towels?"

"They stopped the bleeding until Cassie could fetch Papa." She squared her shoulders. "I've learned a lot since then about medicine."

"What was he bleeding from? Someone punch him in the nose?"

Jules frowned. She didn't appreciate his humor. "The Cassell brothers tried…"

Chauncy placed his hand near his heart. "Cassell brothers? You're too young to know them."

"I remember when they came to Darrow Falls,"

Jules said. "Even then I knew Buck and Clyde Cassell were bad men. They captured Tess and beat Noah. Jem told us how they beat Logan."

Chauncy grimaced. "I'm sorry about that. We thought he was a spy."

"They forgave *you*," Jules said. "Then the Cassells wanted to steal the Confederate gold Blake…"

"Miss Jules, I was in the Confederacy," Chauncy said. "We didn't have any gold."

"When Blake sold his hotel in Memphis, the buyer paid him in Confederate gold. Only it was from a stolen Southern payroll, and they were using Blake to smuggle it past Union sentries. The Cassell brothers wanted it for themselves and shot Blake when he was on the *Irish Rose*."

"I sympathize with your brother-in-law. I had nothing but trouble from the Cassell brothers when they served in my regiment. I underestimated what evil they were capable of, or I would have been more vigilant." Chauncy put his hand over his chest. "They shot me and left me for dead after I caught them stealing our payroll, and it was only paper currency."

Jules touched his arm. "Jessica told us you were in the hospital for a year."

"Theo took care of me," Chauncy said. "In return, I taught him to read and write."

"I'm glad you survived," Jules said. "You're practically family."

"Miss Jessie said Buck was dead," Chauncy said. "Shot in Blake's hotel in Washington City. She said Clyde escaped through a window. You tell Blake I'm grateful he rid this world of one Cassell brother. Maybe the war ended Clyde's life as well."

Jules nodded and opened the door. "I better get to work." She turned to Roe. "Thank you for sending my telegram." She looked at his kerchief. "I'll wash this and return it."

Chapter Eight

Jules hurried across the deck and down the stairs. She hadn't told Chauncy about Clyde being alive. Her mother's words of warning about reacting overly dramatically to a situation silenced her tongue. Clyde had stared at her, knew her name, but had no grievance against her. Besides, she didn't want to worry Chauncy. The man had suffered enough violence in the war and at the hands of the Cassell brothers. She would not repay his immeasurable kindness with a childish fear. He had been relieved to know Blake had killed Buck. Only Blake wasn't the shooter.

She grabbed an apron from a hook on the wall and joined the other women in the dining salon. Because she was late to arrive, Jules had the work station the greatest distance from the galley. The others were nearly done. She grabbed her stack of linens and began covering her tables and arranging the utensils.

She finished her last table when guests began arriving. Jules and the other women reported to the galley. Floyd had been a cook in the Confederate Army. He knew how to make a lot of food from simple ingredients in a short amount of time. Guests had the choice of one menu item. Tonight, the meal consisted of split biscuits topped with a mixture of chicken, carrots, celery, peas, and onions in a thick gravy.

Jules loaded a tray and headed for her tables. She

loaded the next tray with mugs of beer and returned for dinners until all her guests were served. She moved quickly, avoiding outstretched legs or friendly hands attempting to pat her backside when she leaned forward to serve.

A riverboat hauled hungry guests from east to west, north to south, and Jules was in the center of the storm. This was not her grandmother's dining room. Some of the men were veterans, evident from amputated limbs. Others were westerners wearing buckskin and in need of a bath several months ago. A few were dressed in frockcoats and top hats, but that didn't mean they were respectable. Fancy clothes couldn't disguise the uneducated speech or the lack of manners.

The guests didn't waste time with pleasantries or conversation. Once the food was placed on the table, they began eating. Even though she had placed a complete set of silverware at each seat, the men favored eating everything with a knife, licking the blade clean before retrieving another mouthful. The women shoveled the food into their gaping mouths with spoons, belching in appreciation. How they managed to find a pocket of air in their tightly laced corsets to release was a mystery.

Jules joined Lizzy by the bar, waiting for the bartender to fill more mugs with beer. She brushed back a few stray hairs, tucking them into a braid that formed a crown on her head. "How are you doing, Jules?"

"At my grandmother's inn, the guests take time to enjoy the meal."

"These folks behave like field hands, grabbing every morsel tossed their way before someone snatches it," Lizzy said. "Wait until after they're done eating.

Then the fun begins."

It didn't take long for Jules to discover what Lizzy meant. Once the men were done shoving food into their mouths, they filled their cheeks with shredded tobacco. The brown leaves produced a nasty dark juice. Instead of swallowing, the men spat it. Although spittoons were located at regular intervals, the men ignored them, choosing to stain the floor or worse, the ladies' dresses.

Jules was hit more than once.

"They think it's a game," Lizzy said when Jules stopped to examine a large stain on the bottom of her long apron.

"A nasty game."

"It's our turn to eat," Lizzy said. "We better grab a bite." They entered the galley kitchen. A small rectangular table marred with knife marks and stains from preparing food was near the door. A couple of chairs were shoved underneath, and clean plates were stacked on top. A pot of the chicken and vegetables was on the stove.

Floyd removed a tray of biscuits fresh from the oven. "Are you hungry?"

Babs grabbed a plate. "Starving."

Floyd placed two biscuits on her plate and heaped a ladle of food on top. He served the others, and they ate in the dining hall at an empty table. Jules placed a napkin on her lap.

Rita snorted as she tucked her napkin between the buttons on her bodice. "You won't find a man with manners or respect for women in this crowd. Go home to your parlor beaus and marry one of them, Princess."

Jules took a bite. "I don't want to marry any of them."

The others studied her. "Why not?"

"I don't love any of them. Besides, I can't imagine leaving home for what they offer."

"None of them rich enough for you, Princess?"

"The rich ones are the worst. They brag about their accomplishments even though most of them inherited their wealth. They only want a wife to decorate their arm at social events. When they describe the future they envision, it doesn't include my hopes and dreams."

Rita wiped her mouth. "When does any man consider a woman's opinion? I'm lucky if he remembers my name. Don't count on a man to be anything but a disappointment."

"My pa loved my ma," Babs said. "He worked hard for us. Too hard. He was kilt when a tree fell on him. Ma said he was distracted 'cause word had come my brother had died. Then my other brother died. All I've known is death, but I'd like to have some love in my life. Is that too much to expect?"

"I think any man would be lucky to have you for a wife," Jules said.

"Then you're not against all marriage?" Lizzy glanced around, her gaze pausing at the captain's table. Roe was missing. Lizzy had weathered her past better than Rita. She was the sweet to Rita's sour. "Unless you have a babe on the way, there's no reason to rush into marriage. Learn from my mistake. It's better to be a spinster than marry the wrong man."

"My sisters are happy in their marriages, but they chose carefully," Jules said. "Besides love, they looked for respect and equality."

"Equality?" Rita demanded. "In marriage? It doesn't exist. Even if you don't have to wait on him hand and foot, a woman always gives more."

"Rita is right. I was a good wife, but there was no pleasing my husband," Lizzy said. "He didn't notice me unless food wasn't on the table or his clothes weren't washed. Then there was a slap or kick for my mistake."

Babs frowned. "You never loved him?"

"I did at the beginning, but I barely knew him when I married him. I didn't know about his temper or how sensitive he was to criticism. I made the mistake of telling him he should change his shirt because it had a stain on it. He flew into a rage. I didn't know what to do. When I did nothing, he became bolder. After a couple of black eyes and a split lip, I stopped loving him."

"Mama says love can grow or die," Jules said. "Someone's cruelty can crush any tender feelings."

"I kept telling myself I deserved it," Lizzy said. "The pastor said I needed to be a good, obedient wife and lead by example like the Good Book preaches, but I gave a sigh of relief when I no longer had to play that futile role. You can't make someone else happy. You have to find your own happiness." She smiled. "Then you can share it."

Jules turned to Rita. "Did you find your happiness?"

"I'm still searching." Rita leaned forward. "I left the brothel after my sister was murdered. I was so angry, no one dared to stop me. My rage turned to self-destruction when I failed to find her killer. I followed any man who paid for my drinks and offered me a warm bed to share. Then one of them said I should talk to Madame Durieux. She was a spiritualist and claimed she could talk to the dead."

Babs gasped. "Could she?"

"Everything about her was a lie." Rita laughed. "She wasn't even French. Her father had been a traveling medicine man and used her in his cons. But she was clever and married well. After her husband's death, she used her social connections to maintain her wealth. Do you know the difference between a half-dollar prostitute and a hundred-dollar courtesan?"

"No, what?" Babs asked.

"Presentation," Rita said. "Put a woman in a beautiful gown in a fancy parlor, and a man will pay a small fortune to peek beneath her skirt."

"You were a courtesan?" Jules dabbed her mouth as she finished eating. "How was that a good thing?"

"Madame Durieux taught me how to talk and dress to impress clients. I was in control not them," Rita stressed.

"Madame Durieux gave me a job," Lizzy said.

Jules gasped. "As a courtesan?"

"No, I made fancy French meals served with champagne or wine," Lizzy said.

"You know how to make French food?" Babs asked.

"It's all in the sauces. She called me Eliza in front of the guest and taught me a few French words. It was a game to Madame Durieux, and we played along."

Rita laughed. "Remember when that senator spoke French, and you didn't have a clue what he was saying?"

"I thought he was a colonel," Lizzy said. "Of course, he wasn't wearing anything when I delivered dinner."

"We had some impressive clientele during the war,

including officers and politicians," Rita said. "Madame Durieux only targeted men who had secrets to share."

Jules looked around for any eavesdroppers and whispered, "You were spies?"

"No," Rita laughed. "I said Madame Durieux was a spiritualist. We found out information she used to convince customers she could talk to the dead. You wouldn't believe some of the secrets men reveal when they're naked. It was a grand con. Better than anything her father did."

"She sounds like Dicken's character, Fagin," Jules said. "I don't think what you did was honest."

Lizzy laughed. "They make the laws in Washington City, but those who make them don't follow them."

"Madame Durieux opened our eyes to how the world ruled by the rich really worked. She also gave us a purpose," Rita said. "Even though I'd been in a brothel, I was ignorant of the seedier places that sprung up during the war. I thought most of the women worked the sheets by choice or were forced by family like my sister and me, but we found out differently."

Rita's face was grim and she choked on swallowed tears. She waved at Lizzy to continue.

"Demand for prostitutes was high toward the end of the war," Lizzy said. "Hooker had his own district off of Pennsylvania Avenue.

"Those places weren't small brothels that looked out for the women," she said. "They were warehouses of human flesh. The army hired people to go to New York City and offer jobs to young girls traveling alone from Europe. If they owed passage, they bought the debt. All of them were eager to work. Only the job wasn't sewing clothes or working as a maid like they were promised. Once they arrived in town, the owners beat them and starved them."

"They were kept prisoners, locked in their rooms." Rita's voice was hard and mechanical. "After a few dozen men have degraded you, you're willing to do anything to end the nightmare. Only opium makes you more desperate to do anything to satisfy your addiction. Dreams die in the red light district."

"But you still worked as a public woman," Babs said. "Was your dream dead?"

"It may appear like the same work, but it wasn't," Rita said. "My father and the brothel owners beat me down by saying I was worthless garbage, but Madame Durieux lifted me up. She was the first kind human being I had known besides my sister. She made me feel important. Then I met Lizzy, and we formed a partnership."

Lizzy took her hand. "And our lives were important. We saved a few girls."

"Saved?" The two women were grinning. "What do you mean?"

"A doctor would visit the brothels and check for pox," Lizzy said. "We would go as nurses."

"Didn't the doctor know you weren't nurses?"

"He was too busy receiving payment." Rita winked. "We talked to the girls in private and discovered which ones wanted out."

"We had a plan before we visited," Lizzy said. "We would tell them what to do, and we would whisk them to freedom."

"No one stopped you?"

"We used different cons," Rita said. "The best was

telling the owner the girl had smallpox and needed to be quarantined. Then we'd send a notice she died."

"There was quite an outbreak of smallpox in '64," Lizzy said.

"Then the real work began," Rita said. "A dozen baths never quite washes away the shame of having your body stolen. Madame Durieux was good at restoring their hearts. She gave them hope."

"We helped them find family or provided references so they could find legitimate work," Lizzy added. "But when the war ended, the brothels kept a few girls for the politicians and kicked the rest out. They were on their own. We helped as many as we could."

"Until the money ran out." Rita gave Lizzy a sly look. "Told you we should have kept some for ourselves."

"My generous heart." Lizzy patted her breast. "Madame Durieux moved to New York City. She invited us to join her, but con games don't last. We decided to blaze our own trail. We've been working the riverboats all summer."

"How are you making any money if you're not being paid?"

"Tips," Rita said. "Some gentlemen are extremely generous, especially when they're winning at the tables."

"What do you have to do for tips?" Babs asked.

Rita wiped her plate with the remaining piece of biscuit. "Nothing you don't want to. I ran into a man who was an old customer. You can give up that sort of life, but you can't escape it. Too many men have seen you naked. They think they own a part of you, but they're wrong. No one will ever own me again. I made it clear I wasn't for sale."

Jules helped Lizzy gather the plates from their table. The three women were as different as they could be. Rita was hard with a caustic sense of humor, yet she was loyal with a tender heart toward those like her. Lizzy was motherly, hard-working, and kept their spirits high. Babs was a poor girl trying to survive in a harsh world.

Even though she worked hard on the farm, Jules life was pampered compared to their dealings in the world. When she returned home, she would have to thank her parents for being ordinary. She never worried about food or clothing. And if she ever married, it would be a man of her choosing. She was blessed to be so lucky.

Theo joined them and removed his hat. "Miss Lizzy, I need to unlock your room so I can deliver a trunk."

Lizzy looked at the others. "Any of you expecting a trunk?" Their gazes rested on Jules, who shrugged.

"This trunk has belongings left behind by previous guests," Theo explained. "Captain LaDonte thought you could use them to…" He paused. "To supply-ment your wardrobe. Most folks dress up for the games."

"And what's wrong with my wardrobe?" Rita demanded.

Lizzy stood. "Your best dress has more mends and patches than you can count." She glanced down. "So has mine."

"I think it's wonderful you thought of us, Theo." Babs swished her skirt back and forth. "I only have this one dress."

He blushed under her admiration. "I hope you find something you like."

Lizzy removed the key from her bodice.

"I have a pass key," Theo said. "But the captain said I had to ask permission before entering a guest's room unless they were doing something illegal."

Lizzy nodded and returned her key to her bodice. "Put it inside. We'll be along when we finish washing all the dishes."

He nodded.

They gathered the remaining dirty dishes from the guest tables. Jules filled her tray and turned.

Roe walked toward the captain's table. He wore a dark frock coat and gray vest. The clothing was well made and accented his wide shoulders. His hair framed his comely features. He looked around and met her gaze. He frowned and joined Chauncy at his table where he deposited a package tied with string.

"He's not like these mischief-makers." Lizzy had her tray filled with plates. "But that handsome one has a dark shadow over him. You better find out what it is before you set your heart on him."

Jules shook her head. "Oh, I'm not in love with him."

"Too bad. That man could use some love."

Rita glided past her with a tray filled with empty mugs. "Maybe I'll offer him some later."

"No," Jules said. Why had she protested?

Rita jabbed her finger in her face. "You are in love with him."

"I barely know him."

"I've seen stupid plenty of times to recognize it. You can't stop staring at each other."

"Love can be a good thing," Lizzy said. "That spark of interest that grows and ignites into a flame. Just don't let it burn you."

Jules had never been in love with any man. How could she have such a strong affection for a stranger? Roe had been mean and teased her but not in a malicious way like Lara. His was more like a big brother. Did he think of her as a child? And what was the darkness Lizzy spoke of? He'd been nice to send her telegram and buy the items on her list to replace those stolen, and she needed to show her appreciation.

A few biscuits and a hearty serving of chicken remained in the pot. She filled a plate and added a mug of cold beer to her tray before heading for the captain's table.

Chapter Nine

Roe sat at the captain's table and pushed the package toward Chauncy. He was not going to deliver his purchases in person, especially in front of the other women. He didn't want anyone to know he'd been shopping. His family had never favored displays of affection, and Jules was a hugger, even in public. Although he wouldn't object to a private display of gratitude and imagined her young, soft body pressed against his.

When he had described Jules to the women in the stores, they had been eager to help him choose the items on his list. His pockets were lighter due to their expertise. She should be grateful. With some luck, the sheet on his bed wouldn't remain clean tonight.

Chauncy was studying him. Were his thoughts so transparent? He needed to keep his plan to seduce Jules from his former commanding officer. He was protective of the girl and wouldn't approve of his actions. "Do you know there are more than a dozen types of lady's stockings?" He lowered his voice. "The woman at the store wanted to know if she needed garters. How do I know if she needs garters?"

Chauncy chewed on his unlit cigar. "Let's see what you bought." He tugged on the string holding the paper wrapping.

"I spent a small fortune," Roe said. "That woman is

trouble."

Chauncy unwrapped the package. "It's about time a woman gave you trouble."

Trouble. He'd have to be careful. Jules had parents, and her sisters had husbands. He knew Morgan Mackinnon. He didn't want to be on the receiving end of his highlander wrath. He should seek out a woman who wouldn't mind a short-term dalliance and prevent him from making a mistake. This strange desire that had taken hold would pass when Jules left. Then he could resume a celibate life. Or not. He searched the room for a woman who could meet his needs. Even though a few women acknowledged his perusal, none of them stirred him to action. None of them was a strawberry blond with blue eyes that aroused the masculine response normal in a man of his age.

Jules placed a plate before Roe. She leaned over his shoulder and whispered in his ear. "I was getting worried you wouldn't return in time. This is the last of the food."

Roe lifted a fork with shaky fingers. Her warm breath on his skin and her tenderly spoken words had destroyed any vow of ignoring her. "I had to pillage the village for your loot, Princess."

Chauncy spread the paper wrapping to display the purchases.

"Silk stockings." Jules grabbed the pair and rubbed the expensive fabric against her cheek. "Simple cotton would have been enough." She reached for a blue enamel comb. "And these are lovely."

"Your cloak and bonnet are being delivered. I never saw more bonnets in my life. It would have been simpler to take the straw hat off the mule in the street than to narrow the choices to one."

He had meant his words to be harsh, but he choked on any reprimand when she wrapped her arms around his neck, her face against his cheek. Her nearness was unsettling. He craved the physical contact that had been withheld during his life. His father, school masters, and the army had strictly controlled his behavior and any interaction with women. Working for Chauncy had given him a taste of unfettered freedom by comparison, but he didn't socialize with the guests. Until Jules, none of them had piqued his interest. The last thing he wanted was a clinging female, but all words eluded him as he inhaled the scent of her. The dark experiences of the war vanished like distant memories. "Would you keep them for me until I finish the dishes? I won't be long."

Roe nodded. She kissed his cheek and whispered in his ear, "I love what you bought." Her lips were inches from his, but before he could decide whether to kiss her, she was gone, the scent of her lingering on his clothes after she departed.

He turned to Chauncy. "What happened?"

Chauncy removed the stockings Jules had left draped on Roe's shoulder and placed them with the other items on the paper wrapping. "You made some wise purchases."

Roe stared at Jules as she sashayed to the kitchen, leaving him dizzy with watching. "Did I buy her?"

"No," Chauncy said. "My name was in that telegram. We are her protectors, Roe. Remember that when this salon is filled tonight with every reprobate known to man."

"If she's the lamb among the wolves, why do I feel

like I was fleeced?"

He patted him on the shoulder. "Listen to your heart, boy. It won't betray you."

Roe waved his fork at Chauncy. "Did you play matchmaker with Morgan and Miss Jessie?"

"No, they were already in love by the time I met them."

"Well, don't try anything with me." Roe stabbed the flaky biscuit on his plate. "The last thing I need is a wife."

"A wife isn't a burden," Chauncy said. "She's a partner. Someone to share your life with."

"I doubt she would embrace life on a riverboat, and I don't intend to return to practicing medicine."

"She'd make a good nurse."

"She'd keep me awake at night." Roe paused, his mouth open to take a bite. His words echoed in the silence that followed.

Chauncy's eyes widened.

"I meant with worry." He popped the bite into his mouth and chewed.

Chauncy chuckled. "That's what I thought you meant."

After dinner Roe strolled along the deck, enjoying the crisp fall air and the pink and blue skyline reflected in the water as the sun set to create a breathtaking sight that only nature could offer. The lapping of gentle waves on the hull of the boat created a rhythmic pattern that echoed in a quiet beat to the classical song played by the piano player inside the dining hall.

Roe needed fresh air. The image of Jules Beecher in his bed wouldn't disappear. He had prided himself on self-control with women until Jules arrived. How long did a man make love to a woman? As a doctor, others expected him to know the answers, and he'd been embarrassed to ask and expose his ignorance. Kissing was involved and touching. Then undressing and more touching. He was perspiring. A man could perform the basic mechanics with a stranger, but he wanted to impress Jules if the chance arose. That required more than a perfunctory performance. One of his medical books might have advice. He needed to research the subject.

His only experiences with a woman had been a war widow who had reassured him his biological functions worked to maximum potential. She had enjoyed their romps as much as he had before he graduated from medical school and left town. That had been months ago, and he had controlled any needs to seek out the brothels and desperate women in Cincinnati or Louisville until Jules had arrived and reminded him he was a young man who craved physical coupling. One without any connections, complications, or commitment.

Lanterns with etched glass casings were fastened to the exterior post to light the pathway, but in the shadows ahead, a woman leaned against the railing, staring at the colorful river as the final rays of the sunset faded. She was alone. Boldness would be his best weapon. It would hide his nervousness. "You shouldn't be out here by yourself. A man might take you in his arms and kiss you."

She turned. He expected outrage at his bold proposition or a seductive acquiescence. Huge blue eyes stared at him in surprise. "Roe?"

It was Jules. The woman he had been dreaming of

and yet was off limits. Did he defy Chauncy and bed Jules against his orders? Years of obedience overrode any lustful desires. "I thought you were someone else."

"Oh." She seemed disappointed. She stepped into the light of a lantern, and his breath caught in his throat. All words vanished. Her other gowns had hinted at her figure but had not displayed all her charms. The bodice on this gown was cut low to display a fullness that challenged the confines of the scant material. A deep breath and her secrets would be revealed. "That's a lovely gown."

Jules touched the edge of her bodice, her fingertips brushing against the swell of bare flesh. "It's a bit daring. Theo gave us a trunk filled with clothing discarded by former passengers. Rita said I would earn a pocketful of tips with this dress. I hope I can repay you for the items you purchased."

The creamy expanse of pink flesh flowed in seductive curves. They were mammary glands, but his medical analysis wasn't convincing his emotional reaction. He gripped the railing to prevent his hands from exploring the soft loveliness displayed before him.

"Don't you love them?"

Her breasts? The sight had already gone from producing warm feelings to a pounding reaction.

"I think the color is perfect."

They had a lovely pink hue. A blush. Would her skin be as soft and warm as he imagined?

"How did you know blue was my favorite color?"

Blue? He raised his gaze from her breasts to her eyes. "What are you talking about?"

"The combs you bought." She touched a comb that pulled her hair back in soft waves to the crown of her head. Curls cascaded down her back with one stray curl falling across the wide décolletage of her gown and resting on the fullness of her breast. "Where were your thoughts?"

His dream had her in his cabin, his hands removing the combs, her dress, the silk stockings…maybe not them. From the glimpse he had earlier, her legs were firmly curved, leading an intimate path to the crown jewels. His hand itched to explore her body and kiss a blush to her flesh. His heart was pounding, and he gripped the railing. He was battling for self-control and losing. "It's a beautiful gown." Roe struggled to string more than two words together.

"I wonder who left them behind." Jules twirled as the skirt flowed in a circle of color. "Babs didn't have any other gown but the one she was wearing. She was so grateful to Theo, she kissed him."

He struggled to concentrate. "What? She kissed Theo?"

"I think she likes him."

"Theo?"

"Everyone deserves someone to love and be loved," Jules said. "Especially someone as sweet and kind as Theo. Do you know if he's ever had a sweetheart?"

"He's never spoken of one," Roe said.

Jules bit her bottom lip. "It isn't against the rules, is it?"

"What?"

"Theo and Babs?"

"No, but romances aboard any boat tend to be short-lived. At some point one of the lovers disembarks." He frowned. "And Theo is loyal to the

101

captain. You should warn Babs not to set her cap for him."

"A broken heart is better than no heart."

Was she talking about him? "You've lived a sheltered life. You don't know some of the darkness that war creates."

"I've seen the soldiers who have returned. Many of them still suffer from fighting in the war."

Jules saw the victors returning to homes and families. She hadn't witnessed the destruction of the South. She wasn't among the thousands starving the final year of the war. She hadn't seen the cripples in the hospitals and veteran homes. "What do you know about suffering? You spent the war playing with dolls." His words were bitter, and he spat them out.

She stared at the water lapping against the side of the boat. "Broken dolls need extra care."

He snorted. "Isn't it easier to throw away broken dolls?"

She faced him. "Not if you love them." Her tone was serious and concerned.

"You're not talking about dolls."

"Veterans filled our parlor waiting to see Papa. Some of them had shattered bodies, but others had lost something else."

"Their minds," Roe answered. "I saw it in Richmond at the end of the war. Vacant stares, nightmares, screams that chilled a man to the bone."

"The men became better with time. They learned to laugh again."

He snorted. "Show me something funny in this somber world."

Jules pointed at a couple boarding. "What about

them?" The man wore a mustard suit with a black plaid crisscrossing the fabric in a bold pattern. He escorted a woman in a white gown splattered with embroidered green leaves and pink flowers. Her hat had a large peacock feather flowing upward and bobbing with every step.

"I almost bought you that hat." The corner of his mouth twitched. Her reaction was what he had expected. From what he had seen of her wardrobe, Jules had taste.

Jules narrowed her eyes. "You're joking."

"Perhaps, but I don't see you wearing the bonnet I purchased for you. Chauncy said it would protect your nose from peeling."

She pointed to the crescent in the sky. "I don't need protection from the moon."

Was that the real reason? "I've never bought anything for a woman. You can return the items if you don't like them."

She touched his arm, and his body reacted in a wave of muscular contractions. "I love it. And the cloak is beautiful. Everything is nicer than what Edna stole. They must be expensive. I don't know how I'll ever repay you."

He knew a way. His resolve not to kiss her fled as the moon disappeared behind a cloud. The corner was dark. He pressed her back into its shadows. She stumbled, and he caught her, pulling her tightly against his chest. She gasped, and he took advantage of the opening.

He brushed his lips against the smooth flesh of her mouth, suckling the fullness, and sealing his doom. His lips covered hers in a possessive claim, drawing her close. His tongue invaded her mouth, tickling and teasing her response.

She stiffened initially but relaxed as he coaxed her into unfamiliar territory. She kissed him, a tentative tasting. He fought the urge to rush his conquest, allowing her to set the pace. Her lips tasted his, and she pulled him deeper into their tender trap. Thunder roared in Roe's ears, a warning or the primeval cry of man seeking a mate. She shivered in a spasm of delight.

"If you're done playing, we'd like to start the games inside," Chauncy said from the walkway.

Roe turned, blocking Jules. "Of course, Captain."

Jules stepped into the light, an embarrassed look upon her face. Her rosy breast rose and fell with rapid breaths. She touched her fingertips to her bruised lips. "I'm sorry. I don't know what happened." She hurried past Chauncy.

"A moment," Chauncy said, preventing Roe from following.

After she disappeared inside, Roe turned to the captain.

"I am a surrogate father to that girl. I know you're a doctor, but that examination was not for any medical reasons."

"You were the one who pointed out we were star-crossed lovers. I thought you wanted me to court her."

"Courting involves hand holding and reading poetry under a chaperone's supervision. It does not involve removing her tonsils."

Roe laughed. "She has beautiful tonsils."

"Leave the girl alone." His tone was harsh. He saw no humor in Roe's actions.

"She owes me. Nearly fifty dollars for the clothes I

bought."

"She can repay in a different way," Chauncy said. "From what I remember of Miss Jenny's letters, her baby sister sings. I was going to ask her to perform."

He looked at the stage. "You can barely hear the piano player when this room is full. Are you sure she can carry a tune?"

"We'll wait until the audience is drunk. They won't mind even if she sounds like a cat with its tail being stepped upon."

"Do you think they'll toss coins on the stage to shut her up?"

"If she doesn't earn enough to pay her debt, I'll cover it," Chauncy said. "No more playing doctor."

Roe had made the decision to quit medicine, but being ordered not to practice his profession, even romantically, didn't sit well. He saluted. "Understood, sir."

He marched inside. The chandeliers and sconces were lit in the dining salon, giving the room a festive feel. The linens had been removed and sent to the laundry in town. They would pick them up on the return trip. Games were easier to play on the smooth wooden surface, and the tables had been separated for men in the outer area, and the women near the stage to avoid the smoke and spit. If a man didn't have a cigar burning in his mouth, he chewed. Roe had never acquired either habit. The ether used during surgeries was flammable, and his one taste of tobacco had left him sick. His job aboard the *Jenny Lee* required him to be sober. His life lacked any vices. Chauncy could overlook his feeble attempt to seduce one innocent woman.

The memory of her kiss burned and realization

dawned. It wasn't the first time Jules had kissed a man. Anger replaced lust. The chit was experienced, and he was going to find out how she had acquired the knowledge. And from whom. Innocent indeed!

Theo had set up the games, and the waitresses and crew took their designated spots.

The ladies preferred rondo, where letters on cards were used to create words. Each letter was worth a certain point. Keno was also popular with players choosing winning numbers. Jules job was to select balls with a number painted on them from a cage she spun before each selection. Lizzy supervised a faro card game. Rita handled the roulette card game. Babs ran the chuck-a-luck game with an hour-glass cage and three dice.

At the men's tables, games of euchre, seven-up, old sledge, and poker were played. Crew members with enough skill dealt the cards. Roe kept the games honest when possible. Cheating was common, and more than one accusation started a scuffle. He would reveal the gun on his hip and hope the players settled down.

Rita, Lizzy, and Babs wore formal gowns like Jules, but none of them held a candle to the strawberry blond in the shimmering golden dress. Roe wasn't the only man mesmerized by her appearance. A few men had to be reminded to play their cards. Roe's hand rested on the handle of his revolver. He didn't like the way two men at the table nearest the door stared at Jules. If they didn't cool their lust, he might have to threaten them the way Chauncy had warned him about his earlier actions.

He was staking his claim on the woman, and he wasn't going to share. If Jules was innocent, he would heed Chauncy's words and protect her. If she was experienced, as he guessed, he would suggest a payment for her debts they would both enjoy.

Roe joined Jules to collect the money from her game. "You look like you're having fun."

Her eyes sparkled, and her voice had a lilting quality of excitement. "I love playing games."

Why did he convert everything she said to images in the bedroom? "I enjoy games, too. Especially in the dark." Her cheeks blushed.

She handed over the velvet pouch containing the fees to play. "Was Chauncy upset?"

"Why do you ask?"

"He looked angry when he caught us canoodling."

"That had nothing to do with you."

"He's been so nice to my sisters in the past, I wouldn't want him to be disappointed in my behavior."

"Do you always want to please others?"

"Only people I love." She studied him. "Don't you want people to like you?"

"I've always been a bit of a loner."

"All you have to do to make friends is to be friendly."

Her circle of friends had to be enormous. She didn't consider anyone a stranger. "Try not to be too friendly tonight. We have a rowdy crowd." He placed his palm on his revolver.

She covered his hand with her own. Sparks flew so strongly from her touch, he worried the gun would go off. "Have you ever shot a man?"

He managed one word. "No."

A feathery eyebrow rose in disbelief. "Not even in the war?"

He emptied the coins into a leather pouch and returned the empty bag. "I was an orderly."

Her luscious lips rounded as she considered his remark. "You had to collect the wounded from the field?"

He tugged on his frock coat, making sure it covered his trousers. "I saw a great number of broken dolls, Princess. Only I had to throw too many of them away."

Jules touched his sleeve as he turned. "Think about how many you saved."

Chapter Ten

Jules and her co-workers took turns serving drinks, and Theo ran the games in their absence. Rita was finishing her shift and flirted with the men as she filled their empty mugs. She avoided their wandering hands, shifting nimbly out of their grasps.

"Be careful," Theo warned when it was her turn. "They're in a lively mood."

Jules covered her gown with an apron, grabbed a pitcher of beer in each hand, and headed across the floor to the tables where men were calling for more alcohol.

Most of them looked as if they had enough, but she filled their glasses and collected their coins.

"Join me, pretty lady." A man with a closely clipped mustache growled in a low bass. He had substantial winnings in front of him, and by the look of his suit, he didn't count on luck for his wealth. The cuffs of his white shirt were trimmed in lace, and his cufflinks were made from a shiny black stone with a small diamond in the corner. He put his cigar in his mouth and pulled her onto his lap. Jules put the empty pitchers on the table and tugged at his hands.

He laughed at her futile attempt. "Maybe this will change your mind?" He thrust a coin into her cleavage.

Jules screamed. Not a dainty yip of protest but an ear-splitting shout into his ear. "Hands off!"

He dropped her on the floor, and she fell back, her skirt flying upward with the help of her stiff crinoline.

Roe offered her a hand. "I see you're wearing the silk stockings I purchased."

"Does this girl belong to you?" the gambler asked.

"Yes." Roe growled between clenched teeth.

"I don't belong to any man." Jules retrieved the coin from between her breasts and smacked it on the table.

Roe snatched the coin.

"That belongs to me." The gambler pointed to his ear. "She made me deaf."

"You must have been deaf before she screamed or you would have heard her protesting your vulgar behavior."

The gambler pointed at his coin. "But why should I pay you for a little fun?"

"Since you enjoyed a view of her stockings, you can help pay for them." He put the money in his pocket. "Toward your debt, Princess. Now the captain would like to hear you sing."

"Sing?" the gambler demanded. "She'll empty the room if she sings like she screams."

Roe removed the silver coin from his pocket and placed it on the table. "I'll wager no one leaves."

The gambler matched his coin as did others at the table.

Jules looked at the money and turned to Roe. "You haven't heard me sing."

He leaned close and whispered, "Am I going to be broke?"

She could smell shaving soap and a faint musky scent with his closeness. The memory of his kiss stirred an unfamiliar desire. When other men kissed her, she was glad it ended and quickly forgot her suitor, but Roe piqued her curiosity to discover more. She had abandoned propriety when she had returned his amorous kisses with a sweet abandonment she had never shown. Did he think her an easy conquest? Did she care? She studied his lips, lingering and willing his touch. She took matters into her own hands and kissed him on the mouth but retreated hastily before it blossomed into more.

A dark eyebrow shot up in surprise. "What is that for?"

Roe was a cautious man, but he had kissed her, invoking Chauncy's wrath and now was taking a chance on her singing abilities. "For believing without hearing."

She headed for the stage. The piano man had been playing Stephen Foster tunes. Foster had died in January of 1864, and his songs had grown in popularity. *My Old Kentucky Home* had been an abolitionist song but had gained acceptance on both sides during and after the war. They would dock in Louisville tomorrow. The piano player suggested she sing it. By the chorus, the noisy gamblers had quieted.

"Weep no more, my lady. Oh, weep no more, today. We will sing one song for the old Kentucky home. For the old Kentucky home far away."

Her sisters said she sang before she talked, and Jules loved to perform. While Lara Herbruck accused her of showing off, she used her voice to express her deepest emotions in the lilting notes. A hint of sorrow coated the silky sound as she shared Foster's sad song.

Roe stood by the gambler's table, staring at her as

if no one else existed in the room. A slight smile began to form on his lips and increased until his teeth showed in his handsome face. She smiled back as if they shared a secret. No one else existed in the room but them.

When she finished the song, the room erupted in applause. The gambler gathered the coins and bills on the table and shoved them into Roe's hand. Others tossed coins onto the stage.

Roe dumped the coins into an empty beer mug and moved among the tables, accepting money for her performance as he moved to the stage. He handed her the full container.

"Do I keep the money?"

"Those gamblers think I conned them, but you could earn a living on stage."

"No one ever paid me to sing before." She reached inside the mug and withdrew a handful of coins. "I'll only need a few dollars for my trip." She handed him the mug. "You keep the rest until my debt is paid in full."

Roe took the payment. "Do you feel like singing another tune?"

She laughed. "I can sing all night."

Jules sang *Why, No One to Love?* Crewmembers and others aboard the boat who had not been in the salon, gathered in the doorways or outside on the walkway to listen.

"No one to love! No one to love! Why, no one to love? What have you done in this beautiful world that you're sighing of no one to love?"

Theo removed his cap and gathered coins from those too far away to toss them on the stage. Roe joined Jules on stage and took her hand. "Princess Jules," he announced as the audience applauded.

Jules curtseyed. "Do you want me to sing another song?"

"You have a voice that makes the angels jealous, but unfortunately, the men don't gamble when you sing. Why don't you sing again tomorrow?"

"But I need to head for Laurel Holler as soon as possible."

"You can't travel at night, and we won't arrive in Louisville until evening. Part of your agreement for fare included serving dinner and entertaining the guests with games tomorrow night." He took the money Theo had gathered and added it to a second mug. "It looks like your debt is paid in full with plenty left over for yourself."

"I'll need the money to pay for my return passage. I can't expect the children to wait tables for food and board."

Once the games ended, Jules helped the other women gather the dirty mugs remaining on the tables. They split up the duties of washing, drying, and putting everything away.

Lizzy took a mug from her. "How are you holding up?"

"I could drop right now. How are Babs and Rita doing?"

"Babs is teetering, but Rita caught her second wind. She found a gentleman friend."

Jules followed Lizzie's gaze to Rita who was talking to the gambler who had placed the bet with Roe. Rita stood close to his side, her hand resting on his shoulder. His hand encircled her waist, and she didn't remove it. "Rita won't be sharing our room tonight."

"Does she know him?"

Lizzy winked. "She will by morning."

Jules bit her bottom lip. "After what she said in the room, I didn't think she would want to be intimate with a man, even by choice."

"But it is by choice," Lizzy said. "Rita enjoys a romp between the sheets with a man who treats her like a lady."

"I think I would resent marrying a man who has bed a great deal of women before me," Jules said.

"Men don't hesitate to demand a woman is a virgin before marrying her," Lizzy said. "But what happens after the honeymoon? Does her value suddenly decrease? Rita and I had to convince a lot of women they had worth, and it had nothing to do with what men or society demanded. Everyone has talent and special gifts. Would you marry a man who refused to allow you to sing?"

"No, I love to sing. To deny me my voice would be cruel."

"Marriage doesn't always end in happiness," Lizzy said. "Some think love is what goes on in the bedroom, but coupling becomes mechanical when a man pays and chooses from a menu. Love is wanting to spend time with someone in and out of bed."

Jules looked at the doorway. Roe was bidding the guests good-night. "My sister said you don't know if there is any passion until you kiss a man."

"Is Roe the first man to kiss you?"

"No." Jules shook her head. "Most of the men who kissed me, proposed marriage."

Lizzy didn't hide her surprise. "And you turned them all down?"

Jules nodded. "But Roe's kiss was different. It stirred the sort of reaction I see in my sisters when their husbands kiss them. Sometimes when they merely look at them. I didn't think passion would happen to me."

"Passion is a dangerous thing," Lizzy warned. "My husband was all charm and kindness when we were first married. Then he showed his true colors. Take your time choosing the man you have to spend the rest of your life with."

"I'm still not convinced I want to marry. Do you think if a woman is discreet, she could have a lover instead of a husband?"

Lizzy raised an eyebrow. "Your sisters all have children?"

"Or they're expecting."

"There's your answer. When you're fertile, you can't risk bringing a baby into the world without a name and money."

Jules shrugged. "I'm not much of a suffragette."

"Being a suffragette doesn't mean being single and working. It means having the choice to do what makes you happy. That includes marriage."

"What would make you happy, Lizzy?"

"I want a man who talks to me and listens. A man who looks at me and sees me. A man who wants to be with me for the rest of his life. That's love to me."

"It sounds nice," Jules said. "Maybe you'll find someone."

Lizzy looked toward Chauncy, who was locking a strong box. "I wouldn't mind someone like the captain. What do you know about him?"

"His wife died early in the war. He has a tender heart, especially toward women. Don't hurt him,

Lizzy."

"I won't," she promised.

The tables were cleared, the dishes washed, and blankets handed out for a fee to the men who claimed a space on the floor. They were luckier than the ones sleeping on the open deck, especially with the cold night air or if it rained.

Lizzy and Jules joined Chauncy at the bar. Roe was standing guard, his hand on his gun as Chauncy gathered the strong box and his hat.

"You ladies can call it a night." Chauncy looked around. "Where is Rita and Babs?"

"Babs is talking to Theo." Jules nodded over her shoulder where the two young people were talking in low whispers.

"Must be a lovers' moon out," Chauncy said.

"Lovers' moon?" Lizzy smiled. "You sound like a romantic, Captain."

"I'm too old for such nonsense," he said.

"No one is too old for love," Lizzy said. "May we walk with you a bit? It will give Babs some time with Theo."

"I'm climbing stairs," he warned. "It's not as pleasant as a turn around the deck."

"I don't mind if Jules doesn't."

"I enjoy an evening walk before turning in," Jules said.

"A good portion of tonight's money is yours," Chauncy said. "When your sister said you could sing, she didn't exaggerate. Don't tell Miss Jenny, but your voice is the loveliest I've heard."

"I won't, but I will tell her about you naming your boat the *Jenny Lee*. She'll be flattered you honored her."

He showed her a photograph of Chauncy Theodora. "Does she sing?"

"She does," Jules said. "Although she makes up her own words to the tunes."

"I don't have much of a voice, but I like it when others sing. I don't know why, but it touches me here." He placed his hand over his heart.

"Music is like a secret language. It conveys feelings that cannot be put in words."

"There are some great writers who can do the same. I've always been fond of Shakespeare."

"So is my father," Jules said. "That's why he named me Juliet."

"What does Chauncy mean?" Lizzy asked.

"It's French for fortune or gambler." He looked around. "I have the gambler part accomplished. I'm waiting on the fortune."

"I believe you will be a great success," Lizzy said.

They reached the top deck. The captain's cabin and pilot house were near the rear. In between was a sea of bodies, some spread out sleeping, others talking softly in huddled groups, and a few couples were moving beneath blankets. "We have a crowded deck," Roe said.

"It's the cheapest way to travel," Chauncy said as they made their way to his cabin. He unlocked the door and entered.

Chauncy placed the strongbox on his desk and removed a kerchief knotted in a bundle. "Roe said this money belongs to you."

"Could you keep it safe for me until the return trip? I have enough for my journey to Laurel Holler, but I would feel better leaving the money I earned tonight with you."

Chauncy opened the kerchief and looked at Roe. "You took out the money she owed you?"

Roe nodded as he opened the door. "I'll escort the ladies to their room."

They retraced their steps, stopping on the second deck where Theo was waiting with Babs by their room.

"Sorry to keep you waiting." Lizzy unlocked the door.

"We didn't mind." Babs kissed Theo on the cheek. "Good-night."

Lizzy hesitated at the door. "You coming?"

Roe pulled Jules away. "We're going to take a stroll around the deck."

"But…"

Chapter Eleven

Roe captured her arm in his. He needed to talk some sense into her. Jules hadn't changed her mind about going to Laurel Holler. She was unaware of the dangers a woman alone could confront, even on a simple mission of retrieving a few children from a small town in Kentucky. "Why is it so important for you to find your cousins?"

"I have to prove I can be responsible."

"Did you forget to milk the family cow?"

She laughed. "No." She pulled away and leaned against the railing. "I almost killed Papa."

He sensed she was serious and didn't dismiss her remark as foolish, but he didn't agree with her assessment. Jules was incapable of committing any harm, let alone murder. Her nature was too gentle and sweet to hurt another human being even in her own defense. It made her vulnerable, and it also made him desperate in his desire to protect her. He leaned against the railing, next to her, his eyes forward, staring into the lights on the distant shore. "How did you commit this near murder?"

"It was an accident," she defended.

"I'm relieved. I'd hate to have kissed a murderess."

"Your kiss on the deck caught me off guard."

He hadn't mistaken the response. "And you accidently kissed me back?"

She didn't answer, but a warm blush covered her fair skin. He placed his hand over hers. "Tell me what happened with Papa?"

She took a deep breath. He tried not to stare at her rising chest. What horrible deed had she committed to think she had harmed her father? What had driven her to leave the security of her home and risk her life on a perilous journey?

"Do you remember how I told you I broke the wheel in the family buggy racing my cousin, Paddy?"

He nodded for her to continue.

"I left Papa at his patient's home and took his buggy to a party."

"Do you attend a lot of parties?"

"The harvest gathering was my reward for helping Mama put up preserves and do the canning." She showed him the remains of a scab. "A splatter scalded my hand."

He examined the injury. "And I was under the impression a princess lived a life of pampered idleness."

"I do most of the work on the farm. I milk the cows, gather the eggs, and bake the bread." She paused. "I saw the party as a reward for all my hard work."

"Did you have a good time at the soiree?"

"It was fun at the beginning. All my friends were attending, and they wanted me to sing. Lara kept hitting the wrong chords on the piano. I think she did it on purpose."

"Is that the one you called Old Sourpuss?"

Jules reddened.

"She isn't a fan of your talents?" The image of a dour spinster usurped by the charm of Jules made him smile.

"Old Sourpuss is my worst enemy."

Women put a high value on social achievement, and a few weren't above sabotaging the success of others. "Did she ruin the evening?"

"I overheard her telling the other girls that Matt Wheeler and I were intimate in the barn."

Roe gripped the railing. "Were you?"

"Of course not, but he knew I had pink ribbons on my bloomers. Matt must have seen them hanging on the laundry line."

"Then, you better not tell anyone I bought you silk stockings."

Her mood became playful. "Are you afraid your reputation as a moody disdainer of women might be ruined?" She was flirting with him and accomplished at it. With five older sisters, she'd had plenty of tutelage. Was he just another conquest?

"I've worked hard for the silver in my pockets. I have no intention of spending it on gifts for every fair maiden who crosses my path eager to entrap me with her feminine wiles."

His harsh tone sobered her. "I paid you back for all the things you bought, didn't I?"

"Don't worry about it." Roe frowned. "Is Matt Wheeler one of your hometown beaus?"

"No, he does the harder chores for Papa like chopping wood and mucking the stalls."

"I hope you fired him after his scandalous behavior."

She bowed her head. "No. Papa needs someone to do the chores while I'm gone."

"There must be other men willing to do the work."

She gasped and faced him. "You're right. There are plenty of veterans looking for work. Papa could hire any one of them."

"Do you want me to send another telegram?"

"No. I'll deal with Matt Wheeler and Lara Herbruck when I return home."

"Papa won't take care of it?"

"I would never ask anyone else to solve my problems," Jules said. "I'm a grown woman."

That was debatable.

"I had promised to return for Papa by eight o'clock and was gathering my cloak, when I heard Lara's lies." She stomped her foot. "I had to say something, but when I confronted her, she slapped me." Jules touched her cheek.

He'd laughed earlier, but her tale was taking a sinister turn. Old Sourpuss was a bully, and Jules was an easy victim.

"I didn't cry."

"Good girl. Never show fear in the face of your enemies." He patted her hand. "What happened then?"

"After I left, a terrible storm blew in. Not a nice gentle shower but a wretched downpour with thunder and lightning!"

Her arm gestures and facial expressions enhanced the story telling. "The storm spooked Black Knight, and I fell out of the buggy into a muddy field. The dress I had worked on for weeks was ruined. I was cold, soaked, and wanted to cry."

Compared to war, her mishaps had been minor, but tragic for a young pampered woman. He had thought her spoiled, but she was the product of a happy home, a rarity in these times. He loved his parents in spite of their emotional and physical distance. How much more did Jules love her parents, and what event had sent her on this journey? "So when do you threaten Papa's life?"

"He was sick and went out anyway to help a patient. He was going to wait for me, but I was late. When I reached the house, Papa had left. I headed home, and he was walking on the road, soaked and angry. Papa never yells at me, but I let him down. He called me names and said I was spoiled and irresponsible and all my sisters were better than me."

She started to cry, and he handed her a handkerchief. The man she loved was Papa. A simple rebuff spoken in a moment of anger had stabbed a cruel blow to her tender heart. A pang of jealousy erupted. No one had ever loved him enough to risk life and limb to restore a broken relationship. "How did a storm nearly kill him?"

"Papa had been ill with a deep cough and chills, and the rain made him worse. That's why he couldn't make the trip. I had to go. It was all my fault."

Her father was at fault. He had placed guilt and blame on a child. "He's a grown man. Why didn't he wait for you instead of foolishly going out in a storm?"

Jules was shocked by his outburst. "I was late."

Roe leaned in close, his hand resting against the support post. "You were at a party. What did he expect?"

She wiped the tears from her cheeks. "He expected me to be on time."

He shook his head. "He's a strict taskmaster. Too harsh if you ask me." He gauged her reaction.

"Papa?" She was outraged by his criticism. "I never disappointed him before, and everything crashed down at once. I was overwhelmed."

"But he called you a spoiled child."

"He was ill. He didn't realize what he was saying."

"So why do you have to make amends? Go home, and Papa can fetch the children."

She looked hurt. "You don't think I can do it."

"I didn't say that, but you've made mistakes. Look at what happened with Edna Stall."

"She was a thief."

"You shouldn't have trusted her."

"I would prefer to trust people than be a cynic like you." She covered her mouth. "I'm sorry. I shouldn't have said that."

"I am a cynic," Roe admitted. "I don't trust anyone."

She looked at the upper deck. "What about Chauncy and Theo?"

He nodded. "They earned my trust a long time ago."

"If you can trust them, you can trust others," Jules said.

"One of us needs to be wary."

She stood straight, her chin thrust forward. "Do you think I'm a reckless fool?"

"I think you shouldn't go on this trip to Laurel Holler alone. I'm going with you."

Jules gasped. "That would be highly improper."

"Chauncy made you my responsibility, and you don't have to worry about me kissing you again. I promised the captain I wouldn't seduce you."

"Seduce me?" Jules narrowed her eyes. "You're not the first man to kiss me, Roe Greystone."

"I know." He'd been right about her experience.

"How many men have kissed you?"

She shrugged. "Too many to count."

He leaned in close, his voice low. "What is Papa doing during these orgies?"

She gasped. "They were gentlemen who followed the kiss with a proposal."

Roe touched her bare shoulder and stared at the creamy expanse of flesh above the edge of her gown. "I can imagine what they were proposing."

Jules pulled away, a frown on her face and fire in her eyes. "Rita and the others were right. You're not a gentleman. You're only interested in warming your bed with my body. You don't care anything about my feelings."

He jabbed his finger in her face. "My job is to see you return alive to dear Papa and your parlor full of kissing beaus." He stepped back and studied her. "Why haven't you married any of these amorous admirers?"

"Most had been refused by my sisters and hoped for a second chance, but I didn't love any of them. Marriage for marriage's sake is ridiculous." Jules turned toward the river. "Besides, I enjoy living with Mama and Papa."

He stepped behind her. "Until the storm and your fall from grace."

She turned and faced him, her nearness unnerving, but he refused to give her room. "Haven't you loved someone so much, you didn't want any threat of discord to mar your relationship?"

No. He'd never been loved or returned love that deeply. "Then you'll want to succeed. I'll find the children and bring them to the boat."

"That would only prove Papa was right about me."

She headed to her room.

Roe followed. "Then I'll have to escort you, whether it's proper or not." He caught her arm. "But don't expect a proposal of marriage from me, Princess. Any rumors of scandal will be in your imagination."

She leaned against the door to her room. "Then you promise not to kiss me?"

He raised his hand. "I'll obey a vow of celibacy where you're concerned."

Her voice cracked. "Then you have no feelings toward me at all?"

Roe pounded on his chest. "I have a stone for a heart. I've shielded myself from experiencing pain for so long, I can't feel love for any woman."

"What about lust? What about possessing a woman to warm your bed? What about…"

Roe had promised Chauncy he wouldn't seduce her, but his need to connect, to touch was too deep to ignore. He pulled her tight against his chest and savaged her mouth with a hunger that bordered on starvation. He pressed her against the door, panting for breath as his mouth captured hers again and again.

Roe pulled away, examining her flushed features. "Did any of your flower-presenting beaus kiss you like this?"

"No." Jules grabbed a handful of his hair and pulled him close. "And I never kissed them back."

The door opened, and they stumbled inside. Lizzy was in her nightgown and had wrapped a shawl around her shoulders. "What did you do? Tour the city?"

Roe gazed into Jules' eyes. She had matched his passion as a woman and man discovering the promise only experienced by a few couples. This is what caused

Romeo to risk everything for the woman he loved. Jules touched his chest. "You may have to rethink your vow, Roe."

He pulled the door closed. "Lock the door." He waited until he heard the key turn. He had never had trouble ignoring women before. What was it about Jules Beecher that had him in heat like a rutting stallion? He needed to regain control.

Chapter Twelve

Lizzy helped Jules undress, unhooking the back of the gown and untying the skirt. "You ignored all our advice. Are you in love with him?"

"No." Jules covered her face with her hands. "I don't know. It would ruin all my plans."

"Love does that. He must be in love with you."

She dropped the skirt and crinoline to the floor. "Why do you say that?"

"You're not warming his bed."

Jules gathered her discarded clothes. "I wouldn't have gone."

"Oh?" Lizzy laughed and shook her head. "You would have followed him overboard, but he didn't ask."

"He made a promise to Chauncy to be celibate." That had to be the reason.

"Celibate? He needs to do a better job," Lizzy said. "And what was a nice girl like you devouring him like a last meal?"

"I don't know. When he kissed me, I wanted to kiss back. It was so powerful and scary."

"You've got a fever."

Jules touched her forehead. "No, I don't."

"I'm talking about love fever. It starts as an itch that needs to be scratched. Why do you think Rita is with the gambler? Why do people marry? Why do you hear noises from the bedroom that have nothing to do with sleep?"

Jules had heard the sounds of lovemaking between her sisters with their husbands. She had seen the touching and the kissing. Now she understood the silent messages conveyed between lovers. "It's powerful."

"Which is why young ladies have chaperones when they receive gentlemen in their parlors."

Only Roe hadn't called upon her with flowers and candy. He hadn't spoken to her father, seeking permission to escort her to a dance or take her on a buggy ride. Roe was a carefree rogue traveling the Ohio River, and yet, she couldn't ignore the attraction. The memory of his kiss clung to her lips, heart, and areas only marriage would satisfy. Jules pulled on her nightgown and huddled beneath the covers. She stared at the empty bunk.

"Do you think Rita will return before morning?"

"I'm the keeper of the key." Lizzy said. "I'll let her in if she knocks."

Near dawn Jules woke to a scratching at the door. Was it Rita? Why didn't she knock? "Lizzy, I think Rita wants in."

A long, loud snore was her reply.

Jules slid over the side of the bed and landed softly on the floor. She felt along the edge of the bed in a half-sleep stagger to the door as her eyes adjusted to the darkness. The door was locked. She turned toward Lizzy, but the noise had stopped. Soft voices were audible outside, but they faded with distant footsteps. She must have imagined Rita's return. Jules climbed into bed and fell asleep.

Jules awakened to the crew shouting orders to cast off the lines in the early morning hours. The boat jerked from the shore as the paddlewheel rotated and plowed through the water. A shrill whistle shocked any remnant of sleep from her tired body. Her companions had slept through the launch. Rita's bed was empty. She threw off the covers, dropped to the floor, and dressed in a dark skirt and crème-colored blouse. She styled her hair and slipped on her shoes. The morning air was cold, and she wrapped her new cloak around her shoulders. The wool covering had three tiers and was lined with satin.

Roe had said her debt was paid, but his purchases were more expensive than her home-made clothes. She lifted the lid to the hat box and put on the store-made bonnet. It was more stylish than her cloth bonnets or the slouch hat she had worn on the train. The fashionable clothes gave her confidence as she glanced in the small mirror and smiled at her reflection. "No one could mistake you for a child."

Jules headed for the dining hall where food had been placed on the bar for the crew and guests who rose early. She finished breakfast and climbed the stairs to the top deck. The morning air was chilly, and she gathered her cloak about her. Some of the passengers who had paid deck passage remained asleep, but others were awake, sipping coffee or stronger drinks. A group of men were playing a game with dice. Money passed from one hand to the next, creating a fortune for the winner and leaving the other a beggar.

She watched the other boats traveling on the river. It was a larger version of the canal where everyone knew the captains and crew and friendly competitions arose to race against each other. A crewman was perched in the front, surveying the water and watching for any trees or debris. The leadsman cast a lead line to mark the depth of the river.

She moved closer to the stern and leaned against the railing, watching the paddlewheel churn the muddy water of the Ohio River. It was hours before she and the other women would have to prepare the tables for dining. They would feed the guests and dock. Customers would come aboard for a night of gambling and entertainment late into the night. Thursday she would leave for Laurel Holler and fulfill her journey's goal. She would return home with her cousins, confront Matt and Lara about their lies, and her father would be proud she had accomplished her task. Life would return to normal.

But would it? Fear gripped her. What if life at home was no longer enough? Roe had mocked her for attending parties and milking the cows. "Roe doesn't love you." Rita and Lizzy had warned her about men, and one handsome rogue in particular. His kiss had caused her common sense to flee. She'd forget him. She had to. Roe would never travel to Darrow Falls. His life was on the *Jenny Lee*.

"Good morning." Roe leaned against the rail and surveyed her. "I thought you were going to sleep in."

His deep voice caused her stomach to flutter, and she gripped the railing to steady her racing heart. His face had haunted her dreams, and memories of his kiss ignited her body in a primitive call she had never experienced. *Don't look at him. Don't talk about last night.*

She lifted her face to the breeze and inhaled, reminding her heart to slow down. "Don't you love being on the water? I forgot how much fun it was."

He smiled wide, his clean, straight teeth white against the dark growth on his face. He hadn't shaved. "What do you know about boats?"

"My grandfather owns a canal boat."

"The *Irish Rose*."

He'd remembered. "Grandpa transports cargo from Akron to Cleveland and back. My sisters and I helped during the summers, but he's running out of grandchildren for the crew. My cousin Paddy and I are the last of the Donovan and Beecher families. I'm going to miss walking the deck and operating the locks."

Roe looked at the large paddle wheel spinning to propel the boat forward. "The *Jenny Lee* is slightly bigger than a canal boat."

"Thank goodness the deck is bigger than a freighter."

"Isn't the deck on a cargo boat a single plank that connects the top of the cabins?"

Jules walked a straight line. "I learned to be graceful and pirouette without falling off." She twirled and walked toward him on the same line. "A lady lifts her skirt with one hand. Two is vulgar."

"Who taught you that?"

"Colleen." Jules laughed.

"Chauncy listed your sisters. Colleen is after Miss Jenny but before Miss Jessie?"

"Yes."

"Isn't she the troublemaker?"

Jules laughed. "She liked to break rules. She taught us about kissing."

He saluted. "My compliments to Miss Colleen."

She covered her mouth. She wasn't going to talk about the kiss. "We should forget about last night."

"We weren't talking about last night. How did your sister teach you about kissing?"

"She demonstrated on Blake Ellsworth."

"Wasn't he the man shot by the Cassell brothers? You saved his life with towels."

"For which he gave me the gold piece." She sighed. "The one I foolishly lost to Edna Stall."

"Will he be upset?"

"Blake?" She inhaled the breeze and wrinkled her nose at the odd plethora of smells from the river. All the towns upriver dumped their waste into its waters, and only fresh rain washed away the stench. "My brothers-in-law are all good-natured. Even Morgan is friendly, and he had a horrible reputation."

"The highlander temper," Roe said with a smile. "With his fiery hair and booming voice, he struck fear into the hearts of his men, but Miss Jessie never backed down."

Her heart tightened in her chest. "You think highly of my sister."

Roe nodded. "I admired her like most of the men in camp."

It wasn't the first time a man had paid more attention to one of her sisters instead of her, but she didn't want to be second choice. Not with Roe.

"What else did your sisters teach you?"

He had to repeat the question to break through her reverie. "Everything. I know how to play the piano, sew, knit, wrap a wound, birth a baby, and work a lock."

"Did Miss Jessie teach you to shoot a gun?"

Her sister again. "Yes, but I don't like guns. They're horribly heavy to tote around, and they make a loud boom."

"You prefer to soothe the beast with a song than wound him with a bullet?"

"It works," Jules said. "The dining hall had its fair share of unmannered boors, but they were charming when I sang."

"I wouldn't elevate them to gentlemen and ladies."

"The women were presentable."

"None compare to you in that bonnet and cloak."

Jules turned for him to admire her ensemble. "You have excellent taste for a bachelor." Jules stroked the soft wool fabric. "I would never have chosen anything so fine."

"I was at the mercy of the shopkeepers. The ladies of the store saw me coming and played me like a wide-eyed country bumpkin."

She laughed. "I didn't realize you had a sense of humor."

"I lost it," Roe admitted. "The war stole many things."

"But not everything," Jules said. Roe had revealed a small slice of himself, but she wanted to know more. He was guarded and secretive except with Chauncy and Theo. What was he hiding?

"You'll impress your hometown beaus when you return home."

"It will cause plenty of gossip."

"Is that a problem?"

Jules considered the gossipers of town, especially Lara. "Everyone will wonder who my secret admirer is." She shrugged. "Let them."

"You're not going to tell them about me?"

She shook her head. "No. I'll tell them my

belongings were stolen, and I had to replace them. Mama will chastise me for spending too much…"

"Are you ashamed of me?"

Roe looked angry. "I'm trying to protect you."

"Do I look helpless?"

"My sisters are married to Tyler, Logan, Blake, Morgan, and Zach. They think of me as their little sister. They don't need much of an excuse to do bodily harm. They wouldn't like the idea of you buying me clothes, kissing me, and traveling alone with me."

"Morgan traveled alone with Jess, and they weren't married even though he said they were."

Jess again. "He was protecting her."

"And I'm protecting you."

She stomped her foot. "I don't need protection. I'm not traveling with the Confederate Army, I don't know any military secrets, and I'm not Jessica no matter how much you wish I were."

He grabbed her arms and pulled her close. "I'm not in love with your sister. Do I have to kiss you again to prove it?"

"It wouldn't hurt."

Chapter Thirteen

Jules closed her eyes in anticipation of a kiss. He played with her mouth, teasing her to respond. The bell on the deck in the front between the smoke stacks rang, and Jules covered her ears. "What's that for?"

He pulled away. "Trouble ahead. Let's find out what it is." Roe escorted Jules to the pilot house perched above the captain's cabin. Chauncy was behind the wheel. He lowered his field glasses and slowed the boat. "What's going on?"

"A large tree in the way," Chauncy said. "Go see if the crew can shove it aside."

Roe and Jules hurried down the stairs to the lower deck. A group of men were in the bow with long spiked poles. Theo was standing on the stage swung out over the water.

"What is it, Theo?" Jules squeezed forward for a view. Roe put his arm around her waist to keep her from falling in as the men jostled with the poles. She was light in his arms but wiggled about so much, he nearly lost his grip. The woman was a bundle of energy tethered by his subdued demeanor. An uprooted tree floated across the river, blocking the boat's path. Something red was under the water trapped in its branches.

"We might be able to push the tree out of the way," Theo said, "but it's going to take everyone working together."

Several crewmen joined Theo on the stage and plunged their pikes against the bark. One of the men snagged the fabric with a hook on the pole. An arm splashed to the surface.

"It's a body!" one of the men announced.

Roe pulled Jules away.

"I've seen dead bodies before," Jules protested.

"You didn't recognize her?"

Jules turned and stared as more of the body surfaced. A dark mat of wet hair covered the face, but the dress was the same red and black plaid pattern Rita had worn last night. "Rita!" Jules covered her mouth to silence a sob.

Roe pulled her against his chest. "I'm sorry."

Jules reached toward the men. "Be careful with her."

Tears brimmed her lashes. Rita had teased her, but the women had bonded in a short amount of time as they worked side by side. Her concern was sincere. "You should go to your room."

"I'll find a blanket." Rita's limp and lifeless body was hauled onto the stage. "Rita wouldn't want people to see her this way."

Jules disappeared up the stairs. He had expected hysterics, screams, or a flood of tears, but a quiet courage marked her behavior. He had dismissed her as a spoiled child, but Jules conducted herself in the same stoic manner as her older sister. Their father had trained them in medicine, but he had taught them to face a crisis with calmness and courage as well. Tragedy didn't define her, but the war had left a mark on him. He was a coward for wallowing in the past.

He stepped forward and helped the men carry Rita's body to the deck. A crowd gathered, gawking at the sight of a dead woman.

Jules returned with a wool blanket. He helped spread it over Rita's body. A few people voiced their displeasure at being denied a view. "Vultures." Roe scowled, and they fell silent.

The crew had moved the tree enough for the boat to pass. Jules looked at Theo who was securing the stage. "Do you know how she died?"

Theo looked at Roe. "She fell overboard and drowned."

Jules looked from Theo to Roe. "What?"

"No one ever dies of unnatural causes on a river," Roe said. "They all drown."

"Why?" Jules whispered.

"Murder is bad for business." Riverboats depended on hauling cargo and passengers. If word spread that someone had been killed on the *Jenny Lee*, it could affect profits. The crew knew to stick to the story of an unfortunate accident. He looked at Theo. "Better tell Chauncy."

Theo nodded and headed up the stairs.

When he turned, Jules was lifting a corner of the blanket. Roe grabbed her wrist. "What are you doing?"

"I need to know how she died."

"You're trembling." He released her arm. "Let me take a look."

"I'm a nurse," Jules defended. "I know what I'm looking for."

He had given up the profession of medicine. Roe looked around at the curious crowd. "Go about your business." He waited until they were alone and uncovered her head and shoulders. She hadn't been in the water for long. There was little decomposition, but the blood had drained from her body, leaving her skin a grayish white. He lifted her chin. A long, deep cut had been made from ear to ear. "Her throat was cut."

Jules stared. She was pale. It was a gruesome crime. He covered Rita's body with the blanket. "When was the last time you saw Rita?"

"Last night when she left with the gambler. She never returned to our room."

He was the most likely suspect. He helped Jules to her feet. "I'll talk to him." Roe turned to one of the crewmen. "Bud, stay here. Don't let anyone near the body."

The body. It was easier to think of Rita anonymously. The way he had thought of the endless number of patients during the war. It was always harder to cut off a man's arm or leg if you knew his name.

The gambler had a private room on the second deck. Jules followed. She was quiet but calm. He paused by the door to her room. "You should lie down."

"I'm not sleepy." She gasped and rushed to the railing near the dark corner. She wiped her finger against the surface and showed him her shaking finger. "Blood."

He examined the area. More blood was on the upper deck support and beneath the railing. "This is where she was killed."

Jules turned toward the stairs. "Near our room. Someone scratched at the door last night, but before I could answer, it stopped."

Roe examined the doorway. The jamb had been whittled with a knife near the lock. Someone wanted to break in. "Does Rita have any enemies?"

"Lizzy might know." She raised her hand to knock but hesitated. "Let's talk to the gambler first. Do you know what room he's in?"

It was his job to know the paying customers, their rooms, and their needs. Roe escorted her along the walkway and stopped at a door near the stern. He knocked.

Jules crowded beside him. "Stand away from the door."

Her blue eyes widened. "Do you think he has a gun?"

Roe put his hand on his hip. He hadn't expected trouble this morning and had left his revolver in his room. He pushed her away from the door. "If there's trouble, run."

She had a stubborn look on her face. "I'm not going to desert you."

His first opinion of her needed revising. "You're more like your sister than I thought."

"Jess again." She pouted. Even for a beauty like Jules, it had to be humbling having five older sisters, watching them courted and married. She had mentioned her suitors were leftovers from her sisters' refusals. She didn't like being a consolation prize.

Roe raised his hand to knock again, and the gambler opened the door. He was naked. He scratched his unshaven face and yawned. "Are we in Louisville?"

Roe turned to Jules, who was staring. A blush covered her cheeks. He stepped in front of her. "Not yet."

"Then why are you waking me?" He grinned at Jules peeking over Roe's arm. "You're the songbird."

He frowned at Roe. "And you're the con man who suckered me into a bet I couldn't win."

"A gambler doesn't need help making a bet." He stepped forward. "We need to talk. Do you mind putting some clothes on?"

He glared at the sun. "It's too early to rise. Come back later." He limped to the bed. A scar ran from mid-thigh, along his hip, and ended near his waist.

Roe followed him into the room. An empty bottle of whiskey was on the nightstand, and his clothes were scattered on the floor. "What battle were you wounded in?"

"The Wilderness." He crawled into bed and pulled the covers to his chest. "Spent the rest of the war in a hospital." He looked past Roe. Jules stood near the open door. "You want to sing me to sleep?" He patted the bed in an invitation.

"We're here on business." Roe moved toward the nightstand. "Do you have a gun or knife?"

"I'm a gambler. I carry a derringer." He pointed to his valise. "There's a knife in my boot."

Roe opened the valise. The derringer was on top of a clean shirt. It was loaded. The narrow knife blade was clean. No signs of blood. He returned it to the boot sheath.

The gambler arranged his pillows and looked at Roe. "What's going on?"

He wasn't acting like a murderer. He couldn't escape naked, and the knife showed no signs of a violent crime. Roe examined the discarded clothing but found no blood stains. "A woman left the salon with you last night. Her name was Rita."

"Yeah, she was real nice. Kept me company most

of the night." He lifted the empty whiskey bottle and tipped it up for the few remaining drops before putting it down. "I probably should have paid her more, but it's been a long time since I won at the tables. I have debts to pay." He ran his fingers through his gray-streaked hair. "Did she complain about me?"

"No, but do you remember when she left your room?"

He scratched his head. "Early morning. The whistles blew while we enjoyed another romp in bed. When I didn't offer to pay more, she was miffed. She said she was going to her room to sleep."

"She never made it," Roe said. "She's dead."

He leaned forward, his gaze going to his valise. "When she left, she was alive."

His shocked expression was genuine. "How did you pay her?"

"With coins from my winnings."

Rita's death was probably a theft that led to murder. "Thank you for your help. The sheriff will want to talk to you when we arrive in Louisville."

"The sheriff?"

"Do you have something to worry about?"

He squirmed beneath the cover. "My debts aren't all paid."

"All he'll need is a statement," Roe said. "Then you can leave."

Jules exited with him but paused outside. "Do you think he's innocent?"

"No blood in the room, and he looked to his gun instead of his knife when I told him Rita was dead." He walked toward the stairs, retracing Rita's steps. "Maybe she was counting her money, and someone took it."

"First Edna and now Rita," Jules said.

Roe stopped and stared at Jules. "Do you think the thefts are related?"

"They were both murdered the same way."

"You never said Edna was murdered!" A man paused in his walk, glancing from Roe to Jules. Roe took her arm and moved her farther along the walkway and lowered his voice. "How do you know she was murdered?"

"When I refused to pay the rent Edna owed, the innkeeper called the police. When I told the policeman my name, he asked about a letter with my father's name on it." Jules pointed to her room. "I have it in my bag."

She was testing his patience. "What does a letter have to do with Edna's murder?"

"Edna took my reticule, and the letter was inside. When the innkeeper called a policeman, he recognized my name and took me to a dirty alley a block away from the inn." Jules fought tears. "The detective wanted me to identify Edna. She was wearing my cloak. It was soaked with her blood."

Roe put his arm around her trembling shoulders.

She took a deep breath. "Anything not bloodied had been taken by scavengers."

"Not the thief?"

"The detective said a murderer wouldn't take the time to remove her stockings and shoes." Jules paced along the walkway. "Edna was old. He could have grabbed her bag of belongings and ran. Rita was a tiny woman. He didn't have to kill either one."

"The war gave men a taste for killing," Roe said. "And poverty makes men desperate. But it doesn't mean Edna's death had anything to do with Rita's."

Jules leaned against the wall, her hand at her neck. "Both women had their throats cut."

"A lot of men carry knives." He stroked her cheek, trying to calm her fears. "There was nothing tying the two victims to the same killer. The two women didn't know each other."

"They knew me." She trembled beneath his fingertips. She was terrified. She broke away and headed for the stairs. "I need to talk to Chauncy."

He caught her elbow. "Theo informed him about what is going on."

"You don't understand. Edna was wearing my clothes."

"Edna?" Why were women so difficult to understand? "What does that have to do with Rita?"

"I don't know why he killed Rita, but a thief wouldn't have murdered Edna or Rita. Neither one of them looked wealthy. And Rita would have hid her money as soon as the gambler paid her. This was something more." She stopped at her room and ran her hand along the markings on the door. "He followed me here and wanted inside." She looked toward the corner, stained with droplets of blood. "Rita ran into him when she was returning to our room."

Roe pieced together her logic. Someone killed Edna in a dark alley, and Jules thought it was related to her because Edna was wearing her clothes. Rita was walking alone in the early morning hours returning to the room they shared. Coincidence? Likely. "No one has a reason to do you any harm."

Jules was pale and shaking. "He does." Jules hurried up the stairs.

Roe grabbed her arm and pulled her up short when

they reached the top deck. Her breathing was shallow and fast, and it wasn't from running up the stairs. "You're becoming hysterical. Take a deep breath and calm down. No one is trying to kill you."

Her eyes were wide, fearful as she hurried across the open top deck with Roe keeping pace. They paused outside the pilot room. "Who do you think is following you?"

Her lip trembled as she spoke the name. "Clyde Cassell."

One of the men who had shot the captain. A deserter. A mercenary. He patted her hand. "You're overreacting."

"You sound like my mother." Jules clenched her hands. "She thinks I'm overly dramatic." She knocked on the pilot room door. "I feel an obligation to tell Captain LaDonte."

"I don't think he's in danger."

She turned toward him. "Clyde attempted to kill him before."

"That was a long time ago. I think we need more proof Clyde Cassell is behind these crimes besides two dead women."

"How many dead women are required before he is guilty?" Her voice was shrill.

"Calm down."

Theo opened the door. She brushed past him.

"I hate it when no one takes me seriously," Jules said as she stepped next to Captain LaDonte at the wheel.

He turned. "Theo told me the body in the river was Rita. I'm sorry. You and the other women were friends?"

Jules nodded.

"Do the others know?"

She shook her head. "Not yet."

"Theo, you should inform them before someone else," Chauncy said.

"I'd like to tell them," Jules said.

"Theo, stand outside their door. Tell them to stay inside until Miss Jules arrives and don't let anyone speak to them."

"Before you do that, mop the railing area outside the door."

Theo looked confused by Roe's orders.

"There's blood," Roe said. "Rita's blood."

"I understand." He tipped his cap and left them.

Jules took a few deep breaths, but her voice was filled with anxiety. "I'm afraid I've put you all in danger."

Chauncy looked at Roe for an explanation. He shrugged. "She has a theory about the murderer."

Jules smacked her palm against Roe's chest. She was mad. It was the closest she had come to exhibiting any violence. "Roe doesn't value my opinion."

Chauncy frowned as he stroked his beard. "Let me hear it."

"Do you remember how I told you about Edna Stall stealing my belongings?"

"Yes, Roe replaced them."

"Edna was wearing my cloak when she was murdered."

"Murdered?" He looked to Roe. "Did you know she was murdered?"

"Not until a few minutes ago. She thinks the two murders are related because of her. It's ridiculous."

Chauncy signaled for Jules to sit, but she refused. "What does Edna's murder have to do with Rita?"

"Both women had their throats cut," Roe interjected. "A coincidence."

Jules stomped her foot.

Chauncy raised a bushy eyebrow. "You disagree?"

"I saw both of them," Jules said. "It was the same brutal cut."

"We'll inform the authorities and let them know about the similarities," Chauncy said. "Your friends will see justice."

"There is more," Roe said. Her theory about Clyde Cassell was nonsense, and he wanted Chauncy to laugh about it. "Tell him who you think is the murderer."

Jules lifted her chin. "When I was on the train, Edna said my name. A man who was passing, turned, and stared at me. I recognized him and said his name. Clyde Cassell."

"You didn't tell me you saw him." Roe addressed Chauncy, "Why do women leave out important details and wonder why we don't take them seriously?"

Chauncy touched one hand to his heart. "Are you sure it was Clyde?"

"No one forgets his ugly face." Jules' skin was pale, and she visibly trembled. Roe stepped toward her. "I'm going to be sick."

Chauncy pointed toward a spittoon.

Jules bent over the container and emptied her stomach of her breakfast. Her shoulders shook in small convulsions. Roe offered her a handkerchief. Something more was wrong. He helped her to sit in the chair and knelt in front of her. "What else haven't you shared?"

She couldn't catch her breath. "Slow down," he coached.

Once she regained her composure, she spoke. "Rita and her sister worked in a brothel during the war. She said a man cut her sister and killed her right after the battle of Antietam. That's when Clyde and Buck were at the Mermaid's Mirth. I didn't put it together at the time, but she said the man babbled on about his dead brother and a fortune in gold. The Cassel brothers were searching for Blake's gold when Buck was killed. You can't call that a coincidence."

"Are you saying Rita knew Clyde?" Did Rita recognize Clyde hiding in the shadows outside her room?

"She said she would never forget his ugly face." Jules looked at Chauncy. "I think that describes Clyde."

"It could describe many men," Chauncy said. "You were a child during Antietam. Their deaths have nothing to do with you."

Jules stood and smoothed her hands over her skirt as she took several deep breaths. "Of course. I'm so silly." She waved Roe's handkerchief. "My mother always said I overreacted to things. I'm sorry to have worried you." She smiled at Chauncy. "Thank you for tolerating my hysterics."

"Your reaction is understandable with the death of Rita." He patted her hand. "You should rest before we reach Louisville."

"I'll try."

She smiled again, but it didn't reach her eyes. Roe followed her outside. She was hiding something.

Chapter Fourteen

Jules wouldn't burden Chauncy with her suspicions. He had clutched his heart when she had spoken Clyde's name. But she would warn Theo about the danger. He would believe her and take precautions. She walked along the railing of the top deck, reviewing the facts about the two crimes. They were related, and she was the common link. Roe's voice startled her.

"What didn't you want Chauncy to know?"

"Nothing." She shrugged. "You were right. I was imagining the worst. Why would Clyde follow me after barely seeing me on the train?"

"You should never play poker, Miss Beecher."

His gaze penetrated to her soul. She couldn't hide her feelings from Roe as easily as she had disguised them from Chauncy. But would he believe her theory? Clyde didn't know her, but he knew Jess. He had seen her in her sister's old hunting hat, the one she had worn to Antietam when she disguised herself as a male nurse. Clyde had seen a young man in the shadows of the kitchen at the Mermaid's Mirth during the shootout that killed Buck. Their disguises had protected Colleen and Jessica from being found by Clyde. He hadn't been looking for a woman. Until now. She recalled his words on the train. *You ain't no man*. She wasn't brave. She shared her fears. "Chauncy isn't the target. I am."

"Don't start that nonsense. You are the least

threatening person I know."

"I'm a Beecher," Jules said. "We have a long history with the Cassell brothers. There is no love lost between us."

He blocked her path. "What history?"

She needed as many allies as possible to fight Clyde. She had to convince him she was right about her suspicions. "The Cassell brothers were chasers before the war. My cousin Jake Donovan tied them up in a freight car to keep them from hurting a runaway slave my sister, Courtney, helped. Then there was Jennifer and Logan when they were prisoners of Chauncy. The Cassell brothers wanted to kill them, and Chauncy helped them escape. But the worst was at the Mermaid's Mirth where Buck was killed."

"You weren't there."

"No, but Colleen and Jessica were. They shot and killed Buck."

"Your sisters killed him?" Roe looked at the pilot house. "Chauncy thinks Blake shot him."

Jules looked at the river. "It's a family secret. The Cassell brothers are vengeful."

"That still doesn't explain why Clyde would go after you. His fight is with your sisters and their husbands, not you."

"Remember how I told you about the storm the night of the party?"

"Old Sourpuss insulted your honor."

"I lost my bonnet in the wind and took a hat from the bench seat in the kitchen for my trip. It was an old slouch hat Jessica wore when she traveled to Antietam. She had it on when she shot Buck from the kitchen of the Mermaid's Mirth."

"Miss Jessie wore an old man's hat when I met her."

"I was wearing it on the train when Edna called me *Miss Beecher*."

"Miss Beecher." Roe frowned as he ran his fingertips through his hair. "Clyde knew your family name?"

"They met the entire Beecher family when they were in Darrow Falls looking for the runaways. I was nearly eleven years old, and I remember them."

"But you had nothing to do with Buck's death."

"I look like Jess," Jules said. "In the hat, I must have looked like she did in disguise. He thinks I killed Buck. The gold piece in the reticule he stole belonged to Blake. It was the Confederate gold they were looking for. Even a simpleton could put the pieces together."

He believed her. His eyes were filled with concern and a little fear. Not for himself. Roe was no coward. He was worried for her. "I'll be fine."

"Oh, no!" Roe jabbed his finger in her face. "I understand why you lied to Chauncy. You didn't want him to worry, but no lies between us Juliet. No lies."

He had called her Juliet, not princess or Jules. "Then you believe me?"

He grabbed her hand and led her to the stern. "Come with me."

"I don't want to worry Chauncy."

"I'm going to my room."

She stopped. "This is hardly the time to share amorous affections."

He looked surprised. "As much as I'd like to resume our canoodling, I'm going to my room to retrieve my gun."

"Oh, that would be prudent." She waited outside as he entered his cabin. He returned with the revolver strapped to his waist.

"Why didn't your sister shoot Clyde the same time she shot Buck?"

"Hush." Jules looked around and lowered her voice. "According to Rita, Clyde was wounded. Cole and Jess argued about who was responsible for Buck's death."

"There was a reward?"

"No." She frowned at his accusation. "As evil as Buck was, my sisters have carried a heavy burden for taking a life. Only immediate family knew about it."

"Clyde never followed them?"

"Not that I know of, but when he saw me in the hat and Edna spoke the Beecher name, something must have connected in his dark memory of that night." Her legs shook, and Roe's arm encircled her waist. She could take care of herself in ordinary circumstances, but Clyde Cassell was a different matter. She recalled the little girl hugging the deck of the *Irish Rose*, too terrified to move. She needed a distraction. "I should go to Lizzy. She was close to Rita."

"I'll escort you to your room," Roe said.

She placed one hand on her hip and took a flippant tone. "Over an imaginary threat?"

Roe stuck his finger in her face. "I didn't believe you initially, but I believe you now."

She hurried across the upper deck toward the stairs. "You can't shadow me every minute. Don't you have other duties to perform?"

"The captain guaranteed your safe return home. He doesn't want to face your father and explain why he failed."

"Papa wouldn't care if he had one less daughter."

"Just when I thought you were mature, you say something childish," Roe said. "You could run Papa over with a buggy, and he'd forgive you. He loves you. He'd die for you."

She clutched his arm. "I don't want any more people to die."

"Neither do I." He patted her hand. "We'll stop Clyde."

"We?"

"You like to shoulder your own responsibilities, but do you mind if I share this burden?"

Jules threw her arms around his neck and kissed him. "Thank you."

Roe unfastened her hands. "None of that. If I'm going to protect you, I don't need any distractions." He glanced around. "And do me a favor. Don't go anywhere alone. This boat has a lot of hiding places."

They descended the stairs. Theo was standing outside the door. He had a mop in his hand and a bucket on the deck. "They're awake, but they ain't come out yet."

"Go downstairs. We'll have to remove the body," Roe said.

"There's a stretcher in the storage room where I found the mop."

Jules looked at the corner. Theo had cleaned the blood from the railing and deck floor. "Thank you, Theo."

"Didn't want the ladies to see it." He gathered the bucket.

Roe nodded. "I'll join you in a minute."

Jules knocked on her cabin door. Lizzy answered. She was dressed and pinning her hair in place. Babs was seated on her bed. She turned to Roe. "Wait outside."

"Are you sure you don't want me to tell them?"

"I think it would be better coming from me." She closed the door and stood, waiting for Lizzy to finish with her hair.

She put her brush down. "What is it?"

"It's about Rita."

"Don't tell me she ran off with that man," Lizzy said. "She knows better than to trust a gambler to have money in his pocket longer than two days."

"Sit down," Jules said.

"This sounds serious." Babs finished buttoning a dress she had claimed from the trunk.

How did she break the news? "Rita didn't come back to the room because someone stopped her."

"Did someone beat her up?" Lizzy stepped toward the door, but Jules blocked her.

"There's no easy way to say this." Jules took a deep breath. "Rita is dead."

"What?" Babs bumped her head as she jumped to the floor.

Lizzy tried to pass Jules. "No. Rita knows how to take care of herself."

Jules gripped Lizzy's arms. "The crew pulled Rita's body from the river this morning. Her throat was cut."

Lizzy's eyes filled with tears. "Who would do that?"

Jules hugged Lizzy close. She trembled against her. "Rita talked about her sister's killer. She said she had given up looking for him."

Lizzy pulled away, a frightened expression on her face. "In the beginning that's all she wanted to do, but she couldn't find him. I told her he was probably killed in the war."

"Did she describe him? More than saying he was ugly."

"When Rita ran into someone she thought might know him, she would describe him as having a scar on the side of his face and a white streak in his beard."

Jules sat on the lower bunk, her hands gripping her knees. The description matched Clyde Cassell.

"Did that gambler kill her?" Babs asked.

"And I thought he was nice," Lizzy put her hand on the door knob.

"No. We talked to the gambler," Jules said. "Rita left his room this morning. She was killed outside our door. I think it was the man with a scar and white streak in his beard."

"He's alive?" Lizzy asked.

"His name is Clyde Cassell."

Lizzy grabbed her arm. Her grip was tight. "You know him?"

"I saw him on the train. I think he killed Edna Stall the same way he killed Rita."

"But why?" Babs trembled, wrapping her arms around her body.

"He's an evil man. He's killed lots of people over his lifetime."

"Rita always said she'd kill him if she saw him again." Lizzy's face went ashen. "You don't think she tried to take him on by herself?"

"I heard scratching outside the door early in the

morning. It may have been Clyde. If Rita ran into him, she didn't have a chance."

"You said they pulled her body out of the water. Where is she?" Lizzy opened the door. Roe stood by the stairs staring at the deck below. Lizzy rushed forward, and the others followed. Theo was placing a stretcher next to the blanket-covered form.

"No!" Lizzy ran down the stairs before Roe could stop her. She fell to her knees by Rita's body.

Jules had followed close behind her and grabbed her arm before she could remove the blanket. "Don't look."

She stared at her, tears streaming down her cheeks. "I have to know."

Jules nodded. She pulled back the blanket to expose Rita's face.

Lizzy balled her hands into fists. "She was my best friend. I would have fought with her. I would have died if necessary."

"I know." Jules put her arms around her as she sobbed.

"Theo, when we reach Louisville, contact the undertaker and have him make a pine box," Roe said. "We'll give her a proper burial."

Jules looked at Roe. "Thank you." She looked around. "Is there a place where I can prepare the body?"

Roe's eyebrow shot up. "You've done that?"

"Mostly newborns and children," Jules said. "Sometimes the mother helps."

"I'd like to help." Lizzy wiped her runny nose with her sleeve.

"I made space in the storage room," Theo said.

Jules helped Lizzy to her feet. "Why don't we pick out some clothes for her?"

Roe followed. Jules turned. "Our cabin is at the top of the stairs."

"I'd prefer not to let you out of my sight." He placed his hand on his revolver.

"I have an advantage. I know what Clyde looks like, and I know how dangerous he is," Jules said. "You help Theo carry Rita. We'll be fine."

"Scream if you need help," Roe said. "I know I'll hear you."

Jules and Lizzy gathered clothes and personal items to prepare Rita's body for burial.

"What can I do?" Babs asked.

"We'll need water and sponges to wash her body," Jules said. "Theo can help you gather them."

Babs blushed and hurried downstairs.

Jules retrieved her nursing supplies, and they found Roe standing near the storage room. Theo was carrying two large buckets, and Babs had wash cloths and sponges in her arms.

Roe opened the door and lit a lantern to provide light in the closed room. The stretcher was resting on stacked crates and was at waist height. Jules unpacked her medical bag.

"It's a little late for that," Roe said.

"I need to stitch her wound." Jules placed her needles, scissors, and thread on a cloth.

Roe examined a bent needle. "Do you want me to stitch the wound?"

Jules took the needle from his hand. "What do you know about needlework? I can close the gash."

He stared. "How can you be soft and vulnerable

and yet do a job most men would balk at?"

Jules shrugged. "I'm a woman. I do what is necessary."

Theo placed a bucket of water on a barrel and the other on the floor. Babs placed her items on top of a crate. She looked at the blanket-covered body and froze. "I don't think I can help. The last dead person I saw was my mother and…"

"It's all right," Jules said. "The space is small. You can empty the buckets when the water gets dirty and fetch clean."

"I can do that," Babs agreed. She followed Theo outside.

Roe paused at the door. "Are you sure you don't want help?"

"We'll take good care of her." She closed the door and removed the blanket.

Lizzy covered her mouth, and tears dripped down her cheeks. She took a swipe with her sleeve and inhaled a deep breath. "She's a mess."

Rita had lost her shoes and one stocking in the water. They removed the other stocking, her skirt, petticoat, crinoline, and other garments. She wore no bloomers.

Lizzy lifted her arm to wash it. Several slash marks crossed her arms and bruises darkened her skin. "She fought him. Rita had the heart of a lion, but she was built like a newborn fawn. She never stood a chance."

"Are you sure you want to do this? I'll understand if it's too much."

Lizzy dropped a sponge in the bucket and squeezed it. "I'm no stranger to grief. I lost two babies when I was younger. My husband said I had a poisonous womb."

"There's no such thing."

"Kept him from wanting more," Lizzy said. "I didn't mind. It's easier to accept the beatings when it doesn't come from someone who takes you to bed afterward."

Jules had heard the word rape but barely understood the concept of a brutal attack performed in an intimate manner. The act was foreign to all the tales of heroes and lovers. Men were depicted as protectors of women. What barbarian violently forced himself on a woman? What disturbed animal killed without need or reason?

"I had to prepare them for burial. I dressed them in white gowns and booties I knitted. My husband said it was a waste of money, but I wanted my babies dressed in their finest when Jesus took them in his arms."

"We'll make Rita look nice," Jules said.

"She's with her sister now," Lizzy said. "You think they were killed by the same man?"

Jules nodded. "Clyde Cassell is the meanest man I know. He matches Rita's description."

Lizzy looked at the door. "Do you think he's gone?"

Jules debated whether to tell her the truth. Clyde wasn't after them, but they could become victims because of her. "Remember how I said Edna Stall was murdered after stealing my clothes?"

"Yes. That's when Rita told you about her sister."

"She was killed by Clyde Cassell, too."

"Why? Did she know him?"

Jules rinsed the dirty river water from Rita's hair. "No. She was wearing my clothes. Clyde thought Edna was me."

Lizzy dismissed her fears. "Why would Clyde want to kill you? You wouldn't swat a fly."

"He thinks I'm Jessica, my older sister. I look like her," Jules said.

"What did she do to draw his wrath?"

"She killed his brother Buck, the one Clyde was crying about when he went to the brothel where Rita and her sister worked."

"Oh, dear. But that was years ago. Why is he killing people now?"

"Jess was disguised as a man. Clyde was looking for a man."

Lizzy dried Rita's skin. "You don't look like a man."

"I was wearing a man's hat when Clyde saw me on the train. The hat Jess wore the night she shot Buck." Jules squeezed the water from Rita's hair. "I think Clyde was trying to break into our room when Rita returned. She recognized him and…"

"Why would he kill her though? She didn't have anything worth killing for."

"The Cassell brothers were thieves, deserters, slave chasers, and mercenaries," Jules said. "They didn't need a reason to kill. They had their hands into anything disreputable, and they were inseparable until Jess put a bullet in Buck."

"I don't think he's going to wait long enough for you to explain you're not the one who did his brother in."

Jules nodded as she dried Rita's hair. "Not likely."

Lizzy dried Rita's body and rubbed a scented oil into her skin while Jules stitched the neck wound. They dressed her in a white gown they had found in the trunk. Jules styled her damp hair in a braided chignon while Lizzy added rouge to Rita's cheeks and lips.

"She looks pretty." Jules put her arm around Lizzy when she started crying.

Roe knocked and opened the door. "Is everything all right?"

Jules waved toward the body. "She's ready."

Roe handed Theo the buckets of dirty water. He examined the stitches on Rita's neck.

"Is something wrong?"

"This is a running stitch."

"You only need to knot a stitch if it's going to be removed. This stitch is harder to see. That's why I used a crème colored thread."

"I wouldn't have thought of that."

"Did you prepare bodies for burial during the war?"

Roe's voice was low and dark. "No, I delivered the living to the butchers."

"The surgeons had no choice," Jules said. "Shattered bones can't be set. Even if you cut the ends of the bones off, the limb is shortened."

"You never saw the amputees."

"Every town, whether Union or Confederate, has men without arms or legs," Jules said. "Darrow Falls has its crippled veterans. We don't hide them. We're glad they're alive."

Chapter Fifteen

Captain LaDonte docked the *Jenny Lee* in Louisville, and Theo searched for a sheriff and undertaker. Roe stood guard at the salon door as Jules, Lizzy, and Babs prepared the tables for dinner. Clyde couldn't disguise his face, but Roe examined each man as he entered.

Theo returned with twin sisters, Peggy and Annie. They had worked on the *Jenny Lee* before and knew the routine. He called to Lizzy. "You have the key to the room?"

She nodded.

"This is Peggy and Annie. After they store their belongings, they can help serve dinner."

Lizzy retrieved the key. "Follow me."

Roe nodded toward Theo, who followed the women to the room. He had given orders to all the crew that no woman went unescorted and men traveled in pairs. They had Clyde's description, and he had emphasized the threat by reminding them the captain had nearly died at the Cassells' hands. No one else was going to die on the *Jenny Lee*.

His gaze was on Jules as she moved gracefully around the room covering the tables with clean linens and arranging the silverware for dinner. He reminded himself he needed to watch others instead of the woman carefully placing the settings, but his eyes strayed to the slim figure of Juliet Beecher. He was going to protect her, and it wasn't on any order by Chauncy.

The twins and Lizzy returned. Jules handed them aprons, and they loaded their trays with the fish dinner Floyd had prepared.

Chauncy entered the salon with the sheriff. Roe informed him what he knew about Rita and Edna's murders and the probability Clyde Cassell was responsible. Chauncy and Theo confirmed his suspicions and gave the sheriff a detailed description of Clyde.

Roe didn't mention Clyde mistaking Jules for her sister or the role Jessica had in Buck's death. Like Jules, he didn't want Chauncy to worry more than he already did about his passengers. But that made Jules his responsibility. He wasn't going to allow Clyde to harm her. Since she first stepped on the deck of the *Jenny Lee*, Jules Beecher had brought a light into his dark existence. He didn't love her. He couldn't. She was young and beautiful and her kisses vanquished all the nightmares of the war, but he wasn't ready to commit to a woman for the rest of his life. Besides, she only wanted to return home. He wasn't included in her long-term plans.

The sheriff spoke to the gambler Rita had spent the night with and talked to a few crew members who had pulled her body from the water. Satisfied, he shook Chauncy and Roe's hands and left. The undertaker had his men load Rita's body into a pine box and carried it to a wagon.

The undertaker addressed Chauncy. "We'll bury her tomorrow in the pauper's field."

Chauncy handed him several dollars. "Not in the

pauper's field. We'll have a service in the afternoon."

Roe waited for the undertaker to leave. "A service?"

"For Lizzy." His gaze drifted to the older woman serving tables. "She lost a dear friend."

Jules set the mood for the evening with a respectful business-like atmosphere. They engaged in conversations with the customers and served the food and drinks efficiently. No one would guess she had prepared Rita's body for burial or that a mad killer was stalking her. She showed no fear except for a startled gasp when Annie dropped several empty mugs from her tray.

Jules hugged Lizzy as they paused in their work and took her empty tray. Her comfort and joy didn't come from a silly frivolity. Her empathy came from courage to share others' grief and sorrow. No one was alone with Jules in their life. Not even him.

While the dinner guests barely spoke the night before, this group chattered about the dead woman. Few believed she had fallen overboard and drowned. Rumors had blossomed into full-blown tales. The most common was a lovers' spat turned violent. A few claimed it was a suicide because of abandonment. The most cynical claimed the story was a hoax and the coffin had been empty.

Chauncy stopped Lizzy as she passed with a tray of empty plates and mugs. "Why don't you ladies join us for dinner?"

Lizzy signaled the other women, and they joined the captain and Roe.

"What did you tell the sheriff?" Jules asked.

"I told him we suspected Clyde Cassell in Rita's

murder, and there was a similar murder in Cincinnati the day before we left. He wrote down Clyde's description."

"I can't believe she's gone," Lizzy said.

Chauncy patted her hand. "I've made arrangements for a funeral service in the afternoon."

Lizzy beamed. "Thank you."

Jules gasped. "I can't make it."

Everyone looked at her for an explanation except Roe.

"I have to leave at first light to find my cousins in Laurel Holler."

The others voiced disappointment.

"I want to pay my respects to Rita." She looked at Chauncy. "I'd like to sing a hymn tonight if that's all right."

"You can sing whatever you want, Miss Jules."

"Maybe the ladies shouldn't work late tonight," Roe said. The crew hadn't found Clyde, but there were numerous places to hide.

"No," Lizzy said. "I'd rather be in a crowd with eyes watching than in my room worrying." The others agreed. After they ate, they returned to their room to change. Lizzy organized the games and the women. She looked to Chauncy for approval when everyone took their places. He nodded and the games began.

Instead of reducing the number of gamers, the death of Rita increased with the curious morbid. Roe searched the crowd and the doorways for a man who fit Clyde's description as guests entered the salon. Many of the men were stocky with beards. Too many carried guns and knives. But none had a white streak in his beard or a scar on his cheek.

With crewmen guarding the doorways and keeping watch on the deck, Roe turned his attention to Jules. Whether it was her previous experience or the somber mood, the men treated her with respect and kept their hands to themselves while she took her turn serving drinks. She looked up as she gathered the coins and met his gaze. A smile formed on her full lips. His heart bumped against his chest. How could a smile affect him like a schoolboy with all the wonder and joy of a newfound discovery?

"When is Princess Jules going to perform?" asked a man at the table he passed.

Roe took her empty pitchers from her. "Are you ready to sing?"

She nodded.

She was a mixture of child and woman that baffled him. "Are you sure?"

"I love singing. It's my way of sharing how I feel." She joined the piano player, and Roe took up a position near the stage. She sang some Stephen Foster tunes, a few Irish songs that tugged on sentimental heartstrings, and ended with a hymn by Sarah Francis Adams.

"This song is dedicated to a brave woman who lived a hard life. A cruel man shortened her days on Earth. Raise your glasses and say Godspeed to Rita."

They finished their drinks and Jules sang, "*Nearer, my God, to Thee, nearer to Thee! E'en though it be a cross that raiseth me, still all my song shall be, nearer, my God, to Thee.*"

The piano player stopped playing on the refrain, letting her voice be the only sound in the room. *"Nearer, my God, to Thee, nearer to Thee!"*

Roe helped Theo gather the coins tossed on the

stage. "You and your cousins will be able to travel first class when you return home." His words caught in his throat. What would he do when she disappeared from his life?

Chauncy joined them. "Your sister sang that hymn for her husband." He wiped his face with his kerchief. "Brings tears to my eyes every time."

It was dark when the final glass was washed and put away. The boat was lit with lanterns, but few women slept on deck. Men huddled among companions in open areas where they felt a little safer. Roe and Theo escorted the women to their room.

Lizzy unlocked the door. "We have four beds and five women. Which one of us is sleeping on the floor?"

"Jules is leaving early in the morning for Laurel Holler. She'll sleep in my cabin," Roe said.

"Who decided that?" Jules demanded. "I can't share a room with you. What will people think? My reputation will be ruined."

Roe placed a finger against her lips to silence her. "I'll sleep on the deck outside the door. Theo will be outside this one."

Babs threw up her arms. "You don't think the killer will attack one of us?"

Roe rested his hand on his revolver, hoping to reassure them. "I don't know what Clyde will do, but we're not taking any chances."

"I gather I don't have a choice in the matter," Jules said.

"No." Roe wasn't going to argue the point. He wanted Jules safe. "Gather your belongings."

"Don't let anything happen to my girl." Lizzy hugged Jules, and the others followed her example even though they had only met. Jules had the ability to make strangers feel like friends. Most of the men on the boat were in love with her. She didn't love any of them in return, including him. She had a mission. She would return to family and friends once she found her cousins. He ignored any feelings other than a duty to protect her. "Lock the door. Theo will be outside if you need anything."

"I'll fill that basket for you in the morning, Miss Jules," Theo offered.

Jules handed over the empty basket. "Thank you, Theo. My sisters said the basket was magical, but you're the one who performed miracles."

"I'm nothing special, Miss Jules."

"Yes, you are." She kissed his cheek. "Take care of my friends."

Theo beamed, and Roe fought rising feelings of jealousy. She hugged and kissed everyone she met. He shouldn't read anything in her behavior, yet the kisses they had shared were a vivid memory that wouldn't fade. He took the small trunk from Jules. "We have an early start tomorrow."

"Maybe you shouldn't go with me." Her voice trembled. "It could be dangerous."

"I'm the one with the gun," he reminded her. "Besides, the captain ordered me to protect you. I can't do that by remaining aboard the boat."

"I wish I was more helpful. I'm afraid as the youngest, my sisters wouldn't let me do anything dangerous."

"Then you admit you need my help."

"Of course. I'm not stupid."

"We'll find your cousins and return to the boat.

You'll be home in Darrow Falls before your father has time to miss you. He'll congratulate you on a job well done, and you'll be restored to his good graces."

"You're mocking me, but I need Papa to love me."

"I know. I needed my father to be proud of me." It was the reason he had returned to medical school even though he chose not to be a physician. "But we have to stop trying to please others and find our own happiness."

"I doubt any man would have the patience to love me," Jules said. "I'm a lot of work."

Roe chuckled. She spoke the truth.

She pouted. "You don't have to agree."

Some women were worth the trouble. Roe escorted Jules to his room. It was similar to the captain's cabin with a larger bed on the lower level and a smaller bunk on top. A washstand and small desk were the remaining furnishings. He lit the lantern suspended from the rafter. "I'm going to need a pillow and a blanket."

She stepped aside in the small quarters. "Of course."

He removed a blanket and pillow from the top bunk. "I don't think Clyde is a threat anymore. Everyone knows what he looks like. He isn't foolish enough to show his ugly face again."

Her eyes narrowed. "Liar. If you believed that, you wouldn't sleep outside my door."

"Maybe I like sleeping on the deck."

She stepped close. It was unnerving. His fingers tingled to touch her soft skin, to comfort her against any fears. "My sisters have been confronting the Cassell brothers and their violence for a long time. I don't underestimate Clyde, but I won't live in constant fear.

If he wants me dead, he'll find a way."

"Over my dead body."

Jules put her arms around his waist and rested her head against his chest. His breath escaped in a gasp. "Be careful. I wouldn't want anything to happen to you."

"This grumpy old man?"

She studied his face. "You're not so old."

He frowned. "What about the grumpy part?"

Her fingers stroked the growth of beard on his cheek. "You're like a broken doll. Only I can't see the break. How do I mend you?"

"Physician, heal thyself."

She stared at him with those blue eyes that sought so much more than he was willing to share. "That's a funny thing to say."

He turned. "I'll be outside your door. If you need anything, scream."

"Wait." She turned her back to him and pulled her hair forward. "I need you to unhook my dress."

"Me?" His voice squeaked.

"I can't sleep in my clothes, and my ladies-in-waiting are downstairs." She stood still.

Roe examined the seam that hid the row of hooks and eyes. He unfastened the top one. Then the next. "This is going to take a while."

"Pinch the fabric together, and they'll come apart."

A group separated, and he finished unfastening to the bottom of the bodice. The gown opened and fell forward, exposing her camisole and corset beneath.

His hand rested on her bare shoulder, and her skin burned beneath his fingertips. She turned her head, looking over her shoulder. "Thank you."

He swallowed, his gaze locked on hers. How could she trust a stranger to undress her and leave her half-naked without claiming more? Because she respected herself and expected others to do the same. He withdrew his hand and opened the door. "Lock it."

Roe waited until the lock clicked. The woman was a constant temptation. Her skin was smooth and soft to the touch. Her silky hair smelled like spring flowers. Chauncy had given him the task of escorting her to Laurel Holler with the reminder he was her protector. He couldn't kiss her, touch her, or confess his desires. Chauncy had turned him into a eunuch at a time his manliness wanted full expression. No woman had turned his thoughts to mating more often than Jules. She was on the other side of the door in his bed. So close and yet untouchable. It would be a long night.

He set up camp. Roe sat with his back against the door, his blanket wrapped around him. He placed his pillow on his knees and rested his head on it. The distant sound of men shouting and women giggling faded as the night wore on. An occasional footstep drove the sleep from his eyes, but he finally dozed off.

A woman's scream awakened him.

He wrestled out of the blanket's grasp and jumped to his feet. The door was locked. Voices echoed from the lower deck.

Chauncy exited his room. "I heard a scream."

Jules unlocked the door. She had a blanket wrapped around her shoulders over her nightgown. She was safe. "Stay inside," Roe ordered.

"I'll stay here." Chauncy raised his gun. "Go find out what happened."

Roe ran to the stairs where a crowd gathered

around the room where the women were sleeping. "Where's Theo?" He hurried down the steps to the door.

"He's been stabbed." Bud was applying a kerchief to Theo's neck.

Lizzy opened the door. "We heard Theo fighting with a man. Babs made me open the door, and she screamed. The crewman yelled for us to stay inside."

"Bring me your towels!" Roe ordered.

Babs and Lizzy returned with the towels from their room. Roe placed one over the bloody kerchief and pressed against Theo's neck. "Go back inside and lock the door."

"I want to help," Babs said.

"I was on watch," Bud said. "I was coming around the stairwell and heard the scuffle. I had my knife and waved it at the man with a scar on his face. Then the door opened, and the woman screamed. It happened so fast."

"Do you know where the man went?"

"Jumped over the side, but I didn't hear a splash."

"Bring the stretcher from the storage room. Then organize a search party."

Roe applied pressure and waited for Bud and the other crew members to return. Theo waved toward the basket, and Babs picked it up. "Let me see that." Babs waved the Beecher basket with shaky hands. Several slats were cut or broken.

Babs clutched the basket. "Is Theo going to be all right?"

Roe didn't dare examine the wound. He needed to maintain pressure, but Theo had lost a lot of blood. He needed to reassure her. "Theo is strong."

Babs followed as the crewmen transported Theo to the upper deck on the stretcher. Roe kept his hands pressed on the towel against Theo's neck.

Chauncy saw them coming and opened his door. "Put him in here."

They placed Theo on the captain's bed, and the crewmen stepped back. "We'll search the boat."

"Search in groups," Roe cautioned. "He's dangerous."

Roe turned his attention to Theo. He lifted the bloodstained towel. The cut was high near Theo's jawbone. Blood wasn't squirting from the wound, so the knife hadn't penetrated deep enough to reach the arteries, and the largest jugular veins appeared intact. His trachea hadn't been touched. He replaced the towel and applied pressure. How had Theo warded off Clyde? His knife was still in the sheath on his belt and his gun holstered. Clyde must have surprised him before he could react.

Babs stood nearby, clutching the damaged basket. What had Jules said about it being magical? The battered carrier had saved Theo's life. He turned to Chauncy. "I'll need water and bandages."

Chauncy lifted a pitcher. "I have water. No bandages."

Roe turned to Babs. "Put that basket down and come here."

Babs stared at Theo on the bed. "I need you to press down on this towel. Slip your hands beneath mine and don't let up."

Babs hesitated but obeyed. "Press hard," he instructed. "I'll be back shortly. Don't let up."

The door to Roe's room was locked. He pounded

on it. "It's me!"

Jules opened the door. She had put on a work dress and long apron. She had her medical bag. "I heard Theo was hurt. I want to help."

"Wait for me." He knelt on the floor by the bed and reached underneath. He pulled out a dust covered leather bag.

Jules frowned. "Why do you have a doctor's bag?"

He opened the door. "I was a butcher during the war."

"You said you were an orderly."

"I graduated to a bloodier occupation."

Chapter Sixteen

Jules stared at the bag in Roe's hand. He was a doctor. Why hadn't he said anything? The dust covering the black leather had been accumulating for months. He had called himself a butcher. Would he be able to help Theo?

Chauncy was clearing furniture out of the way as Babs stood by the bed. Her hands were stained with blood seeping through the towel pressed against Theo's neck. She turned as they entered. "It won't stop bleeding."

Roe put his bag on the end of the bed and grabbed a fresh towel from a stack Chauncy had placed on a chair. "Step back."

Jules watched as Roe expertly examined the wound. She peered around his shoulder. The gash was smaller than the ones she had seen on Edna and Rita. The blood didn't squirt with the beat of the heart. No artery had been cut. Theo could survive if he didn't lose too much blood. She set her bag on the desk and removed the items she would need. Her father's training became automatic. She threaded several needles and laid them on a clean towel. After filling a basin, she set it on the table by the bed. She tossed a washcloth into the water and wrung out the cloth. "I have needles and thread ready." She looked at the dusty medical bag. "Do you have any cauterizing rods?"

"In a round box."

Jules opened the hinges. She had expected the instruments to be dust covered like the bag, but they were clean and shiny. She removed several items before finding the container with metal rods and porcelain handles. "How many do you need?"

"At least four," Roe said. "I'll need a candle and more light."

Chauncy lit another lantern and placed it on a hook in the ceiling. He placed a candle on the nightstand and struck a match, touching the flame to the wick.

Theo blinked his eyes. He was awake. "Don't move, Theo," Jules warned.

Roe pressed against Theo's neck with one hand and held him down with the other. "It's Doctor Greystone. You're going to be all right, Theo. Everyone is safe. I'm going to take care of you. I need you to trust me."

Roe's voice was soothing and reassuring. Theo visibly relaxed. "I'll need to put him out to stitch the wound."

Jules had basic nursing supplies but nothing in her bag to put someone under. "Do you have any ether?"

"I have chloroform in my bag."

Jules searched the contents.

"It's a green bottle."

She found the chloroform and a nose applicator.

He released the pressure on Theo's neck and blood surged, staining the cloth and his hands. "I can't let go." Roe looked at her. "Do you know how to apply the chloroform? You'll have to be my hands until the bleeding stops."

"Yes." The initial inhale caused convulsions. "Can

you hold him so he doesn't jerk around?"

"I'm going to need your help." Babs and Chauncy held Theo as Jules placed the applicator in Theo's nose and added chloroform to the cotton on the end of the device.

Roe held Theo's neck firm as he reacted to the first drop. He relaxed into a deep sleep with the second drop. Jules corked the bottle and set it aside.

"I want you on my left side," Roe said. Jules took her position.

"What do you want me to do?" Babs asked.

Roe nodded toward the needles. "Put those on a tray and have them ready for Jules. She's going to need all of them. Keep the scissors ready." Babs stood next to Jules.

"I'm starting with the deepest part of the cut and working upward," Roe said. "Chauncy will be on my right heating the irons." He turned. "I'll keep switching them out to keep them hot."

Chauncy heated the first iron in the candle flame. Jules took a needle in her fingers. When Roe released the pressure on Theo's neck, blood flowed. He tossed the soiled towel into a porcelain chamber pot with the other towel and grabbed a clean one, packing it into the wound. He used the wet cloth to wipe away blood so he could see to work.

Roe cauterized several vessels. The smell of burnt flesh filled the cabin. Chauncy heated one rod while Roe worked with the other. Once the vessels were cauterized, Jules began binding the two edges together. A knife wound was easier to close than a gash from stone or brick. The severed flesh was smooth. She bound the opening and knotted the thread for easy removal. She grabbed the scissors from the tray shaking in Babs' hands and snipped the threads. "Tell me what happened, Babs."

"It was awful." Her voice trembled. "We heard Theo shoutin' outside our room and screamin' in pain. Lizzy wouldn't open the door, but I made her. It was the devil himself jabbin' his knife. Theo warded him off with your basket." She glanced at the battered carrier on the end of the bed.

The slats were cut or broken where Clyde's knife had damaged them instead of Theo's body.

Roe grinned at her. "Your magic basket saved Theo's life."

He could smile while performing surgery? Or maybe that was when he was happiest.

"Poor Theo fell to the deck," Babs continued. "I screamed, and the man jumped over the side. Lizzy made me go inside until Mr. Greystone arrived." She looked apologetic. "I mean Dr. Greystone."

"Mister," Roe corrected. "I'm not doing this because I was a doctor. I don't have many friends." He looked at Theo. "I can't afford to let one die."

Jules had admired her father's skill as a physician, but he had never spent time on a battlefield where minutes could mean the difference between life and death. It was evident Roe had learned his doctoring knowledge where a calm efficiency was required. He waved off the last cauterizing rod, and Jules finished the last stitch.

Roe stared at his bloody hands. "I swore I'd never practice medicine again. So much for keeping a promise."

Jules offered him a clean towel. "But you saved

178

Theo's life."

"It'll take more than Theo to balance the scales of death and butchering in my career."

"You're young. I'm sure you'll tip them in your favor."

"Oh, no," Roe said. "This was a mistake. I never intended to practice medicine again. If it had been anyone else but Theo, I would have left my bag under the bed gathering dust."

Jules looked at Chauncy. He didn't believe him, either.

"Roe was a talented physician during the war," Chauncy said.

"Yeah, I could make arms and legs disappear with a swipe of a saw."

Jules folded a bandage and placed it over the stitches. "He might tear his stitches open if he moves his neck."

Roe searched his bag. He found a short board and wrapped it with a roll of cut cloth. He placed it against the side of Theo's neck and head, securing it across his forehead and neck. "That should stabilize his head."

Babs stared at Theo as he began to stir. "Is Theo going to be all right?"

"Yes." Chauncy offered his hand. "Let me escort you to your room."

She took a last glimpse and followed Chauncy outside.

Roe tugged off Theo's boots and carefully removed his coat.

"Do you need help?"

Roe handed her the bloodied jacket. "This is ruined."

"I'll see what I can do." Jules scrubbed the stains with a stiff brush and placed it on the back of the chair to dry.

Roe was slipping Theo's trousers off. "Don't look. Theo would die of embarrassment if he knew you saw him in his short pants."

Jules turned away and laughed. "I think Babs would take offense more than Theo. She's staked a claim on him."

"I noticed. I've never known Theo to have a sweetheart. I hope he knows what to do."

"Most couples figure it out." Jules washed her needles and meticulously dried them before inserting them into a length of thick cloth. "Are you done?"

"Not yet," Roe said.

She wiped the dust from Roe's valise. "It's a beautiful bag."

"Filled with saws and scalpels and all manner of torture. I might as well be a sadist during the Spanish Inquisition." Roe tapped her on the shoulder. She turned. Roe had placed Theo's clothes on the end of the bed and covered him with a blanket.

"Why don't you want to practice medicine? Why are you running a riverboat when you could be saving lives?"

"Saving lives? When was hacking off men's arms and legs considered saving lives? I attended medical school after the war ended because I promised my father I would finish my education, but I'm a doctor in name only."

"You could cure people and heal them as a doctor."

"Do you enjoy being a nurse?"

"Yes. I enjoy helping my father with his work."

"Then you can keep my bag." He pointed to it. "It's yours."

The medical instruments were high quality. "I couldn't accept such an expensive gift."

"All I'll do is shove it under my bed and forget it."

"You can't do that." She packed his instruments in their compartments and closed the bag. "I'll take it. Thank you."

Chauncy knocked, and Roe opened the door. "The crew checked everywhere. No one saw anyone resembling Clyde," he said. "He's long gone by now."

The words were meant to reassure her, but Jules didn't underestimate the hatred of Clyde Cassell. She turned when Theo made a guttural sound. The chloroform was wearing off. She took his hand. "It's all right, Theo. You're going to be fine."

He opened his eyes and whispered a hoarse reply.

"Don't talk," Roe ordered. "And get some sleep."

He touched his neck. "Clyde?" he murmured.

"No sign of him," Chauncy said, "but I have guards on the women. We'll keep them safe."

He relaxed against the mattress and closed his eyes.

Jules yawned.

"You should get some sleep," Roe said. "We have a long trip tomorrow to Laurel Holler."

Jules clutched the bed post. What if Clyde was waiting for her to leave the boat? What if he attacked them on her journey? "Are you a good shot?"

"Not as good as your sister, but Clyde is a big target."

Jess again. Roe didn't understand the dynamics of siblings. She had lived her entire life in the shadows of her sisters. She loved them, but having endured listening to compliments of her sisters' virtues and accomplishments from former suitors, she longed to have a man solely focused on her.

She looked up and caught Roe staring at her. He had a quirky grin on his face. "I have no interest in Miss Jessie."

Could he read her thoughts? "What does that matter to me?"

"Every time I've mentioned her name, you've reacted the same way. You have no reason to be jealous."

She raised her chin. "I'm not jealous."

Roe examined blood on his shirt. "I need to change clothes." He gathered the medical bags and opened the door. "We only have a few hours until dawn." His blanket and pillow were outside his door. "I don't know how much sleep I'll get on the deck."

"You won't be able to protect us if you're exhausted," Jules said. "There are two beds in the room. Take one."

Chauncy chuckled from the open doorway. "Odd as it sounds, I agree. In separate beds," he emphasized.

Roe gathered his blanket. "You trust me?"

"You two could drop where you stand. Exhaustion is a good chaperone." Chauncy motioned to Roe. "But a word first."

Roe opened the door to his room. "Go inside, and I'll wait until you're in bed."

She took the medical bags from him and entered. She had dressed hastily to help Theo and reversed the process, climbing into bed. "Come in!"

Roe locked the door and tossed his blanket and pillow on the higher bunk. "You took the best bed."

She moved the candle burning beside the bed. "I'm the guest."

He removed his coat and hung it on a wall peg. After pouring water into the wash basin, he removed his soiled shirt.

Jules peeked from the security of the bed, the covers pulled to her chin. Small scars covered his right shoulder and side. "What happened to your back?"

He looked over his shoulder as if he had forgotten the injury. "Canister explosion." He faced her as he dried off. "I covered a patient to protect him from the shrapnel. War gives birth to these horrific weapons of annihilation. Who would think of packing small metal balls inside a metal shell and have it explode into a fury of destruction? The metal shards cut into a man's flesh, and the balls shatter and splinter bones. Unable to mend what is left of the carnage, the damaged limbs have to be removed."

"There was no other choice," Jules said, trying to ease the pain in his voice.

"It never made the crippling operation any easier."

She leaned on her elbow to see him better. "Why do men go to war? Why do they find pleasure and glory in killing and maiming one another?"

"War is unnatural, and there is no reward." He removed his boots. "We're ordered to kill against all the virtues we've been taught since birth, and we wrestle with the decisions made in battle for the rest of our lives."

"Like broken dolls."

He nodded in agreement.

"How long did you serve with Chauncy and Theo?"

"I was drafted at the end of '62. Just in time for Chancellorsville and Gettysburg."

But he was a doctor. "How old are you?"

"In years or experience?" He rubbed the stubble on his jaw. "I'm twenty-two going on fifty."

The math didn't add up. "How can that be? It takes four years of college and two more in medical school to be a doctor."

"I finished high school when I was fifteen. My father was a professor and expected me to excel at my studies. I finished my college exams before reporting to duty. I enlisted as a private, but Chauncy promoted me to a lieutenant and assigned me to the medical corps. He doesn't know how many times I've cursed his name for that decision."

His words were spoken in humor. He loved Chauncy. He was like a father to him. "Are your parents alive?"

"They escaped to England when I warned them the South was losing the war. I thought about joining them, but my father sent money instead. He wasn't a very affectionate man, and I guess it was his way of showing his love. Some of it paid for the *Jenny Lee*. The rest paid for my year in medical school."

"Only one?"

"For most medical students the second year is spent learning on the job with an experienced doctor. One of the surgeons from the war was teaching and realized I had learned my trade on the battlefield. He passed me on my final exam."

"You worked hard to accomplish your goal. Why abandon medicine?"

"I like this job better." He looked around. "I'm a

third owner of a riverboat."

"You have a gift, Roe. I know. I've observed my father's work long enough to know he would be envious of your skill."

He ran his fingers along the top of his medical bag and pulled away as if burned. "If you're done chattering, I'll like to climb into bed."

He thought of her as an ingénue and her life had been sheltered compared to his, but he had the talent to be more than he was claiming in life.

He wrestled under the covers and tossed his trousers to the end of the top bunk bed. "You can put out the light."

"Goodnight." Jules blew out the candle.

Roe's deep voice echoed across the darkness. "Why does it distress you when I mention your sister?"

Distressed? "Why do you think I'm upset?"

"Don't play coy, Juliet. I've studied your expressions and can recognize the various tones in your voice. I know when you're agitated even when you hide it behind your smile."

She rolled onto her back and stared into the shadows. "I've had to listen to praises for my sisters from other suitors. I've been compared to them all my life. Even Papa found me wanting."

"And you think because I mentioned Miss Jessie, you'll never be first in my heart," he concluded.

Exactly. "Your arrogance is only rivaled by your conceit, Doctor Greystone."

He chuckled. "You are the first person, male or female, to describe me with those words. You don't know how humbling it is to be the youngest of your classmates. I was always trying to prove myself."

"You proved your skill tonight with poor Theo fighting for his life. I never understood the tragedy of war so clearly. What could be worse than watching life ebb from your friend and being helpless to stop it? But you knew what to do to save him."

"And you were a capable nurse," Roe said. "You helped to save the life of a friend. Theo will be pleased with your needlework."

"I'm sure he'll be happy to be alive." She waited a heartbeat. "Do you think Clyde is still on the boat?"

"They searched and didn't find him. Cowards like Clyde hide in the shadows. We'll leave early and be far away before he crawls out from under the rock he's hiding beneath."

He was trying to reassure her, but Clyde was relentless. A quiet sob escaped her lips.

"Damn."

Her bed creaked from Roe's weight as he joined her. He pulled her close, his arms offering comfort. "I'm only going to hold you."

Her hand sought his face and caressed his cheek. "I'm scared."

He pulled her close. "So am I, Juliet."

Chapter Seventeen

Roe cuddled his pillow, savoring the warm softness as the first minutes of wakefulness stirred his brain. His body didn't want to relinquish the warmth of his bed. He stretched, his hand stroking the smooth curves of a warm body beneath his fingertips. His hand rose over the roundness of a feminine hip, dipped to a narrow waist, and slid upward claiming the fullness of a woman's breast. Realization hit him in the gut. Jules!

She turned toward him, trapping his arm beneath her twisted nightgown as his hand cupped the swell of firm tissue.

His thumb slid across smooth flesh, arousing her nipple to a hard peak. His hand was pinned, fluttering with nervous energy, and the more he struggled to free his fingers, the more he stroked her skin, arousing both of them.

Jules opened her eyes. Her blue orbs widened as their gaze met. Instead of a scream, her lips dripped with sarcasm. "Lose something?"

"Your gown is twisted around my wrist." His excuse was lame, and his voice too husky to hide the pleasure in his accidental journey.

Her voice was skeptical as she fought morning sleepiness. "How did your hand find its way beneath my nightgown?"

He matched her playful banter, masking their

embarrassment. "It strayed while I was asleep."

"You should put a harness on it."

He chuckled. "If you turn away, I will reclaim my roving fingers."

She turned, her hips wiggling against his tormented body, and his short pants strained to contain his anatomy's amorous reaction.

Jules tugged on her gown, and he withdrew his arm as his fingertips traced the curve of her body and found freedom. He waved. "My hand apologizes for its rakish behavior."

"Well, it should." Jules tossed off the covers exposing long shapely legs. She stood on the floor, smoothing her gown in place.

Roe stared at her figure, visible beneath the thin cotton.

She placed a hand on her hip, emphasizing the curves beneath. "What are you staring at? You're a doctor."

He stammered an excuse. "The only patients I saw were flat chested and hairy."

"Is that why you were giving me an examination?"

"You're too healthy to be a patient."

She slammed her pillow on his body. "Cad!"

He wrestled her into the bed and pinned her against the mattress. "I never slept better than last night."

She looked around. "I miss sharing a bed."

"Who do you sleep with?"

She laughed. "I slept with one of my sisters until last year when Cass married. It was nice on cold nights to cuddle with someone."

"Any time you need a warm body, I'd be happy to volunteer."

Jules rose from the bed and gathered her clothes. "I hope you remember to behave when the children are around." She tossed him his trousers.

He sat on the edge of the mattress, the covers covering his thighs and groin. "I should go alone." Her mutinous stare didn't deter him. "You don't have to tell your father I helped you. You can take full credit for finding the children."

"I can't lie to Papa."

About anything? "You're not going to tell him about sharing my bed, are you?"

"If he were to ask…"

"Trust me, Juliet, your father won't want to know."

Her eyes widened. "Did something happen I should be aware of?"

He looked at the exposed sheet. It was clean. "No."

She relaxed. "I appreciate your offer, but they're my cousins. My responsibility."

He had tried. Clyde was out there somewhere, waiting. He attacked at night so if they reached shelter by nightfall, they should be safe. "We need to leave soon. We're already behind schedule."

"I didn't know we had a schedule."

"I was in the military. It's hard to break the habit." He shook his trousers. "I'll dress first. Turn around."

"Why should I have to turn around?" She spun, her nightgown billowing with the movement. "You're not naked like the gambler?"

"No." He put on socks and his trousers. "You should have closed your eyes. What would your father think about you staring at a naked man?"

"He was awfully hairy."

He swatted her on the butt.

She rubbed her backside. "What was that for?"

"Next time close your eyes."

"You don't have hair on your chest."

"It's all on my head." He shook his thick hair and rubbed his hand across the growth on his jaw. "And my face. I need to shave."

"You do that while I dress." Jules stepped into her bloomers and pulled them on beneath her nightgown. "Keep your back turned."

Roe soaped his face and sharpened his razor. He stared into the small mirror above the washstand and saw Jules in the reflection. She yanked off her nightgown and slipped on her camisole. Her back was turned, but the sight of naked flesh was more than enough to return his arousal. He forgot about shaving.

She stepped into her corset and pulled it into place, straining to reach the strings in the back and yanking them from top to bottom to tighten the lacings.

"Here." Roe pulled on the bindings until her body was secured in the stiff garment. "I don't know why you wear this thing. Your waist is smaller without it."

"It's considered immodest to go out in public without one," Jules said. "You better worry about yourself. I can manage the rest." On the bed she had spread a corset cover, crinoline, petticoat, and travel outfit, the one she had worn on her arrival on the *Jenny Lee*.

Roe concentrated on his reflection in the mirror. He stroked downward, removing the soapy stubble. He wiped the dirty blade on a towel and was almost done when a movement caught his gaze. Jules was brushing her hair. The reddish-blond tresses snapped and curled with the movement of her brush like flames shooting from a fire. He nicked his face. "Ouch!"

"Are you all right?" She reached his side and examined the damage. "I would think a doctor would have a steady hand."

He dabbed at the wound with a washcloth. She was oblivious to the torment she was inflicting. He washed off the residue of soap and put on his shirt and pulled up his suspenders. A trip required a vest and coat. He added his holster and gun. He put on his hat and looked around. "Where is my medical bag? I need to check on Theo."

Jules opened her travel trunk. "Do you need to pack anything? I have plenty of room, and it would be more efficient to take one bag."

"He grabbed a clean shirt and socks and tossed them inside."

"That's it?"

"A day to get there, a day to get back. What more do I need?" He opened an ammo pouch. Inside was an extra cylinder for his revolver with lead balls and powder loaded in the chambers and a box of percussion caps to ignite the gunpowder.

Jules looked around.

"Forget something?"

"Where's my basket?"

"You left it in Theo's room. You weren't planning on taking it on this trip, were you? It's beyond repair." He opened the door, looked around, and they exited. Roe knocked on the neighboring door. It was a little after dawn with rays of light peeking above the treetops.

"Chauncy greeted them with a revolver in his hand."

"Trouble?"

Chauncy holstered the gun. "I'm being cautious." He looked at Jules. "How did you sleep?"

"Like a baby."

"Baby?" He looked at Roe.

"She slept like a baby. We didn't make one."

"I trust you slept in separate beds."

"Of course," Jules lied.

Theo was sitting up in bed weaving reeds into the magic basket.

"What are you doing?" Jules asked.

"Fix basket." His voice was a hoarse whisper. He showed Jules his handiwork.

The old basket was worn and damaged. "Is it worth saving?" Roe put his bag on the end of the bed and examined Theo. His skin had recovered its natural color, and his eyes were clear.

"Oh, yes," Jules studied the basket where Theo had replaced the broken slats. "It's always gone on my sisters' journeys. After saving Theo's life, it's more magical than ever."

Theo nodded in agreement.

"Who am I to argue about magical baskets?" He looked at Chauncy for support but found none. He believed in the powers of the food hamper as well.

"Let Jules work on it while I examine you." Roe unwrapped the bandages holding the splint in place. "I put this here to keep you from moving your neck, but once the wound begins to heal, you can remove it."

The stitches had held, and there was minimal spotting on the bandage. He replaced it with a fresh one and replaced the splint. "What do you remember about the attack?"

"I had fallen asleep by the door." Theo paused and swallowed. "I'm sorry."

Roe handed him a tin cup of water. "Drink slowly. I fell asleep at my watch, too."

Theo took a deep breath and continued. "I sensed someone nearby and woke with a jerk. The basket was by my head. I grabbed it and blocked Clyde's knife slash."

Jules looked up from her repair work and smiled. Theo beamed and returned to his story. "We tussled, and he cut me." Theo touched the bandage. "I don't remember much after that."

"Babs screamed and scared Clyde off," Chauncy said.

"Was Babs hurt?"

"No. She helped take care of you after we carried you upstairs."

"I remember that part." Theo's face darkened. "Did you find Clyde?"

"We searched, but he was gone," Chauncy said.

"You are to rest, don't talk unless necessary, and I'll take the stitches out in ten days." Roe closed his medical bag and looked at Jules. "What's the prognosis on the basket?"

Jules slid a slat into place. "Good as new. I can pack food for the trip."

Roe shrugged. "Who am I to travel without the magic basket?"

Jules headed for the door. "I need my cloak and bonnet."

"I'll get the trunk," Roe said.

"Let me put your medical bag in it," Jules said. "We might need it."

"We?" Chauncy looked concerned. "I thought Roe was going alone…"

Jules lifted her chin. "I made a promise to Papa to find my cousins and take them home. I won't break that promise."

Roe patted his revolver. "I'll keep her safe."

"You'll need my help." Theo struggled to throw off his covers.

"You stay in bed and rest," Roe said. "Doctor's orders."

His eyes widened. "You practicing medicine again?"

"You are my one and only patient, Theo."

Chauncy stepped outside his door and signaled Roe to wait as Jules entered the neighboring room. "Do you think it's a good idea for her to be on the road?"

"If I go alone, she's stubborn enough to follow on her own, and that's more dangerous," Roe said. "We'll travel during the day. But the sooner we find the children and return to the *Jenny Lee*, the better I'll feel."

He handed him a bag of coins. "You'll need money for night accommodations." Chauncy looked at the closed door. "Keep her safe, Roe. She's family."

"Family?"

"I'm her surrogate father."

"When you reach Cincinnati, send a telegram to her father telling him she'll be home soon with the children."

"I'm not going to Cincinnati."

"What?"

"You can be back by tomorrow night," Chauncy said. "I'll give the crew the day off after loading the cargo, and we'll wait for you. I'll send a telegram today telling her parents Jules and the children will be home by Sunday. Monday at the latest."

So soon? He tried not to think about Jules' departure. Roe knocked on the door. Jules opened. "Why did you open the door without asking?"

She frowned. "Who else would it be?"

"I could have been Clyde."

She dismissed his concern with a wave of her hand. "He wouldn't knock."

Keeping her safe would be harder than he thought. He grabbed the travel trunk. She fastened her cloak and tied her bonnet. They had been items in a store window, but Jules made them works of art adorning her figure and framing her face.

"What are you staring at?"

"You look nice."

"A gentleman I know bought these for me." She gathered the repaired basket. "He has excellent taste, don't you think?"

He had always thought men were fools to buy expensive gifts for women, but her appearance was as much a boost to his pride as it was to hers. Roe lifted the trunk. "Let's eat and be on our way."

Chapter Eighteen

Roe and Jules reached the summit of the slope of the bank and turned to look at the *Jenny Lee* docked on the river. He sensed her apprehension. "Are you sure you don't want to change your mind? I can find Laurel Holler."

"How does that prove I'm a responsible adult?" She turned and headed toward the edge of town. Roe followed. Her baby doll looks made it easy to think of her as a child, but she had proven her maturity in her tender care of Rita's body, her unflinching steadiness stitching Theo, and her casual acceptance of spending the night together. Her teasing had heightened his growing attraction. It would be difficult to keep his hands off her, but his undivided attention was needed to protect her from Clyde. He was out there somewhere, waiting for an opportunity. Roe wasn't going to give him one.

They found the livery away from the congested downtown, but a sign with the words *closed* hung on a nail by the door. A couple of horses were in the paddock and a buggy was in the yard.

Jules looked around. "Where do you think the owner is?"

"We could borrow a buggy and horse and leave a note." Roe's suggestion was met by an alarmed look. Jules was honest to a fault. "I'd pay," he defended.

"Let's try over there." Jules knocked on the door of a nearby house. A woman answered. Her hair was loosely braided and her dress wrinkled. She looked beyond Jules. "I thought you were my husband."

"Is your husband the blacksmith at the livery?" Roe asked.

"Yes, I'm Ellen Dunne. Our son is sick, and my husband, Ryan, left to find a doctor. Only it's been hours." She searched the empty yard, and her shoulders slumped.

Jules looked at Roe. "Would you help?"

He frowned. He had told her he didn't want to practice medicine, but she had packed his bag in the trunk he carried. "I've never worked on children."

"Children are miniature adults, Doctor Greystone."

Ellen gasped and her face was filled with hope. "You're a doctor?"

Roe wanted to deny his occupation, but the woman was in distress. How difficult could it be? He probably had a bad cold. "Yes. Do you want me to look at your boy?"

She stepped aside. "Please. You're an answer to my prayers. He's been in so much pain, and there's nothing I can do to ease it."

They entered the house. Dishes were stacked in the dry sink. Clothes were tossed on a sofa, some folded, and others in a pile. In the corner was a double bed. A young boy was propped on several pillows. He moaned.

Roe placed his hand on the boy's forehead. It was warm but not hot. No fever. "What is the boy's name?"

Ellen twisted her apron in her hands. "Bryan. He's eight."

Roe lowered the covers. A poultice was placed on

Bryan's bare shoulder and chest. "What happened?"

"He fell from a tree. He complained about his arm hurting. I tried every home remedy but nothing works."

Roe placed the trunk on the floor and retrieved his medical bag.

"He'll be gentle." Jules reassured her with a smile.

She had more confidence in his abilities than he did. He removed the poultice and examined the boy's arm and shoulder, which was swollen. He cried out in pain.

"His shoulder is dislocated," Roe said. He pressed along his side. "Ribs are bruised but don't appear to be broken." He examined from his shoulder to his neck. Bryan winced. "Clavicle is broken but not separated. When he fell, was he unconscious for any length of time?"

"No," Ellen said. "He ran inside. He'd torn his shirt and thought I'd be mad. He complained about the pain, but I didn't worry until later."

He looked at Jules. "Why don't you take Bryan's mother outside? See if her husband is returning."

Jules looked at the boy's shoulder, met his warning gaze, and nodded. "We'll go for a little walk."

Roe needed to pop Bryan's shoulder into the socket. It wouldn't be safe to put a little boy under using chloroform. The pain would be short-lived but intense. He waited for the women to leave. "Bryan, do you know how to make a Rebel yell?"

"Sure."

"When I count to three, I want you to give out the loudest, fiercest Rebel yell you can."

Roe positioned his hands on the boy's wrist and elbow and counted. On three the boy yelled, and he tugged on the arm and rotated the shoulder until the ball joint popped into the socket. The yell turned to a scream but stopped as quickly as it started.

His mother ran into the house. "What are you doing to my son?"

Jules was close behind, her hand restraining Ellen from moving any closer. "It had to be done."

Bryan's shoulder was back in place, and Roe eased him to a sitting position. "He's a brave soldier."

"Did you hear my Rebel yell?" Bryan grinned.

Ellen visibly relaxed. "Is that all?"

"No." Roe searched his bag. "Do you have a length of cloth? I need to make a sling for his shoulder."

Ellen searched through the laundry on the sofa and lifted a yard of cotton fabric. "Will this do?"

"Perfect." Roe folded the cloth and wrapped it around Bryan's shoulder and back. "See how I tied this? He'll need to keep this brace on for eight weeks. You can wash it if it gets too dirty, but put another one on. It'll keep the collar bone in place until it heals."

"Is it a bad break?"

"In a boy his age, it's not a break," Roe said. "More like a splintered crack. No climbing trees or rolling around." He wrapped the arm that had been dislocated against his chest. "I don't want him moving this arm either. I don't want his shoulder popping out of the socket again."

Bryan examined the wrapping. "I look like a mummy."

Roe laughed and messed his hair. "The pain will be worse if you don't follow instructions."

"I'll make sure he takes it easy."

"Ah, Ma," Bryan complained.

"Eight weeks." Roe held up his fingers. "Then you can return to a normal life."

"What about school?" Ellen asked.

Bryan grinned. "I get to miss school?"

Roe looked at Ellen. Keep him home a few weeks, but he can return to school as long as he doesn't play with the boys in the yard."

"But it doesn't hurt no more," Bryan said.

"If one of your friends jerks your arm, it'll hurt," Roe said. "Eight weeks."

The door opened. A big man filled the doorway. "The doctor was busy. He couldn't come with me." He looked around. "What's going on?"

"It's all right, Ryan," Ellen said. "This is Dr. Greystone."

"A doctor? A real doctor?"

Roe closed his bag. "Your son will be fine. He dislocated his shoulder and broke his collar bone."

Ryan gripped his hand and shook so hard, Roe had to flex his fingers when he was done. "Thank you. How much do I owe you?"

"What we need is a buggy to rent," Roe said.

"Of course. I'll hitch one up."

"We'll need a double seater," Jules said. "Do you know how far away Laurel Holler is?"

"It's about five or six hours."

"Then we better leave," Roe said. "We want to get there before dark." Roe carried the trunk to the buggy and loaded it in the back.

Ryan hitched the horse. "Where did you learn doctoring?"

"I learned in the war," Roe said.

"Are you a sawbones?"

"That's one of the nicer titles I was called."

Ryan threaded the reins. "I didn't see many battles. I kept the horses shod and made repairs to guns and swords."

"And you made it home."

"That was my goal. How long are you going to need this buggy?"

"A couple of days. We're picking up three children in Laurel Holler." Roe reached for his purse. "How much do I owe?"

"You took care of my boy. How much do I owe you?"

Roe extended his hand. "Why don't we call it even?"

He shook his hand. "Fine with me." He looked at Jules. "You said you were picking up three children? You look too young to be parents."

"My cousins," Jules said. "Their parents died recently."

"Then I won't keep you."

Jules turned back toward the house. "I forgot my basket."

Ellen came out the door with the hamper on her arm. "I packed some sandwiches and fruit for your trip."

Roe helped her board. "The magic basket never goes empty."

Jules grinned. "It has many powers, Dr. Greystone."

Roe took his seat. "Is this the only road to Laurel Holler?"

"There's a couple turnoffs, but if you stay to the left when you come to a fork in the road, you'll reach

Laurel Holler," Ryan said.

Roe allowed the horse to travel at a leisurely rate. The road to Laurel Holler began wide and well-worn but narrowed to a dirt path that ascended steep hills and descended into rocky ravines. They crossed creeks and streams. "You shouldn't have told them I was a doctor."

"I'm sorry." She fumbled with the basket. "I know you don't want anyone to know, but Ellen was in so much distress and poor Bryan. You helped him when no one else could."

"Don't fret. I'm not mad. I couldn't let the boy suffer."

"You told me how you became a doctor, but why did you choose to practice medicine?"

"I wanted to be a professor like my father. I had my nose in a book most of my life. Then my little sister became ill. We had a self-taught doctor. He tried his best, but she died in my mother's arms. My parents never recovered from her death, but I made a vow to study medicine and help the sick."

"What's changed?"

"The war interrupted my plans. Instead of medical school, I journeyed to the battlefield. I wasn't prepared for the brutality. In books they glamorize wars with traditions of honor and gentlemanly manners. Men don't line up, bow, and fire a shot to claim victory. No, they rip and tear a man apart with bullets so big they either shatter bones or rip holes through him."

He gripped the reins tighter to steady his hands. "Others told me the battlefield would be a better tutor than the formal training of a medical school. Hands on experience."

Roe shuddered. "My first battle was Chancellorsville. It was in the woods or what was left of the trees. I started as an orderly, gathering the wounded with their broken, battered bodies writhing in pain. We were ordered to carry the men in gray out first. Those in blue begged for help, a drink of water, or a bullet to end their suffering. I knew how to stitch wounds and wrap bandages, but I had blissfully been unaware of the cruelty of men toward their fellow man. I had never supported slavery, but there had to be a better way of ending it than the slaughter I witnessed."

"Tyler and Logan blamed the politicians," Jules said. "They failed to do their job. The Declaration of Independence says *all men are created equal,* but from the beginning, the chosen leaders ignored their own words."

"And when they couldn't convince us with poetic phrases their cause was just, they drafted us to fight, knowing we would defend our homes. I didn't belong to the Confederacy. I belonged to Virginia. The men bleeding and dying were Virginians. I had to help them."

"Morgan Mackinnon believed the same thing. You were with him at Gettysburg."

"There were so many wounded the doctor handed me a saw. Men would come in with gaping holes where bones once existed. The surgeon in charge would order an amputation. I'd cut and saw until I was covered in blood. It didn't matter if I lost a few." Roe looked at his hands. Blood had covered them. "The Wilderness and Spotsylvania were massacres. The time between battles wasn't months but days. We couldn't keep up with the flow of broken bodies. Cold Harbor was the last before we set up camp in Richmond and waited for the end."

Roe turned away, fighting back the nightmare. "You think the amputations are over, but the winter was cold. Fingers and toes turned black and had to be removed. Men wasted away to skeletons. But instead of surrendering, starving men marched toward the promise of food that the enemy kept just out of reach. Those able to walk, deserted, heading home to whatever was left. Others surrendered for a meal. Then we reached Appomattox Courthouse, and Lee surrendered. We thought we were heading for a prison, but Grant pardoned us, and Lee told us to go home."

He shook his head. "My home was gone. My parents were living in England and didn't want me to join them."

"Why not?"

"The South patterned itself after English society. Titled aristocrats owned the land, and the servant class catered to their every whim. My father, once a respected professor, was reduced to hired help on an estate. I think he was ashamed of his lowly status. He sent me money to finish my education, and I returned to the place I felt most comfortable in—the classroom. I knew more about surgery than most of the instructors. They taught from books or lessons on cadavers. It's not the same when a man is screaming and begging you not to cut off his arm or leg."

Jules placed her hand on his thigh. He fought not to react. "But you saved their lives."

"Saved for what? I saw the results of the endless surgeries. Men without arms or legs or both. How many were cripples because of me? No, I'm a butcher. My medicine left remnants of a man behind."

"Don't you think that a man who has the courage to fight in a battle has the courage to live even maimed and crippled?"

"What about my courage?" Panic seized him. "I had nightmares about arms without bodies reaching for me, legs chasing after me. I couldn't do it anymore. The memories were too real."

"But you saved Theo's life, and you helped Bryan."

"I had no choice with Theo, and Bryan was simple. I didn't have to cut off his arm."

"I didn't know," Jules whispered. "I won't tell anyone."

"You spoke of broken dolls, Jules. I'm one of them."

She smiled. "Then I'll love you more."

She said the words easily, but he wasn't deserving of love. Blood stained his hands, and darkness crippled his heart. He hadn't earned the right to happiness. What if his despair overshadowed her bliss? He couldn't rob her of the joy of living because he refused to participate. "Tell me about your miserable childhood."

"Miserable? I had a wonderful childhood," she countered.

He chuckled. She had led a blessed life. The normal upbringing had fortified her for the trials and dangers Clyde had introduced into what should have been a carefree outing. "Cheer me with tales of six sisters growing up in Darrow Falls, Ohio."

"You asked for it," Jules warned with a smile so bright, any darkness vanished in its glow. Jules shared stories about her sisters and cousins. She had a large family and an abundance of love. His own life had been sparse of both. Her cheerful voice entertained him on the journey. Only when she spoke of her cousin Jake Donovan did her words become sad. Killed at Antietam, Jake had left a hole in their family. She recovered with tales of Little Jake Ellsworth whose antics kept everyone on their toes. It was late in the day when she paused in her narrative. "I don't know what else to share."

"Then sing a song, Juliet. Sing something to vanquish the darkness from my soul."

"There once was a troop o' Irish dragoons cam marching doon through Fyvie-o and the captain's fa'en in love wi' a very bonnie lass and her name it was ca'd pretty Peggy-o."

"That's a Scottish folk tune."

"Morgan taught it to me. Would you prefer something Irish?"

"No, I enjoy anything you sing." He paused. "You're Irish?"

"Juliet Donovan Beecher. I'm English, Irish, and German."

"I'm English with a highlander thrown in. That's why I liked Morgan. My great-grandfather kidnapped a bonnie lass and married her after she gave him a son."

"Afterward?"

"The dates are a *wee* murky, but the family Bible says he was born before the wedding vows. Rumors say after he saw the boy, he claimed him as his."

She frowned. "Then he only married her for the child's sake?"

"There were seven more children." Roe winked. "I think they got along well enough."

"My father doesn't enjoy drama in his life," Jules

said. "Colleen had a reputation for trouble, but Jessica gave Papa gray hair. He was not happy when Morgan secretly married Jess. Although he had to forgive him. A major in the Confederate Army couldn't visit Ohio during the war."

"It might have caused a few problems," Roe agreed. "What does he think about Morgan now?"

"Morgan won Mama over. Papa couldn't complain after that." Jules sang several verses of *The Bonnie Lass o' Fyvie-o* before they reached the town.

Chapter Nineteen

Laurel Holler consisted of a store, church, saloon, and two rows of homes framing the dirt street. None of the buildings was marked as a jail or Town Hall. Jules read the letter from the sheriff. It was sparse in its contents. "We should stop and ask for directions."

"There's only one road." Roe pointed. "How could we get lost?"

"Do you know which house belongs to the Bauers? I don't. The children are supposed to be with a neighbor. Which one?" She pointed toward the store. "The storekeeper probably handles the mail. He should know where they are."

Roe stopped the buggy in front of the store. He helped her maneuver the small metal step. She grabbed the basket. "Do you plan to shop?"

She lifted the lid. "We need more food. The children might be hungry."

"You don't argue with a man. You wear him down with reason." Roe escorted her inside the store. The interior was dark but warm from a fire in a pot-bellied stove in the center of the room. Jules raised her palms to the stove to warm them.

"Bit chilly today." The storekeeper rolled toward them in a wheelchair. Both legs had been amputated above the knees. Jules looked at Roe, who was staring at the man. Did he feel responsible? She removed the letter from her skirt pocket. "I'm Jules Beecher. I'm looking for the Bauer children. I'm their cousin from Ohio." She opened the letter. "Sheriff Marvin Peel wrote that George and Maria Bauer had died. I'm here to take the children home."

"I'm Spencer Wade of Wade and Sons." He waved his arm around the store. "I knew the Bauers. They were good folks. I sold his shoes."

Roe raised an eyebrow. "George Bauer was a cobbler?"

"Yes, he always joked I was his worst customer." Spencer waited. "You're supposed to laugh, young man."

Roe attempted a smile. "Mr. Bauer had a strange sense of humor."

Jules turned to Spencer. "Who took the children in?"

He frowned. "I don't know. I haven't seen the children since the sheriff brought their parents' bodies into town, and they were buried in the cemetery."

Roe looked around the room. "Do you know what the couple died from?"

"A sudden illness," he said. "Maybe the sheriff took the children to the orphanage."

"Orphanage?" Jules looked at Roe. "That would be awful."

"She's read *Oliver Twist*," Roe said. "Where's the sheriff?"

"Sheriff Peel rode to Possum Creek. One of our local boys stabbed a man in a fight. You'd think they'd had enough of fighting in the war. Some men became meaner from the experience. I don't…"

"When will he return?" Roe interrupted.

"Don't know." Spencer stared at Roe, who turned away.

Jules folded the letter and shoved it into her pocket. "Do you know where the Bauer farm is located? Maybe the sheriff left a note or a neighbor knows something."

"You head toward the church, and there's a path along the cemetery that leads out to the Bauer Farm. About ten miles."

Roe stared out the window. "The main road doesn't reach it?"

"That's the long way. You can't take the shortcut after a rain, but it's been dry for at least a week. The creek will be low enough to cross. If you don't find a message at the house, you could stop at the Widow Kallie Moore's place. She's the nearest neighbor. It's the next house up the road on the same side but be careful. She has a mean dog tied to the porch, and she don't like strangers. Her three boys were in the Confederacy. None of them returned home."

"How awful," Jules said.

"Hopefully, she knows where the sheriff took the children," Roe said.

"I hope it wasn't an orphanage," Jules said.

He patted her shoulder. "We'll rescue them before they have to beg for more gruel."

She pouted. "You don't take me seriously."

"I'm the voice of reason for your tender heart." Roe lifted her chin and gazed into her eyes. "The children are fine. Wherever they are, we'll find them."

Jules looked around the store for something to eat. "If the sheriff returns, tell him we're looking for the children."

"I will." He paused. "Will you spend the night at

the Bauer house?"

"I'd prefer not to," Roe said. "Is there a boarding house in town?"

"No," Spencer said. "But I have a spare room upstairs. My older son and wife are visiting her mother. She's growing frail, and they're helping her move in with us. That's going to be her room."

Jules chose a chunk of cheese and a loaf of bread. "I'd like to buy some groceries."

Roe grabbed smoked sausage and added it to her pile. "We'll take these things."

Jules glanced around for anything they might need. She pointed to a blanket on a high shelf. "We might need that for the children. It's chilly on the road."

The storekeeper took Roe's money. "You need a blanket?"

He looked at the high shelf. "How do I reach it?"

The storekeeper whistled. A tall, lanky boy ran into the room. "What is it, Pa?"

"This couple would like to buy one of our blankets."

He grinned and slid a ladder on wheels along the top shelf until it lined up with the blanket. He scurried up and grabbed it. "This one, sir?"

Roe looked at Jules, who nodded.

The boy retrieved it and handed it to Jules. "One enough?"

"I have my new cloak to prevent any chill." She turned to Roe. "What about you?"

"My coat is warm enough." Roe waited as Jules packed the basket. "We should be on our way."

Spencer wheeled around to block their path. "Is something wrong, young man?"

Roe backed away. "What do you mean?"

"I'm good at reading people, and you're hiding something. You're avoiding eye contact. Don't you like looking at cripples?"

Roe stared out the window. "I saw plenty of them during the war."

He spun his chair to face him. "You're young. Where did you serve?"

Roe threw his shoulders back and looked him in the eye. "Third Corps from Chancellorsville to Appomattox Courthouse. Do you want to see my pardon?"

"I thought you were in the Union. I wore grey, too. I was with Joe Johnston until Atlanta. Lost both legs to the sawbones."

Roe stared at the wheelchair. His face was pale. "You must hate doctors."

"The doctor didn't shoot me. Artillery blast scattered debris everywhere. My legs looked like Swiss cheese. I screamed plenty when they carried me in and put me on the table. I could see a wheelbarrow filled with arms and legs. Scary sight. It gave me nightmares for months."

"I know," Roe said.

Spencer searched him. "You don't look like you're missing any limbs."

He swallowed. "I'm a broken doll on the inside."

"Doll?" He turned to Jules. "Do you know what he's talking about?"

"Did you ever wish the doctor hadn't saved your life by taking your legs?"

"Jules," Roe growled.

"Honest question deserves an honest answer,"

Spencer said. "Sure, I wanted to die at first. Self-pity about what might have been is a cripple's worst enemy. But my wife worked hard to keep the store running in my absence. And I'm lucky. I have two boys to be my legs. And I get to see them grow up. The alternative would be worse. Plenty of graves on the countryside for those who didn't return home."

Jules extended her hand. "Thank you, sir. Some doctors think they're butchers."

He stared at Roe. "You're a sawbones?"

"I was," Roe admitted. "I quit after the war."

"Too bad. We have a shortage of doctors in these parts." He turned to Jules. "Is he any good?"

Jules smiled. "He's an excellent doctor." She lowered her voice. "But it's a secret."

"Not with you around." Roe grabbed her arm.

"You should listen to your wife, Doc," Spencer said. "Then the only broken dolls would be your patients."

Roe didn't look back and rushed Jules to the buggy. He tossed her aboard and took the reins.

Jules squirmed in her seat. "Are you angry with me?"

"Do you intend to interfere with my life in the future?"

She smiled. "That depends."

He smacked the reins on the horse's rump. "On what?"

Her voice was barely above a whisper. "If I'm in your future."

"I don't want to be a doctor. I don't want to be a husband. I'm only doing this because Chauncy ordered me." He met her gaze. "Don't expect me to be your

Romeo."

He had rejected her. "I hate Romeo, and I hate Shakespeare, and I... Oh, no!" Romeo Greystone. She'd heard that name before. Her hand covered a gasp.

Roe grinned. "You figured it out, huh?"

"Dr. Romeo Greystone." She hid her face in her hands and groaned. "Jess mentioned meeting a doctor named Romeo. She was teasing me, and I flew into a rage. Then she said we would never meet because you were a Southerner."

"Just because we share their names, doesn't mean we have to be star-crossed lovers," Roe said. "No more than I have to be a sawbones."

"But why did we meet? And why did you save Theo's life? We have little control over our futures."

He frowned, tugging on his hat to keep the breeze from blowing it away. "Your mother was right. You are overly dramatic."

"At least I have emotions. You're rigid and stoic no matter what happens."

"I'm trying to keep you alive. I can't become emotionally attached to you."

But she was falling in love with him. "Why not?"

"Do you want Clyde Cassell to sneak up on us while we're canoodling in the back of the buggy?"

Jules turned to the empty seat in back. "Why would we canoodle in the back seat?"

"More room to play doctor."

She faced front. "You don't want to be a doctor."

"At least we agree on one thing."

They passed the church, and he stopped the buggy by the cemetery. Two fresh graves had been dug. No marker. "Your cousins?"

"Must be."

"Do you want to put flowers on the graves?"

She searched for any late blooms but saw none. "I don't have any. I'll say a quick prayer, instead." She bowed her head, and Roe waited before urging the horse onward.

The road was a rutted path with few homes. The simple dwellings were spaced far apart. Some had been abandoned during the war and remained vacant. Those that were occupied remained in disrepair with a few scrawny chickens scratching for food in barren yards. A woman worked in the field to harvest the last of the crops and prepare for winter. Two gaunt children stared with haunted, hungry looks on the edge of the yard as they passed on the road.

"You'll have your cousins to feed," Roe said when Jules reached into the basket. She stared at the children. "First rule of war is survival."

"The war is over," she reminded him.

Roe pulled on the reins and handed her his knife. "Cut off a slice of the bread for each of them and add cheese and the sausage. Then we get out of here before they tell all their relatives we have food."

Jules made sandwiches and handed them to the boy and girl standing by the road. "How far to the Bauer house?"

The boy pointed, his mouth full as he chewed. Roe urged the horse forward as Jules looked back. "I wish I could have shared more."

"Didn't you share with Edna Stall, and she emptied your basket?"

A sob escaped her throat. "They're children."

Roe stopped the horse. "Do you want to go back?"

Jules shook her head. "No, but if we don't eat it all, I'm giving them the rest."

"Make me a sandwich before you give it all away," Roe said. "Your generosity is going to make you poor."

"Helping others never leaves you poor."

Roe sulked. "You make it difficult to be cynical. Don't you ever complain?"

"All the time, but I do it with a smile so no one notices." She held the sandwich in one hand. "Give me the reins so you can eat."

He handed her the leather straps and took the sandwich. It disappeared with a few bites.

"Do you want the reins back?"

"No." Roe placed his hand on his revolver.

Jules looked around, searching for any signs of Clyde. They hadn't passed a house for some time.

It was late in the day when they reached the empty dwelling. A sign painted with the name *Bauer* was nailed to the front fence to identify it. The house was one story made of hewn logs. A stone fireplace was on the north side. No animals moved in the yard. No lights were glowing from inside. Jules knocked, and the door swung open.

"Let me go first." Roe pointed his revolver and entered the front room. A board creaked beneath his steps. "Bring the lantern from the buggy."

Roe stood in the middle of the single room as Jules raised the light. The main room had a table and benches on each side. The pantry shelves were empty except for a crock with the remnants of lard and a stack of empty pie tins. Jules opened a cupboard beneath the dry sink. A slop bucket and a couple of dirty rags remained.

The two bedrooms were empty except for the bed

frames and corn husk mattresses. No linens and no clothing remained. "If they were transported to the orphanage, why take blankets and bedding?"

Roe holstered his gun. "I think we need to visit Kallie Moore."

"Let's go before it gets dark. We don't want to scare her."

Chapter Twenty

Kallie's house was half a mile up the road. The storekeeper was right about the dog. A brown mastiff with a scarred black nose and huge paws greeted them from the porch with bared teeth and ferocious growls. When Roe stepped from the carriage, the dog lunged toward him but was pulled up short by a length of rope that strained against the hound's weight.

Jules trembled as he lowered her to the ground. "Do you think that cord will hold?"

Her blue eyes were wide with terror, fixed on the canine. "Are you afraid of dogs?"

"Terrified. I was bit as a child. Lara Herbruck said I had rabies and would go mad." Her eyes never left the beast straining at its leash. "She offered to tie me to a tree."

"What sort of person torments a frightened girl?"

"Why do you think we called her Old Sourpuss? She's Jessica's age but always picked on me. She thought it was funny when I would cry."

Roe put his arm around her shoulders. "Bullies target someone weaker."

"That's why I need to face my fears." She squared her shoulders. "I'm not a little girl anymore."

The dog barked and lunged, causing the porch support to crack under his weight. Roe jumped and pulled her back with him. "A little fear is good."

She looked around. "Do you think there's an outhouse nearby? My bloomers are going to be wet."

"You could squat in the tall grass on the side of the house."

"Don't do anything until I return." Jules froze when the door was yanked open.

A woman, who had to be Kallie, stepped onto the porch. She smacked the dog with the butt of a musket as big as her. "Sit, you mangy cur!" He whimpered and squatted, eyeing the old woman. Kallie had gray hair twisted into a ratty chignon. The thin strands accented her wide, sharp cheekbones. Her leathery skin sagged on a bony frame. She raised the musket and aimed it at them. "Git off my property," she ordered in a voice that scratched like sandpaper. Kallie's dress was faded and patched with squares of mismatched material. She spat a stream of tobacco juice that erupted the dust in the yard.

"We're looking for the Bauer children," Roe called out, looking into the interior of the house for any signs of the youngsters.

"I'm their cousin, Juliet Beecher."

"Beecher! I knew them Bauers were abolitionists."

"Do you know where they are?" Jules stepped forward, and the dog lunged, baring his fangs. Jules backed into Roe.

He placed his hand on her shoulder and moved her behind him. "Call off your dog."

"I don't know nothin' about no children," she said.

"They were your neighbors." Jules pointed. "Just down the road."

"Those Yankee lovers didn't die soon enough." She spat another stream of brown juice. "He made shoes for the Union while our boys went barefoot."

Kentucky had been a border state split in its loyalties. Spencer had said none of Kallie's sons returned home from the war. "Did your boys serve in the Confederacy?"

Her sagging shoulders straightened, and she tossed her head back. "You bet."

"I was in the Third Corps under General Jackson and General Ewell."

She stared at him, measuring him for truth. "My boys served under General Longstreet." A smile creased her face briefly before hatred returned to her eyes. "Two were killed at the Devil's Den in Gettysburg. The eldest died at Spotsylvania. They're all gone. All dead. I got nothin' now!"

Jules grabbed the basket from the buggy. "We have some food we'd be happy to share."

"I don't want your charity."

A noise echoed from inside the house. Roe stepped forward, but the dog lunged, inches from his leg. "Is someone in there?"

"My addlebrained nephew," Kallie said. "The war left him a slobbering idiot." She turned and shouted through the open door, "Shut up, you, or I'll make you shut up!"

"Maybe I should look at him," Roe said. "I'm a doctor."

"He don't need no doctor." Kallie raised her voice. "He needs a switch and a kick in the pants."

The woman was hiding something. "Did the sheriff come by for the Bauer children?"

"Now that you mentioned it, he said something about taking the Bauer brats to the orphanage in

Louisville."

"Brats?" Jules protested.

"He said I could take whatever I wanted from their house." She spat again. "I hope you don't think you deserve any of it."

Roe recognized the defiance. They weren't going to win Kallie's friendship. "We're only interested in finding the children."

"Then you've come here for nothin'."

Roe looked around. "Anybody else come by?"

Jules stiffened against him. He caressed her shoulder to ease her fears. It was unlikely Clyde had beat them to the area. He didn't know they were looking for the children.

"Nobody comes up this road but them that lives here. Only got one neighbor up the road, and he don't like strangers, neither." Kallie raised her gun.

Jules clutched his arm. "Oh, Roe, we have to find them."

"We have a couple hours of daylight. We can return to town and wait for the sheriff to return," Roe said loud enough for Kallie to hear.

"You do that. Ain't nothin' here but an old woman and an idiot boy. We've talked 'nough. Git before I have to make my gun talk for me."

"Thank you for your help," Jules said. "Good night, Miss Kallie."

"You don't have to be polite to the old biddy." Roe motioned for Jules to board the buggy. He stood between her and the armed woman and then joined her.

"Mama always said honey attracts, and vinegar sends people away."

"You're loaded with honey. All it's going to do is

stick you in a mess."

Jules lowered her voice. "I think she's hiding something."

"I know she is."

"Then why didn't you press her for answers?"

"Her loaded gun and her big dog," Roe said. "You still need to use the weeds?"

Jules nodded. "More than ever."

Roe turned the buggy around. They moved down the road far enough for the woman to disappear inside the house. He pulled on the reins and pointed to the field beside Kallie's home. "Those weeds high enough?"

"Don't look." She stepped to the ground.

"Go pee." He searched the other side of the road. He needed to empty his bladder.

****

Jules jumped to the ground and headed for the tall grass. The wind was blowing towards her from the house. She was downwind of the dog. If she was quiet, he might not hear her. She squatted and did her business. From her hiding place, she could see the yard behind Kallie's house. Laundry was hanging on the line. Kallie headed for the back yard with a large basket. Jules remained still, staring through the blades of grass. Kallie yanked the clothespins from the line and gathered a sheet. On the line behind it hung two pairs of short pants and a girl's dress. They had to belong to Caroline and her brothers, George and William. Kallie had lied.

Jules waited for Kallie to carry her laundry inside. She snuck to the side of the house and listened for the dog. She had gone undetected. The bedroom window had no glass. A tattered curtain covered the opening. She peeked inside. Two boys were on a bed asleep. A girl stood by the door, listening.

"Caroline," Jules whispered.

The startled girl turned, and her blue eyes widened. Jules raised her finger to her mouth when she made a noise. She signaled her to come closer. "I'm your cousin, Juliet Beecher. I've come to rescue you."

"Were you the one Mrs. Moore was talking to?"

"Yes. Did you make the noise?"

She shook her head and glanced over her shoulder. "Mrs. Moore locked the door and ordered me not to make a sound." She turned toward the door. "But when I heard voices, I thought it might be someone to help, but you left."

"I'm here now."

"She has a gun."

And a big dog. "Why are you staying with Mrs. Moore?"

"She told the sheriff she would take us in. She was nice at first, but then she made us work in the garden digging potatoes and other chores." Caroline raised her palms to show blisters raised on her small hands. "My brothers are too little to do the hard work, so I do most of it." She glanced at the bed. "They're wore out most days."

"You better not be asleep, you worthless chit," Kallie screamed from the other room. "I need you to iron the laundry."

Caroline's eyes widened. "You better go before she sees you."

She couldn't risk one of the children being hurt by Kallie's gun or dog. "We'll come back after dark for you and your brothers. Be ready to leave through this window."

Tears sparkled in her eyes. "Promise?"

Jules nodded. "Don't say anything not even to your brothers. We don't want Mrs. Moore to suspect anything."

Caroline glanced over her shoulder. "I know how to be quiet."

"What are you doin'?" Kallie's footsteps echoed across the floor. Jules flattened herself against the wall of the house as the door opened.

"I'm coming, Mrs. Moore."

"You step lively, or I'll take a switch to you."

"Yes, ma'am."

"I see your worthless brothers are asleep."

"They worked hard today."

"Worked? When they're bigger, they'll pull their own weight. Until then, you have to work twice as hard to make up for them."

"Yes, ma'am."

"Come on. If you burn anything, I'll put the iron to your flesh."

Jules bit down on the finger in her mouth to keep from screaming. The woman was a monster. She could rescue the boys now, but that would leave Caroline at Kallie's mercy. She ran toward the tall grass. The dog began barking. He had heard her, but she didn't slow. She ran to the buggy and joined Roe. "What took you so long? I was ready to send out a search party."

Jules caught her breath. "Move the buggy."

He hesitated. "Why is the dog barking?"

"He probably smelled my fear. Please, go!"

Roe slapped the reins on the horse's rump. "You

look sick."

"The children are inside," she gasped. "I saw their laundry on the line, so I snuck to the window. She's making them work for her like slaves."

Roe stopped the buggy. "Then we have to go back for them."

"Not against a dog and a gun. Besides she has Caroline with her in the main room. I had time to tell her we'd come for them after dark when Kallie is asleep. We can sneak them out through the bedroom window."

Roe squeezed her hand. "She wouldn't dare harm them."

She wanted to believe him.

They returned to the Bauer farm and hid the horse and buggy in the barn. George Bauer's cobbler workshop was on one side of the small structure. On a long bench were stands for metal shoe forms sorted by size. In a long box were sharp blades to cut the leather uppers and awls for making the holes for the lacings. A sewing machine joined the upper pieces and a peg machine drove wooden pegs into the soles and heel to anchor them to the leather uppers. A box contained several pairs of finished shoes. They were different sizes but few were brogans, the footwear worn by the military.

"Kallie accused your cousin of making shoes for the Union."

Jules lifted a pair of ankle-high shoes. "These look like brogans."

"It's a popular style, but the military contracted the making of the uppers and had the soles and heels put on separately by companies in the East," Roe said.

"That's what they did with the uniforms," Jules said. "They cut the jackets and trousers from wool in Columbus and sent the pieces to women to sew. My sisters and I sewed hundreds. When we were done, we shipped the finished uniforms to Columbus for distribution."

"George was making the entire shoe." Roe examined the machines. "Did your cousin buy these machines after the war?"

"I remember Grandma Bauer talking about someone making triple the number of shoes." She looked around at the neatly organized shop. It was untouched. "It must have been George."

"Then he was successful after the war." His voice was oddly worried.

"Isn't that a good thing?"

"Not to his poor neighbors."

"Kallie called the Bauers Yankee lovers."

"Kallie is an angry woman." Roe examined an unfinished pair. "Did your father mention what your uncle and aunt died of?"

"No. Sheriff Peel wrote they had died suddenly." Jules placed her hand on his forearm. "What do you suspect?"

He dropped the shoe in the box and looked around. "Seems odd the house is stripped of everything, but the workshop hasn't been touched."

Jules shrugged. "Nobody wanted his shoes."

"They could sell the finished ones for two dollars a pair."

Jules stared at the box filled with at least a dozen pairs. "You don't think that old woman had something to do with their deaths?"

"Envy can be a motive when your neighbor is successful and happy and you're not."

"I don't care how bitter Kallie Moore is, she couldn't be capable of murder. Could she?"

"She's holding three children as prisoners," Roe said. "She could be capable of anything. We spent four years killing each other in a war. The right circumstances can motivate the best of people to do horrific deeds."

"I think the sheriff would have noticed if Kallie shot George and Maria."

"There are less obvious ways to kill someone. Poison is often the choice for women, whether murder or suicide," Roe said.

"Poison?" Jules and her sister were familiar with the poisonous plants that grew in Ohio. There were several to choose from. "Wouldn't they have noticed a burning or strange taste?"

"Perhaps Kallie visited with a gift of muffins made with a poisonous plant."

Jules shook her head. "But the children didn't die."

He frowned. "Then she put it in coffee or wine. Something the children wouldn't eat or drink."

Jules shook her head. "Why would she kill them?"

"I hope I'm wrong, but your light hasn't dispelled all the darkness in my soul," Roe said. "I don't trust that woman. Maybe Kallie didn't commit murder, but she took the children and not out of the goodness of her heart."

"Are you going to share your suspicions with the sheriff?"

"It's difficult to prove murder with the bodies buried." Roe closed the barn door. "But Kallie is dangerous. As soon as it's dark enough, we rescue the children."

Jules entered the cabin through the kitchen door.

"No lights," Roe said. "Kallie may check to see if we headed back to town."

Jules waited until her eyes adjusted to the semi-darkness. Two bedrooms were attached to the main room, which consisted of a kitchen and dining area. Roe walked the length of the room and opened the front door. He disappeared outside.

Jules peered out into the darkness. "Roe!" she hissed. A rock hitting something echoed from the roadway. Had Clyde knocked Roe unconscious? A shadow loomed in the doorway. It was Roe. She hugged him, holding on. "What were you doing?"

He closed the door and secured it with a rusty bolt. "Here." He handed her a piece of wood with the *Bauer* name painted on it, the sign she had seen on the fence.

He didn't say why he had removed it. "I don't think Clyde knows we're heading for the Bauer farm."

"The name is in the letter," Roe reminded her.

"I don't think Clyde can read."

Roe checked the doors and windows to make sure they were secure and entered the bedroom of George and Maria. "I need a nap." Roe stretched out on the cornhusk mattress on the bed.

"What should I do?"

"Wake me if you hear anything."

She sat on the corner of the mattress. "Fine protector you are."

"Then figure out a rescue plan."

"Me?"

"You spoke to Caroline. She trusts you. I trust

you." Roe yawned. "You think of the best way to get them out without waking the dog or Kallie."

"I can do that." Jules spread the blanket from the buggy over him and paced back and forth. The floorboards creaked with each step.

"Think quieter," Roe growled from the bed.

Chapter Twenty-One

Jules should have slept in the children's room, but she wasn't brave enough to be alone. She stretched beside Roe and wrapped her cloak around her body. She closed her eyes, but sleep eluded her. Even if Kallie wasn't a murderess, she was mad with hatred. She needed to figure out a rescue plan that wouldn't result in anyone being hurt or killed. Keeping the children safe was her priority. She played different scenarios in her mind until she settled on a plan.

Jules wasn't asleep. She was in a twilight between sleep and wakefulness. She inhaled and sighed, cuddling against the neighboring warm body. Someone kissed her. Tender lips plucked at hers, deepening to a more passionate display of affection. She opened her eyes. "Roe?" she mumbled through bruised lips.

"Who else would be kissing you?"

"It's dark. I wanted to make sure." She touched his face, memorizing the contours and lines beneath her fingertips. "Why did you kiss me?"

"That's how you wake a princess in a fairytale."

"I hope this adventure has a happy ending."

"What fairytale doesn't have an ogre or wicked witch in it to make things interesting?"

"Must we have both?"

He placed a comforting arm around her. "Did you think of a plan?"

She snuggled against his body for warmth. "I'll watch the front door while you rescue the children out of the bedroom window."

"But they know you."

"I can't carry the boys if they're asleep or we have to run," Jules said. "But I can throw a piece of sausage at the dog to keep him quiet."

"That little piece of meat isn't going to keep him satisfied for long."

"Getting the children out of that house is the most important thing, Roe. If I get bit, you can stitch me up."

"I know you're brave, but that brute will rip you to pieces. We ignore the dog unless she unleashes him. I'll lift you in the window, and you hand the boys to me. I'll get them out with Caroline, and then you run with the children, and I'll guard the rear."

"How can you fight off the dog and Kallie? I'm not leaving you behind, Roe."

He rested his hand on his revolver. "I have my gun."

Jules rolled to her side. "Have you ever killed anyone?"

"I was in a war."

"You were a doctor."

"If it comes to killing a mad woman so you and the children can escape to safety, I won't hesitate to shoot."

"Let's hope it doesn't come to that."

"No matter what, once you load the children in the buggy, you take off. I'll run and catch up."

Jules wasn't going to leave Roe behind. He had become too important. And it wasn't for protection against Clyde or Kallie. Although Roe might deny it, he was capable of compassion and deep tenderness. She had witnessed it in his treatment of Theo and of Bryan. Lizzy had warned her of a darkness in him, but Roe was letting light back into his life. He was letting go of his past and, hopefully, reaching for a future. "Run fast."

The sky was cloudy, hiding the moon and stars, and would help them approach undetected. They left the buggy on the road out of view. Roe locked the brake against the wheels to keep the horse from running away. "Don't forget to release this when you escape."

"You'll release it," she reminded him. Jules lifted her skirt and removed her crinoline hoop. Its absence would make it easier to climb in the window. She placed it in the back of the buggy wedged beside the trunk. She pulled the back of her skirt between her legs and tied it at her waist, creating loose pants.

Roe's eyebrows rose and a faint smile decorated his face. "What fashion style is that?"

"The style that's necessary to climb in and out of windows."

He left his hat on the seat and turned up the collar of his coat to hide his white shirt. "Did you sneak out of your home often?"

"No, but I climbed trees, and it keeps the hem from snagging on branches."

"I never pictured you as a tree climber."

"As the youngest, I had to help pick the fruit off the highest branches. After I lowered my hem, I thought my climbing days were over."

Roe checked the revolver in his holster. He handed her a few rocks from the road, pocketing a few. "How is your aim?"

"I'm an excellent rock thrower." Jules placed the stones in her pocket. It might not stop the dog, but a well-aimed stone could slow him down. She removed what was left of the sausage from the basket, wrapped it in a kerchief, and handed it to Roe. "For the dog."

"How old are your cousins?"

"The boys are four and six. Caroline is nine."

"I hope they know how to run fast."

They approached the house from the field. An animal scurried through the tall grass. Jules slammed her hands over her mouth to keep from crying out. Roe pointed toward the house. A light was on in the main room. Kallie wasn't asleep.

His mouth was close to her ear. "Do you want to wait?"

Kallie's vicious threats against Caroline had haunted her. "No."

Roe pointed to the sky. "We need to hurry. The moon wants to peek out from those clouds."

They emerged from the tall grass. Roe stepped on a twig. It snapped. They froze. "Why isn't the dog barking?"

Roe withdrew his revolver. "Something is wrong."

"Don't dogs sleep?"

"Not that one."

This was their best chance of getting the children away from Kallie without the old woman firing a shot. Jules dashed across the open yard and peered into the window. "Caroline," she whispered. No one answered. "Caroline." She heard a noise. Was it from the children or from the other room? Roe joined her by the window. "What's wrong?"

"I think they're asleep."

"Are you sure they're in there?"

Jules placed her hands on the window sill. "Boost

me up."

He glanced around. "I don't like this. If I say duck, hit the floor."

Grab the deck. She had done that before when the Cassell brothers had shot at her grandfather's canal boat. She remembered the fear and her legs shook.

Roe holstered the gun, made a foothold with his hands, and lifted her to the window. Jules climbed inside, landing with a soft thump on the wooden floor. She waited, expecting the door to fly open and Kallie to appear in the opening, her gun aimed at her or the children. The bed was to her left, and she crawled on her hands and knees, peering over the top.

She touched the nearest sleeping form. A long braid lay on top of the covers. She put her hand over Caroline's mouth and shook her shoulder.

The girl jerked awake, struggled to scream, and scratched at Jules' hand. "It's me, Juliet, your cousin."

The girl stiffened. Caroline's arms encircled Jules' neck, nearly choking her. A sob escaped her throat. "You came."

"I promised I would." Jules pulled back the covers. Caroline wore a dress, and her brothers wore their shirts and trousers. They couldn't bother with hats or coats. "We have to hurry." She carried the youngest, William, to the window and handed him to Roe, who put the sleeping boy over his shoulder. Caroline woke George, hushing him to be quiet. She led him to the window, and Jules handed him out.

"Our shoes!" Caroline ran to the bed and knelt, reaching beneath to gather their footwear.

"We'll buy new shoes." Jules tugged at the back of her dress.

"But Daddy made them."

Caroline dropped one. The thud echoed in the quiet stillness. Jules placed her hand on Caroline. "Don't move." Light streamed in through the window. The moon had broken out of the clouds. She looked at the door, waiting for Kallie to burst into the room.

Jules grabbed a pillow, tore off the covering, and helped Caroline put the shoes inside. She dropped the bag out the window and helped Caroline climb onto the sill. Roe urged the girl to drop into his arms.

With the children safe, Jules crept toward the door. Something was wrong. A light showed through the crack around the ill-fitting opening. She glanced back. Caroline was being lowered to safety. She gauged the distance. She could run and dive out the window if necessary.

Jules peered through the sliver of an opening between the door and frame. Kallie lay sprawled across the table top, her pale face turned toward her, staring. Jules jerked to attention, every nerve on edge, her urge to flee battling curiosity.

Kallie's eyes were open but vacant. She didn't move. Her hair was loose, the thin strands fanning over the table top like a lacy shawl. Blood drooled from her lips. Her bodice was torn and amidst the pale white skin was a line of red, the source of a bloody stream that flowed across the surface of the table and dripped on the floor. Had the dog attacked its owner? She held her breath, listening for any sound of the animal.

A shadow passed between Kallie and her position behind the door. Familiar odors of whiskey and tobacco mixed with dirty sweat and blood drifted from the main room. Roe hissed at her to join him. She backed away, treading lightly, but the floor boards creaked beneath her weight.

"Juliet," Roe called softly.

Jules backed toward the window, afraid to turn away from the door. A thunderous thump startled her as the door swung open with a force that strained the hinges. A light behind him, the stocky man stood in the opening waving a bloody knife in his hand. "Who's in here?" The voice sent chills down her spine. It was Clyde Cassell.

"Duck!" Roe shouted.

Jules fell to the floor and shots rang out above her. The door slammed, and Clyde barricaded himself in the other room.

"Come!" Roe shouted.

Jules didn't need urging. She scrambled to her feet and dove out the window, knocking Roe to the ground. She jumped to her feet and raced Roe to the road. "Where are the children?"

"I sent them to the buggy."

Her heart pounded as fear drove her. She didn't dare glance toward the house to see if they were being pursued. "That was Clyde Cassell. He killed Kallie."

"Are you sure?"

"There was blood everywhere." She stumbled on the uneven ground and grabbed Roe's hand to keep from falling. He held on. "He killed her just like Edna and Rita."

An awful thought nagged her. "Do you think he killed the dog?"

Roe kept his gun in his hand, glancing over his shoulder. "That would explain why he didn't bark."

They reached the buggy. Caroline was helping

William board. "I heard a gun."

"We're fine." Jules lifted the children into the seat as Roe stood guard. She arranged the blanket over their laps. "Hold onto your brothers."

Roe pulled the brake and waited until Jules was in her seat, the reins in her hands.

"Go!" Roe ordered as he jumped aboard.

Jules slapped the reins on the hindquarters of the horse. Her hands shook. The clouds were thinning and the moon provided enough light to see the road as she urged the animal to hasten their departure. Roe pointed his gun in the darkness behind them. "Is he following?"

"I don't see anyone, but don't stop until we reach town."

"Are we going to die?" Caroline asked from the back seat.

Jules couldn't see her young cousin but recognized the fear in her voice.

"You're safe now," Roe said. "We won't let anything happen to you."

He had included her as a rescuer. It stiffened her spine, and she clucked at the horse to maintain its speed. She slowed the animal as the distance increased and homes appeared more often.

Chapter Twenty-Two

The town of Laurel Holler was asleep when they arrived. The moon and stars cast the buildings in dark shapes against the lighter sky. The temperature had dropped, and the children huddled in the back beneath the blanket. Jules stopped the buggy in front of the store. Her shoulders ached from the tension and fear of fleeing Clyde Cassell. Her hands had blisters from gripping the reins, and tears of fear dampened her cheeks.

Roe holstered his gun. "I hope Mr. Wade meant it when he offered a room for us to stay in. It's too dangerous to spend hours on the road in the dark to reach Louisville."

Jules nodded, unable to speak without betraying her fear. She turned to the children. Caroline stared back, her arms around each of her sleeping brothers. "Are you all right?"

She nodded.

Roe jumped from the buggy. "I'll wake the storekeeper."

"No, guard the children." Jules climbed from the buggy, untied her skirt, and knocked on the door of the shop. Austin, wearing a nightshirt, answered.

"We need a place to stay until morning," Jules said. "Your father said he had a room we could use."

"Who is it?" a tired voice shouted from a back

room.

"It's them folks who bought the blanket, Pa."

Spencer Wade rolled in from the back room in his wheelchair. He wore a nightshirt and had a blanket draped over his stumps. "Come in, folks."

Roe had the boys in his arms, and Caroline tagged behind him with her bag of shoes. "Is the sheriff back?"

"Came in at dusk. I wouldn't wake him unless it's important."

Roe hesitated. They hadn't told the children about Kallie's murder. "It's important."

Spencer Wade looked at his son. "Go fetch the sheriff, Austin."

"Where can we put the children?" Jules asked.

"You found them, huh?" Spencer waved upstairs. "First room at the top of the stairs on the left."

"Let's put them to bed, and then we can talk," Roe said. "There are horrors a child doesn't need to know."

Spencer lit a candle and handed it to Jules. "I'll start a pot of coffee."

Roe carried the boys, and Jules took Caroline's hand. "Do you want me to carry your shoes?"

She clutched the bag in her other hand. "I'm not a child," Caroline said in a soft whisper. "Mommy said I was her big helper."

"She was right. You helped your brothers reach the buggy."

"I told them the dog would catch them if they didn't run." Her voice shook. "I don't like dogs."

"Not all of them are mean like Kallie's dog." She tightened her grip. "A dog once bit me, but that didn't stop my sisters and me from getting a dog of our own. Old Blue was a good dog."

The room had one bed. Roe plopped the boys on the mattress and removed their trousers.

Jules turned down the covers and slipped William beneath. George crawled in beside him. "Where are we?"

"You're in Mr. Wade's store," Jules said.

The boys fell asleep immediately. Caroline fumbled with her dress, and Jules helped her. As Caroline climbed into bed, the candle illuminated her back. Bruises marred her shoulders. "Did Mrs. Moore beat you?"

Roe examined her back, and she winced. A dark scowl marred his expression.

Caroline relaxed in the bed. "She likes to use a switch, but she didn't break me."

"No, she didn't." Jules had seen children beaten by parents, school teachers, and employers. She couldn't fathom why they thought thrashings and punishment would make anyone work harder. All it did was instill fear. That was the real reason.

Jules stroked Caroline's blond hair from her face. "You're named after my grandmother. She's your grandfather's sister. Her name is Caroline Josephine Bauer Donovan. We call her CJ. My sisters and I have names that start with C or J. There's Courtney, Jennifer, Colleen, Jessica, Cassandra, and me. I'm your cousin, Juliet. Only most people call me Jules."

"Mommy called me Liny."

Roe knelt beside the bed as Jules tucked the girl in. "Liny, how long were your parents sick?"

"Not long. Daddy had an awful stomach ache and threw up. He couldn't work. Then Mommy became sick."

"Did they have a fever or rash?"

"No, but Mommy said her mouth burned and always wanted water," Caroline said. "They couldn't get out of bed."

"Did anyone visit before they became ill?"

"Mrs. Moore visited every day. She said she was going to get the doctor, but she never did." Caroline frowned. "She took us to her house and locked us in the room. She said if we left the property, the dog would chase us down and eat us."

"What did she tell you about your parents?"

"She said they were gone, and we were to obey her and do as we were told." Caroline sobbed. "When are they coming back?"

"Who?"

"Mommy and Daddy."

Roe pulled Jules aside. "I never had to explain death to anyone," he whispered. "During a war, dying was too common not to understand."

Jules nodded and knelt by Caroline. "They can't come back. They're dead." Jules took her hand. "That means God needed them in heaven, but they can look down and watch over you."

"Now?"

"Always." Jules placed her hand on her chest. "And you can feel them in your heart so they're never completely gone."

Caroline released a sob. Had she hoped her parents would return? Had that kept her going under Kallie's brutal assault? "I want my Mommy."

Jules caressed her cheek as tears dropped onto her hand. "I'm sorry, Liny. I'm so sorry."

Roe waited for her to stop crying. "Did Mrs. Moore

give your parents anything before they were sick?"

"She served coffee. She was nice then," Caroline said with a yawn. "She said I was a hard worker for helping my mommy."

"I bet she did," Roe said. "You and your brothers get some sleep. We're leaving for the boat in the morning."

Roe and Jules backed out of the room and closed the door. "I know I should feel sorry the old woman is dead, but no one had the right to kill that little girl's parents."

"Then you think Kallie murdered them?"

"Two healthy young people don't suddenly die of stomach aches, and a burning mouth could be from a poisonous plant. But if Kallie did murder them, she won't murder anyone else." Roe stopped at the bottom of the steps.

"Do you think we should have warned her about Clyde?"

"Who would have thought she was in danger with her gun and dog?"

"Why would Kallie allow Clyde inside her home? How did he find us?"

"You said he was a chaser," Roe said. "Men who can track runaway slaves, can find anyone."

"Do you think your shots hit him?"

"That's why I need to go back to the house with the sheriff."

Jules grabbed his arm. "What if Clyde is there?"

He patted his revolver. "We'll be armed."

Spencer rolled into the store area with a tray loaded with a pot of coffee and cups. Roe poured a drink. "Do you want one?" he asked Jules.

She shook her head. "I want to sleep." She sighed. "At least try."

Roe handed her his cup after a sip. "I'll retrieve your trunk."

She wrapped her cold hands around the hot cup, the aroma filling her head with memories. Her father drank coffee in the morning. Every day he worked to provide for his family. It was a big responsibility. One she was only beginning to grasp. When he was sick, he couldn't work. If he didn't work, he wasn't paid. Although they weren't poor, her parents, like many homeowners, could lose everything from an illness or death. If her father was still ill when she returned, she would work to pay the bills. She had to make amends and ease any distress she had caused them.

Roe returned with their belongings and carried them upstairs. Austin and the sheriff arrived as Roe was coming down the steps. Sheriff Marvin Peel was an older man with a belly straining his waist band. He hadn't bothered to put on a tie or vest. He didn't look happy about being awakened in the middle of the night.

"I hope this isn't some prank." Marvin accepted a cup of coffee from Spencer and glared at Roe. "What is so darn important it couldn't wait 'til morning?"

Roe put his arm around Jules. "Kallie Moore was murdered."

"What?" Coffee splattered from his mouth through gaps in his teeth. "Who are you?" Marvin placed his cup on the counter and rested his hand on his revolver.

"Roe Greystone and this is Miss Jules Beecher."

"Beecher," he repeated. "I know that name from somewhere."

"The Bauer children are my cousins. My father

wrote you."

"Dr. Sterling Beecher is your father?"

She nodded. "Yes, sir."

He looked around the store. "Why didn't he come?"

"He became ill, and I took his place." She searched her skirt pocket. "I have your letter."

He glanced at the letter, but his hand remained on his gun. "So what makes you think Mrs. Moore was murdered? Did you have something to do with it?"

Roe stepped toward him. Like many veterans, he didn't fear confrontation, and his voice had a hint of anger. "No, it was Clyde Cassell."

"Never heard of him," Marvin said. "Why would he want to kill Mrs. Moore?"

"He wants to kill me," Jules said. "He hates women, especially ones named Beecher."

"Your family are abolitionists?"

"They were, but that's not…"

"Is this Clyde fellow a Confederate?"

"Yes," Roe said. "So am I."

Marvin studied him. "Then why are you traveling with a woman named Beecher?"

"The war is over."

"Kallie Moore lost her three sons in the war. She was never the same."

"Don't make excuses for her," Roe said. "She could have…" Jules touched his arm, and he stopped.

"We don't know for sure," she whispered.

He nodded. "I fought for Virginia. I'll never forget the battles or the men who died, but I won't wallow in self-pity and blame. Clyde Cassell was a deserter and murderer. He shot his commanding officer, and he's killed at least four women. Don't let your misplaced sympathies cloud your vision."

Marvin retrieved his cup and sipped. "Why don't you tell me what happened from the beginning."

Roe and Jules filled him in on the history of the Cassells and the Beecher dispute.

The sheriff thought about their words. "Doesn't sound like much of a reason to kill someone."

"Clyde doesn't need a good reason to kill," Roe said. "Clyde and his brother were chasers, mercenaries, and thieves. They didn't hesitate to inflict harm if anyone attempted to stop them."

"You said brothers? Where's the other one?"

"Buck was killed in 1862." Jules swallowed the fear in her voice. "Clyde might blame the Beechers for that, too."

"You killed him?"

"Me?" Jules gasped. "No, I'd never harm anyone."

"Buck was killed in a shootout during a robbery," Roe summarized. "Clyde is the one you have to worry about."

"What is he doing here?"

Jules trembled. "He followed me."

"To the Bauer house?"

Roe put his arm around her shaking shoulders. "No, we didn't see him there. It was empty, and I mean empty. Someone removed all the food, dishes, and linens."

Marvin frowned. "It wasn't like that when I collected the bodies."

"Kallie claimed you gave her permission to take what she wanted."

"I never said anything of the kind to her."

"Why didn't you bring the children to town?" Jules had trouble controlling her anger. "How could you leave them with her?"

"Mrs. Moore had already taken them in."

"It didn't occur to you that she might be dangerous?" Roe was nose to nose with Marvin.

"She can be mean to strangers, but she'd never hurt anyone."

"There's a little girl upstairs with welts on her back," Roe said. "That woman not only beat that child, she may have murdered her parents."

"What?"

"Do you know what George and Maria died from?" Jules asked.

"Mrs. Moore said they had influenza."

"Is she a doctor?" Roe's voice dripped with sarcasm.

Marvin raised his voice. "Are you?"

Roe paused before extending his hand. "Dr. Roe Greystone at your service."

The sheriff stared. "A real doctor?"

"Some called me a butcher during the war, but I have a paper stating I can practice medicine."

"Mrs. Moore said the Bauers were ill for a couple of weeks. Said it was influenza. They were throwing up and had swelling around the face. She said she took care of them until they died. Then she drove into town and told me what had happened. When she offered to take the children, I was grateful. Not many people can take in three children." Marvin paused. "I found some letters from a Caroline Donovan at the house. She was an aunt of George, and I wrote her."

"My grandmother," Jules said. "That's when my

father wrote you."

"Did you tell Kallie that Dr. Beecher was coming?" Roe asked.

"No, I don't get out to her place much." He studied Roe. "What makes you think the Bauers didn't die of natural causes?"

"Has anyone else had influenza?" Roe asked.

Marvin reflected on his question. "No, but some folks are hardier than others. Where's your evidence, young man?"

"I don't have any. Kallie may be innocent and just a good neighbor, but I find that hard to believe. After we stopped at the Bauer house, we drove next door to Kallie's place. She wouldn't let us in. Said the children weren't there. She said you had taken them to an orphanage."

"Orphanage?" The sheriff finished his coffee and handed the cup to Spencer. "I only put that in the letter to get a timely reply. When Dr. Beecher wrote, I figured the children could stay at the Moore place until he arrived." He swiped his mouth with a kerchief. "Why would Mrs. Moore lie?"

"That's what made us suspicious," Roe said. "Kallie showed us the barrel of her gun, and we left. Miss Beecher had to…"

"I visited the weeds along the property to take care of personal issues," Jules said. "I saw children's clothing hanging on the wash line behind the house. I crept toward the bedroom window and talked to Caroline. She said Kallie was forcing them to work."

"It's normal for children to do chores."

"In addition to the bruises, she had blisters on her hands." Jules fought a sob. "I hope you don't mistreat children like my cousins have been abused."

"No, but you should have come for me."

"The children might be dead if we hadn't gone last night." Jules steadied her voice. "We waited until dark and returned. Roe lifted me into the window, and I passed the children out."

The sheriff looked at Roe. "Where's the part about Kallie being murdered?"

"The dog didn't bark," Roe said.

"What's a dog have to do with murder?"

"That dog won't let you near the place without making a ruckus," Austin said. "I hate making deliveries there."

Jules pointed at the boy. "That's right. We thought it odd the dog didn't make any noise. I saw a light in the next room and peeked through the crack. I saw Kallie on the table, staring at me." Jules fought back tears. "Blood was all over, dripping on the floor."

The sheriff turned to Roe. "What were you doing during this? Did you kill her?"

"Do you see blood on me?" Roe demanded. "I was outside the window, helping the children escape. I sent them to the buggy in the road and called for Jules. That's when Clyde Cassell broke through the door, and I shot at him."

"Did you kill him?"

"No. He escaped into the other room. We took the opportunity to run." Roe let out a deep breath. "When we arrived, we asked Austin to wake you."

"I'll hitch a wagon and fetch the body," the sheriff said.

"I'd like to go with you," Roe said.

"If she's dead, what can you do, Doctor?"

"Look for any evidence I hit Clyde."

"Nothing nastier than a wounded animal," Spencer said.

"I agree," Roe said. "I wouldn't want you to find him alone."

Marvin wiped his brow and put on his hat. "I appreciate the help. I'll be out front in ten minutes. Be ready."

Chapter Twenty-Three

Roe searched the shelves and cases of the store. He couldn't let the sheriff travel to Kallie's place alone, but he wouldn't leave Jules and the children in any danger. He looked at the boxes behind the counter.

Spencer wheeled his chair after him. "What are you looking for?"

He looked Spencer in the eye. "Do you have a gun?"

"What's wrong with the one you're wearing?"

"I'm not leaving Jules unprotected."

Spencer nodded. "I have my muzzleloader from the war."

"No revolver?"

He spun his wheelchair around and rolled toward the back room. "I received a Colt revolver last week for a customer." He returned with a wooden box on his lap. He pried the lid with a knife. "Will this do?"

Roe examined the gun. He presented it to Jules.

She raised her hands. "I'm no good with a gun. I jerk too much when I pull the trigger."

Roe handed the gun to Spencer. "Are you too tired to keep watch?"

"Are you expecting this Clyde fellow to come here?"

Roe glanced at Jules. "No, but he's too dangerous to take any chances."

Jules frowned. She suspected the truth, but he wasn't going to voice his suspicions and add to her fears. Clyde Cassell was out there in the dark. He may have seen her in the bedroom and recognized her. He'd killed too many women not to take precautions.

Spencer examined the new gun. He pointed to a shelf behind the counter. "There's powder and bullets on that shelf."

"I can load it," Roe offered as he retrieved the box of conical lead balls and tin of black powder.

Spencer refused to surrender the revolver. "I remember how to load a gun."

"I know what you're doing," Jules said. "But I'm too scared to tell you I'm not afraid."

Roe put his arm around her and kissed her forehead. "I'll be back in a couple of hours. Go upstairs and sleep."

"Not likely." She touched his sleeve. "Be careful."

Roe didn't want to leave her, but if General Robert E. Lee had taught him anything, it was to surprise the enemy. Clyde wouldn't expect an attack. But he wanted Jules and the children to be safe during his absence.

"Up," he ordered, escorting her upstairs.

She turned. "I know you promised Chauncy you'd be a gentleman, but if you don't kiss me, I'm going with you."

"I'll tell him you threatened me." He kissed her on the lips, lingering when she didn't resist, responding when her arms wrapped around his neck and her body sought comfort. He reassured her with his lovemaking. He had fought every urge to touch her when they shared the mattress in the Bauer house, faithful to Chauncy's admonition to treat her like a sister. But only the presence of the children crowding the bed kept him from taking Jules into the bedroom and giving her his full attention.

He waited until she had locked the door before returning to the main floor. Roe gathered his hat and checked his gun. "I don't have to tell you how important she is to me."

Spencer patted the revolver on his lap. "I'll protect her with my life."

Roe looked around. "Where's Austin?"

"He's hiding your buggy and horse in the barn. No need to advertise you're here."

Roe stepped outside. The sheriff drove a small wagon with short sides and no canvas. He had thrown a few blankets on the seat and was sitting on them. A rifle was placed on the floor at his feet.

He climbed in beside him. "I see you brought some blankets to cover the body."

Marvin grunted and urged the horses forward. "You said you were a doctor. Do you know anything about boils?"

Roe wasn't surprised by the inquiry. Doctors were asked medical questions all the time. Many of them outside the office, the patient too embarrassed to be seen officially. "Where is it?"

He shifted on the bench seat. "On my backside. The first one appeared a couple of days ago, but I think there might be more. I almost didn't return to town because of the pain of riding."

Boils were common and spread if untreated. "How often do you bathe?"

"Once a month, most of the time."

"You need to bathe more often," Roe said. "To

treat the boil, soak clean cheesecloth in hot water and place a thick wad over the boil several times a day. Allow the pus to drain onto the cloth. Throw it away or burn the gauze. Don't touch it. Cover the boil at all other times with dry gauze. And wash your hands after touching the boil. Otherwise they'll spread, and if you think one boil hurts, wait until you have a dozen."

"Thanks, Doctor." He lowered the brim of his hat. "I couldn't tell my wife about them."

"Why not?"

"I thought a lady friend gave them to me."

"Those sores would be on the front not on the backside," Roe said. "And there's no cure. It's not a pretty way to die. You might want to think about being faithful to your wife."

"She don't show much interest in me," he mumbled.

"You take a bath more often, and that may change."

He chuckled. "I guess I didn't think about being pretty for my wife." He became serious. "Besides the scar, what does this Clyde fellow look like?"

"I've never seen him, but others say he's a stocky man with long brown hair and a beard with a white streak," Roe said. "He carries a revolver and Bowie knife. He prefers the knife for killing. He slices the neck, deep and deadly. Don't let him near you."

Roe searched the trees and road as they traveled back on the familiar path. No sign of Clyde. They passed the Bauer farm. It looked as deserted as before, but Roe asked the sheriff to stop. He looked around the house and barn. No signs of anyone. He grabbed the box of finished shoes from the barn and placed them in the wagon. They stopped at the Moore place next.

Roe followed the sheriff to the yard. The dog was sprawled in a pool of blood at the end of his rope. Marvin lifted the dog's head. "His throat is cut."

The door was ajar and light from a lantern spilled out through the opening. Bloody footprints faded inside the cabin. Both men had their guns ready. Kallie was where Clyde had left her sprawled on the table. Her skirt was bunched around her waist, exposing her skinny bare legs. The sheriff lowered the fabric.

Roe examined Kallie's face and neck. "Same wound as Rita. If he was planning to kill her, why…"

"Yeah," the sheriff growled. "Mrs. Moore was mean, but she didn't deserve this."

"What if she poisoned the Bauers?"

"You have no proof. I won't have a dead woman's name slandered."

"I know it won't make any difference, but I'd like to know the truth." Roe searched the kitchen area. A coffee pot rested on the stove. A fire had died only recently. The white embers emitted heat. A cloth bag contained coffee. He sniffed. He wet his finger and dipped it into the ground beans. It burned his tongue. He spat. "I think I found the poisoned coffee." He closed the bag and shoved it into his pocket.

"How do we know for sure?"

"I'll feed some to a rodent and see if it dies."

The sheriff picked up a tin cup in the dry sink. "It's not poisoned. Mrs. Moore drank some."

Roe took the cup. A small amount of brown liquid was in the bottom. It smelled like the coffee in his bag. "That doesn't make sense. Unless…"

"What?"

"Clyde drank the coffee, but I doubt one cup would kill him." He grabbed the lantern and examined the floor. Blood stained the opening in the bedroom doorway and droplets trailed across the floor to a stack of folded laundry. Blood stained several pieces of clothing that had been discarded on the floor. "I must have hit him."

Marvin joined him. "What do you think will kill him first, the poison or the bullet hole?"

"He's too mean to die a quick death." Jules and the children were in danger. "We should get back to town."

"We load Mrs. Moore and her dog into the wagon first."

"Why the dog?"

"I know he was a mean cur, but I don't want to leave him here for the coyotes to rip apart."

They wrapped Kallie in a blanket and carried her to the wagon. While Marvin wrapped the dog, Roe looked around. In the pantry, he found a collection of medicinal herbs and roots. Some of the plants were poisonous. Kallie's room contained a new quilt on the bed. In the children's room he saw a trunk. It contained the children's clothing and personal items.

A photograph of a couple was on top. It must have been George and Maria. They were young with a future before them. George had worked hard to build a life for his family. He had stood by his convictions against slavery. He had seized an opportunity to make more shoes after the war.

Kallie had lost her sons in the war and any chance at wealth in the aftermath of the Confederate defeat. She couldn't fight the United States government so she had turned her anger to an unsuspecting neighbor. A crazy woman had destroyed the Bauer's dreams. He grabbed the quilt from Kallie's bed and examined the corners. Maria Bauer had stitched her initials in the fabric. She added the quilt to the trunk of Bauer belongings. One more memory to ease their loss.

"Help me load the trunk," Roe said when Marvin joined him. "The children will need it."

Roe secured the door and joined Marvin. "Spencer said Kallie's boys were killed in the war. Did she have any other family?"

Marvin slapped the reins on the back of his team. "None I know of. After her boys were killed, she kept to herself. I can't believe she killed the Bauers. She complained about their sympathies to the Union, but I didn't think her hatred ran deep enough for murder."

"We can afford to give her the benefit of the doubt. I took a box of finished shoes from George Bauer's workshop. Sell them and use the money to pay for her burial."

Marvin looked shocked by his gesture. "Why?"

"She was a tortured soul," Roe said. "I can sympathize with that. The war created a lot of broken dolls. Some of them couldn't be fixed. We have to forgive others who are plagued by demons. We have to forgive ourselves."

Marvin turned the wagon around in the yard and headed toward town.

The trip had taken longer than he had anticipated. A lightness in the eastern sky signaled dawn, but somewhere in the shadows lurked a wounded Clyde.

Chapter Twenty-Four

Jules stretched tortured muscles in the chair where she had fallen asleep. A pale light filtered through the sectioned window and decorated the floor boards with lighter colored squares. Morning had arrived, and the children were stirring. She looked around at the unfamiliar surroundings. They were at the Wade's store. How long had she slept? She looked out the window. A fog rested above the frost-covered ground. Where was Roe?

She had slept in her clothes and smoothed the wrinkles with her hands.

"I have to pee," George stated.

Jules looked for a chamber pot. After they emptied their bladders, Jules helped the boys and Caroline wash and dress. She poured the water from the wash basin into the chamber pot and placed a lid on it. She grabbed her cloak and carried the pot downstairs with the children following.

Spencer was seated in his wheelchair, asleep. His hand rested on the revolver on his lap. "Don't wake him," Jules warned. She entered the back room. Most of the space was used for storage, but in a small space to the side was the kitchen and pantry. A door next to the stove opened to the yard. A box for wood was within arm's reach. A pump was located farther in the yard, and an outhouse was near the creek flowing behind the store. She fastened her cloak, opened the door, and searched for any signs of life. She carried the chamber pot to the outhouse. She pulled on a rope fastened as a handle and yanked the door open. A wooden bench with a hole was placed over a pit in the ground. She emptied the chamber pot, holding her breath until the foul task was completed.

Something moved in the dark shadows of the small compartment. A large black snake lowered its head from the ledge of the roof and startled her. She yelped and jumped back, tripping over her skirt and falling to the ground. The chamber pot rolled across the yard.

"What's wrong?" Caroline asked from the porch.

Black snakes were harmless, but Jules had reacted like a frightened child. She scrambled to her feet and snatched the handle of the pot and its lid. "I'm fine. Just clumsy." She smiled and walked slowly to the pump. She filled the pot, emptied it, and rinsed it again, using the repetition to calm her nerves. She left the pot to dry in the yard and washed her hands.

She smiled at the children who backed up to allow her to enter. "Are you hungry?"

"I'm starving!" George announced.

Jules draped her cloak over a chair and added wood to the stove. After lighting the fire, she searched for flour, buttermilk, and lard for biscuits. She mixed the dough, kneaded it, and pressed it into a circle.

"I can cut the biscuits," Caroline said.

Jules handed her a round cutter. "There must be eggs around here somewhere."

George pointed outside. "I see chickens."

Hens were strutting down the plank of a chicken coop to search for grubs and bugs in the morning grass.

She grabbed her cape and a small basket.

"Can I help?" George asked.

After the snake in the outhouse, Jules didn't want the children to leave the safety of the house. "Can you find a bowl and fork while I'm gone?"

He nodded.

Jules fastened her cloak and crossed the yard, glancing side to side, looking for any signs of trouble. Clyde would be stupid to be in town. He was more likely lurking in the woods or hiding in an abandoned building.

She stood outside the door to the coop. The boards were hand hewed with large gaps between them. She peeked in an opening and didn't see anyone lurking inside. A small piece of wood nailed to the wall kept the door from swinging open. She turned the wooden handle, and the door creaked.

The nesting boxes were on each side of the building. She grabbed an egg from the nearest one and put it in her basket. She found two in the next box and added them to her collection. She stepped deeper into the chicken coop, the small quarters already warm from the morning sun streaming through the cracks in the walls. Her movements stirred feathers lining the nest, and she sneezed.

A grunt no chicken would make was uttered beneath the boxes. A well-worn boot with a hole in the sole slid into view. She backed away toward the door. Clyde Cassell emerged from the gap between the nesting boxes and the floor like a slithering snake ready to strike. He was dirty, his hair caked with feathers and cobwebs. His clothes were rumpled and stained. Whether it was blood or dirt, she didn't wait to determine. She screamed and threw the basket of eggs at him before running toward the house.

Caroline was standing in the doorway, a wooden spoon in her hand. "Get the storekeeper!" The girl disappeared inside.

Jules slipped on the wet grass. She braced her fall with her hands. Clyde grabbed her cloak and tugged. Jules screamed as loud as she could. The fastener choked her, and she scratched at her throat. "Don't kill me!" She rose to her knees to escape.

A stream of tobacco juice stained the grass beside her. "I just want to chat with you for now." He stomped on her butt, pinning her to the ground.

A sharp pain radiated from his weight on her hip bone. He was too strong to escape. What was taking Caroline so long to fetch Spencer?

"Look at me!" he ordered.

She leaned on an elbow and twisted her body to obey. His dirty boot was braced on her hip and stained her cloak with mud. The hem of his checkered pants was frayed, and he wore no socks. His coat was faded and military. Probably stolen from a dead soldier. A haversack hung across his chest. He reached into the cloth bag and threw her beaded reticule on the ground by her face. "Is this yours?"

She didn't answer.

"Is this the bag your friend stole from you?"

"Edna was not my friend." Jules stared at the familiar purse. "But you didn't have to kill her."

"I thought she was you."

Jules closed her eyes to the image of Edna's body in the bloody alley. Clyde wanted her dead.

"Where did you get the gold coin that was inside?"

Jules opened her eyes. Thick fingers gripped the handle of his long Bowie knife. The morning sunlight reflected off the metal. She stretched out of his reach, but he held her firmly in place, pinned beneath his boot. "Blake gave it to me."

"Blake Ellsworth? The owner of the Mermaid's Mirth?"

She nodded. The shiny blade was hypnotizing as he waved it before her eyes. The edge was razor sharp, and blood stained the surface near the hilt. Hers would be the next to flow from the sharp cut of his knife. Would her life end quickly or pour out slowly in an endless cry for mercy?

"Why did he give you a gold coin? What did you do for him?"

"It was for helping to save his life after you shot him on the *Irish Rose*."

"That was Buck. It was supposed to be a warning shot." His chuckle turned into a growl. "Then you shot Buck in the leg."

"That..." she bit off her reply. While Jess had shot Buck, she had clutched the deck in fear. She had been too scared to determine the shooter's identity. "Does it matter?"

He spat another stream of tobacco juice on the ground inches from her face. Blood was mixed with the brown liquid. Beads of sweat were on his forehead even though the morning air was cold. "I heard ya singin' on da boat. Ya sing real perty." His words were slurred.

Who cared how she sang? "Why did you kill Rita?"

"Who?"

"The woman on the *Jenny Lee*." She needed to

keep him talking and buy time. Where was Spencer?

"She attacked me. Said I killed her sister." He grimaced in pain. "I can't remember all the people I kilt."

"And Kallie? The woman up the road?"

"She thought I was her son." He laughed in a way that sent chills down her spine. "I showed her I was no kin."

Bile rose in her throat, and Jules fought the urge to empty what little contents were in her stomach.

A shot rang out. Jules screamed. Spencer was in the doorway. He rolled his wheelchair into the yard where he waved his revolver.

Clyde yanked Jules to her feet and against his chest. "You go ahead and shoot!" he shouted at Spencer. "Kill us both." He backed away, pulling her with him to use as a shield. His knife was pressed against her throat. He lowered his voice. "This ain't the end of our talk."

She stumbled as she walked backwards, bumping into him and tangling with his feet. A sharp pain pierced her neck, and she gasped. He threw her to the ground.

Shots rang out. Jules lay face down, afraid to move, waiting for death to take her. A throbbing radiated from her throat. Clyde must have cut her, but why were her thoughts so clear?

"Juliet." It was Roe's panicked voice. He rolled her over, staring into her face. He was kneeling, examining her for any injuries. "He cut you. It isn't deep."

She touched her neck. Her fingertips were covered with warm blood. He pressed his kerchief against the wound. "Hold this."

"I thought he killed me. I thought I was dead."

The expression on Roe's face said the same thing. He picked her up and carried her to the house against her protest. She could walk.

Spencer rolled his chair back. The sheriff arrived, slowed by his age and weight. "What happened?"

"Clyde Cassell was here."

Spencer pointed. "He took off toward the woods."

Marvin headed in that direction as Spencer backed into the store.

Jules looked around. "Where are the children?"

Spencer pointed to the ceiling. "I sent them upstairs and told them to lock the door. Austin is standing guard on the steps."

Roe placed her on a stool near the counter. Her cloak was muddy and her skirt torn along the hem. Roe lifted the kerchief and examined the wound. "It won't need stitches. Nothing worse than a shaving nick."

It had to be more serious. "I want to see." She pointed at a hand mirror on display.

Roe handed it to her, and she removed the kerchief. The bleeding had slowed. The cut was small and shallow. She had fared better than the other women who had crossed Clyde's path. "I wonder why he didn't kill me."

Spencer handed Jules a glass of golden brown liquid. "Drink this."

She recognized the smell of whiskey, but obediently sipped. The fiery liquid burned her throat, and she coughed. The warmth helped to dispel her fear.

Roe knelt in front of her, and his hand rested on her knee. His eyes were filled with concern. "What happened?"

Jules pointed outside. "I was gathering eggs to feed the children, and Clyde was hiding beneath the nesting boxes."

Footsteps echoed on the stairs. Austin had a broom in his hands. "Is he gone?"

"Yes," Spencer said. "Why don't you gather the eggs for breakfast?"

"Make sure it's safe," Jules cried, unable to hide the fear in her voice.

Roe put his arm around her trembling shoulders. "We saw Clyde run into the woods."

"I'll watch for any trouble." Spencer wheeled his chair after his son.

As soon as they were gone, Jules broke down as the near-death experience became too much to bear. Roe picked her up and placed her on his lap as he sat on the stool, letting her cry. His comforting arms soothed away her fears, and she calmed her breathing.

Caroline's voice echoed from the staircase. "Can we come down now?"

Jules wiped the tears from her face. "I don't want them to see my crying."

"Brave girl." Roe put her on her feet. "Go wash your face, and I'll get them."

Jules stepped around Spencer at the back door and peered out into the yard. Austin was heading toward them from the chicken coop. No signs of Clyde. She walked to the pump and splashed water on her face. She dabbed at the cut on her throat and pressed the kerchief against it like a bandage. She buttoned the collar on her dress to secure it. Austin waited for her at the door and handed her the basket of eggs.

When Roe escorted the children into the kitchen,

Jules was busy frying eggs and baking the biscuits.

"Why did we have to hide in the bedroom?" Caroline asked.

Jules turned the eggs. "There's a man causing trouble."

"The man with the scar?"

How much had Caroline seen at Kallie's house? "How do you know him?"

"He visited after I fell asleep last night, and his yelling woke me up," Caroline said. "I peeked through the crack in the door. He was so scary that I ran back to my bed and pulled the covers up over my head."

"If any of you see him again, run," Jules said. The boys looked at each other as Caroline nodded.

"Are you sure you should tell them that?" Roe asked.

"They have to know he's dangerous," Jules said.

"Don't worry." Roe knelt in front of the children. "We'll keep you safe."

Spencer pulled William onto his lap. "These boys look like they can handle any trouble."

George puffed out his chest. "We sho' can."

"Thank you for making breakfast," Spencer said. "With my wife and other boy absent, I've done most of the cooking, and it's barely edible."

"How long will they be gone?"

"They're due back in two days. They have to sell what they can and pack the rest. We didn't want my mother-in-law living alone anymore."

"Family is important," Jules said. "You were kind to let us invade your home."

"As much as we appreciate your hospitality, after we eat, we'll head for Louisville." Roe leaned close, his mouth brushing her ear. "Don't let the children go outside."

She kept her voice low. "Do you think Clyde will return?"

"We have Kallie and her dog in the wagon out front," Roe explained. "We don't want them to see her."

"Did you find any poison in her house?"

"In the coffee." Roe turned to Austin. "Do you have any mice in the barn?"

"Sure. What do you want with mice?"

"I only need one. Do you think you can capture it?"

"The barn cats catch them all the time."

"I need one alive."

"They like to play with them first. I'll rescue one."

"What do you want with a mouse?" Jules asked.

"To test the coffee for poison."

"What difference does it make now?"

"I think Clyde drank some."

"He was sweating, and his speech was slurred," Jules said. "What do you think he drank?"

"Kallie had a collection of home remedies in her pantry. It could have been any one of them." Roe followed Austin outside.

Jules served breakfast to the children and Spencer. After washing at the pump, Roe and Austin joined them. What Roe didn't eat, Austin finished.

"I can fix more," Jules said.

"You'll be here all day if you want to fill Austin up," Spencer warned.

Roe wiped his mouth. "Get the children ready to leave. I'll load the buggy for the trip."

His eyes were tired. "You've only had a short nap

since we've started."

"I won't sleep until we're back on the *Jenny Lee*."

The sheriff returned as they prepared to leave. "He disappeared into the woods, and I lost his trail. Do you think you hit him?"

"Not from the bullet I fired," Spencer said as he wheeled into the room. "I didn't want to hit Miss Beecher."

"The doctor found blood at Mrs. Moore's cabin," Marvin said.

Roe frowned. "He was strong enough to attack Jules. It must have been a flesh wound."

"I'll move the wagon," Marvin said as he opened the door. "And I'll make sure the Bauers have a marker for their grave."

"You should know that the mouse died," Roe said as he handed Jules her cloak and bonnet.

Marvin looked confused. "What mouse?"

"The one I fed this coffee to." Roe removed the bag from his pocket and handed it to the sheriff. "She poisoned the Bauers. It doesn't matter now except knowing the truth, but I'd clean out her pantry and bury everything in it."

Marvin looked at the children in the other room. "I should have checked on them."

"We can't see the future, and there's no sense in beating ourselves up about the past," Roe said.

Jules took his arm. "You don't sound like a broken doll any more, Dr. Greystone."

"But I have plenty of cracks." He glanced out the kitchen window. "Daylight is wasting."

Austin handed Jules her basket. "I filled it for your trip."

"Don't say it," Roe growled. "I'm not ready to believe in magical baskets that never go empty."

Chapter Twenty-Five

Roe helped Jules pack the children in the back seat and cover them with the blanket. The sun was shining, but the air was crisp. Jules took her seat, and Roe handed her his gloves. "You're driving." He placed his hand on his revolver. "Everybody ready?"

Jules waved at Spencer, Austin, and Marvin. "Why can't the sheriff ride along with us?"

Roe leaned close, a smile tugging on the corners of his mouth. "He has a boil on his ass."

Jules scrunched her face in disgust. "I'm glad I didn't see that."

"Huge puss-filled mountain ready to explode."

Jules closed her eyes. "Ugh! Stop that!"

He laughed, a strange sound to his ears. "He only described it. Some things even a doctor wants to avoid seeing." Like the images that haunted his dreams.

"Where are we going?" George asked as he huddled beneath the blanket.

"Home to Darrow Falls."

"Is it far?" Caroline asked.

"We're going to travel on a big boat and then a train," Jules said.

"A train?" George asked.

"We've never ridden on a train," Caroline said.

The road was well-traveled, and Jules urged the horse along at a fast clip. Daylight didn't dispel the heavy cloud of fear hanging over them. Roe searched for any signs of danger, but the road was lined with trees and shrubs along the edge that would aid Clyde in a surprise attack. The children were becoming restless on the long trip, and Jules couldn't hide her anxiety. He needed to distract her so she wouldn't worry. "Why don't you teach the children a song?"

Jules smiled, and it was as if the sun broke through the clouds. She had that effect on him.

She glanced over her shoulder at her cousins. "Do you know 'Polly Perkins of Paddington Green?' It's a song from England."

They stared with vacant expressions. "That looks like a no," Roe said.

"I'll teach you the words." Jules began the chorus and followed with a verse. "*She was as beautiful as a butterfly and proud as a Queen, was pretty little Polly Perkins of Paddington Green. She'd an ankle like an antelope and a step like a deer. A voice like a blackbird, so mellow and clear. Her hair hung in ringlets so beautiful and long. I thought that she loved me, but I found I was wrong.*"

Her voice was sweet and lighthearted, and the children followed her lead. They could have been traveling to a picnic. They had learned several verses by the time they reached Louisville. Roe joined in toward the end, caught up in the lively tune.

When they arrived at the blacksmith's shop, a group of people were gathered around the livery and house. Some were on blankets. Others sat in the grass.

Jules gripped Roe's arm. "It looks like people have been hurt. You don't think Clyde beat us here?"

The crowd lacked the panic a madman on the loose

would create. "This reminds me of wounded gathered around a hospital tent on the battlefield waiting to be seen by a doctor."

Her eyes widened. "You?"

Roe groaned. "Ryan must have told everyone about how I helped his son."

"You could make a run for the boat."

She was joking, but it was his decision. She wouldn't force him to do the right thing. That gave him the freedom to choose his own path. "Chauncy won't depart until tomorrow morning," Roe said. "We have time to help out."

"You want to take care of them?"

"I took an oath to help those who were sick. I've neglected it too long." He raised his hand. "Maybe they won't notice how my fingers tremble."

Ryan greeted them as they stopped by the fence of the livery corral. Roe propped his foot on the front of the buggy. "What's going on? Are you having a party?"

Ryan removed his hat. "I only told two people, but word spread about what you had done for Bryan, and people started showing up."

Roe tipped his hat back. "What do they want?"

"They want a doctor to heal them."

Roe looked around and let out a long whistle. "Aren't there any doctors in Louisville?"

"Too many of them are tonic peddlers who leave you near death's door rather than cure you," Ryan said. "When it looked like you weren't returning soon, I sent a man to fetch a doctor, but now that you're here, we won't need him."

"I'll take care of as many as I can before I board the *Jenny Lee*, but I need your help," Roe said. "Any of the men you know have guns?"

"Are you expecting trouble?"

Roe nodded. "Post them around the yard. If they see a stocky man with a scar on the side of his face, he's dangerous. Tell them to keep their distance and alert me."

"A lot of men have scars."

Roe motioned with his fingers. "A long slash with a white streak in his beard."

"We have veterans who can stand guard and watch for him."

"Veterans? Which side did they serve?"

He pushed his hat back to reveal his eyes. "There's only one side now."

Jules shook her empty basket. "The children are going to need something to eat."

"Ellen will take care of them. We need you to take care of the clumsy fellow."

"Clumsy?"

"He cut his leg with an axe. Arrived about an hour ago."

Roe helped Jules and the children out of the buggy. "Where is he?"

"In my house."

"I'm going to need hot water, towels, and bandages." Roe grabbed his medical bag and handed Jules her bag. "I bet you wish you were back home in your parlor entertaining your beaus."

"Sipping tea is highly over rated." She laughed. "But I did enjoy receiving the presents."

He tugged on the edge of her cloak. "Anything as nice as this?"

She gazed into his eyes. "No."

Her blue eyes conveyed so much more. He wanted time alone with Jules. He looked around at all the people. He wasn't going to find any.

Ryan called to his wife, who was stirring a large kettle hooked to a tripod over a fire. She left her post and herded the children to a neighbor's house. Jules waved to reassure them as she entered Ryan and Ellen's home. Several people gathered around the bed where Roe had taken care of Bryan a day before.

"Step back," Ryan ordered as the crowd parted, and Roe stepped closer.

Jules removed her cloak and bonnet and put on an apron. She arranged her supplies. She looked up and caught him staring. "If they had nurses like you in the war, I never would have quit medicine."

"What about Jessica?"

"Who?" Jules was still jealous of her sister, but Roe was in love with only one Beecher sibling. He removed his coat and tossed it on a chair. He rolled up his sleeves and tied an apron around his waist. It was time to work. "Let's have a look."

The man was covered with a blanket. His face was pale and beads of sweat dampened his hair against his forehead. He babbled incoherently. Roe lifted the blanket covering his legs.

The dirty bandages covering the wound were soaked in blood, but worse was a tourniquet someone had tied below the knee. It had slowed the bleeding but cut off circulation to the lower limb. The toes and foot were black. "Who put the tourniquet on?"

"I think he did to stop the bleeding," Ryan said.

"How long ago did he cut himself?"

"This morning," Ryan said. "His wife drove him

into town and saw the crowd of other patients. He's bad off."

Roe looked around at the curious gawkers who had gathered in the small house. "Everyone wait outside." He looked at Ryan. "Except you. I need a slop bucket. And find his wife."

"How bad is it?" Jules asked.

He removed the soiled bandages and exposed an uneven gash that had nearly severed his leg and exposed the broken end of one shin bone. Red lines marked his skin. Blood poisoning. "I need to amputate." A cold dread filled him. "Like old times."

Jules touched his arm. "You have no choice, Roe. He'll die if you don't."

"It doesn't make it any easier. When was the last time you assisted in an amputation?"

"Last winter. A man had frostbite, and Papa had to cut off three toes."

"This man will call me a butcher when he wakes and he's missing his foot," Roe said.

"If you don't amputate, will he wake up?"

"Let's see if there's any hope." Roe released the tourniquet and blood squirted from the wound. Even without the constriction, blood didn't reach the foot.

"I can tie off the arteries unless you want to cauterize them," Jules said.

"Tie off the big ones." Roe retied the tourniquet and unpacked his bag. He unrolled a leather bundle. Several scalpels were nestled in separate sections, their sharp edges ready to slice through flesh. He gripped the handle of a saw. The sound of metal scraping against bone echoed from past memories. His hand shook. He gulped air.

Jules didn't see his panic. She was arranging his medical instruments on a clean towel. He handed her the saw. She gazed into his eyes. "You can do this, Dr. Greystone."

He didn't want to disappoint her. She believed in him even if every memory was shouting at him to run. Run away.

A woman entered with Ryan. "This is his wife." She stood at the end of the bed staring at her husband.

Roe had walked away from the surgeon's table and the profession of doctoring to avoid butchering. Soldier after soldier had passed beneath his hands. He had cut and sliced, sawed and stitched, leaving a remnant of the former occupant brought to his table. He recalled Spencer Wade's words.

I have two boys to be my legs. And I get to see them grow up. The alternative would be worse. Plenty of graves on the countryside for those who didn't return home.

He turned to the woman. She was worn out like many of the women who had shouldered more than their share of responsibilities during the war years. Her face lacked emotion, her mouth set in a grim line.

"The foot is gangrenous, and he's showing signs of blood poisoning. I have to amputate."

She gripped the post of the bed, her knuckles white. "I know."

"You don't have to watch, but afterward, I want to show you how to care for the wound so it heals properly."

She nodded. "He was drunk when he did it."

"Does he drink a lot?" Jules asked.

"More than I'd like," she said. "He's a mean drunk.

He was swinging the axe at the dog and missed. The fool didn't even feel it. I tried to stop the bleeding. I found the neighbor, and he helped me load him in the wagon."

"Do you give me permission to remove his leg?"

"Me?" She stared at her husband and then Roe. "Will he die if you don't?"

"Yes."

Her eyes filled with worry. "Have you done this operation before?"

"Too many times to count."

"He ain't much, but I don't have nobody else. You take his leg. If it's God's will, he'll live."

Jules put her hand on the woman's shoulder. "Better wait outside. We'll send for you when the doctor is done." Jules turned to Roe. "She took the news better than I thought."

"A tough life will make you accept whatever fate throws at you. I wonder if we're making her life harder by saddling her with a drunken cripple."

"Tell him he has to give up drinking or die," Jules said.

"Drink won't kill him."

A sly smile appeared on her pretty lips. "Papa warns men all the time about drinking, especially to men who beat their wives or children when they're drunk. Men listen to a doctor when they won't listen to anyone else."

"Your papa lies to his patients?"

"He took an oath to save lives. He didn't take an oath to tell the truth. That's only in the courtroom." She raised a dainty eyebrow over a knowing smile.

"I'm liking your papa more and more," Roe said.

"Maybe you'll meet him some day."

Meeting Dr. Sterling Beecher terrified him. If he disapproved of Roe, he couldn't ask Jules to choose between her family and him. Not when he wasn't sure of her answer. He loved her but did they have a future together? He shook off the warring thoughts and turned to Ryan. "I need more lanterns." Roe searched the kitchen and found a wooden cutting board which he placed under the patient's leg.

Ryan stopped hanging lanterns from the rafters above the bed. "What do you need that for?"

"The bed is too soft for cutting off his leg. This will give me a firm surface."

"Don't tell Ellen about the board." He looked at the patient. I'm not a queasy man, but do I need to hold him down or something?"

"No, I have chloroform." Ryan looked relieved.

Jules threaded her needles and cut lengths of thread to tie off the bleeders.

Roe removed the bottle of chloroform from his bag. "Let's make sure he stays asleep."

Jules placed the applicator in the man's nose, and Roe applied a few drops to the cotton. The man convulsed and then relaxed. She handed Roe a scalpel.

He stared at the blade gripped in his fingers. "I'm not shaking."

"You sound surprised."

"I always thought I couldn't cut into a man again." He turned the blade in his fingertips. It was an extension of his hand. "Let's finish this gruesome task. The hard part will be when he wakes and wonders why he only needs one shoe."

"Let's hope he has a sense of humor like Spencer

Wade."

Roe returned her smile before he turned to the patient. The first cut was the hardest, but memory from constant repetition returned. He cut around the leg, allowing extra skin so he could fold the flesh over the bones and allow shrinkage. He turned up the skin, baring the muscles and bones. Jules handed him the saw, and he moved the blade back and forth in the familiar grating rhythm that had haunted so many nights.

Jules tied off the arteries and cauterized the smaller bleeders. She wrapped the gangrene limb in a towel and placed it in the slop bucket. Ryan stared at it, covered his mouth, and ran outside. Jules stitched the wound, leaving a hole for drainage.

"You seem to know what you're doing, young man."

An elderly man stood at the end of the bed watching his work. He had a medical bag in his hand.

"Are you a doctor?"

"Dr. Payne." He extended his hand.

Roe wiped his hand on his apron and returned the greeting. "Dr. Greystone." He nodded toward the patient. "Do you know how to take care of an amputation?"

"I've done my fair share," he said. "More than you, young man."

"I wouldn't bet on that." Roe handed his instruments to Jules. "Did you serve in the war?"

"No, I was too old." His eyes widened, and he looked at the amputation. "You were in the army?"

"Third Corps."

"You planning on practicing medicine in these

parts?"

"I'm a part owner of a riverboat. If I practice medicine, it'll be from port to port."

Jules looked up from cleaning his instruments in a pan of hot water. She looked surprised by his words, and a little worried. He wanted to reassure Dr. Payne he wasn't infringing on his territory. "If these are your patients, I'll gladly step aside."

"I have trouble keeping up now that I'm older," Dr. Payne said. "I appreciate your help."

Ryan returned with the patient's wife. Jules showed the woman how to wrap the wound and how to check for any signs of gangrene or blood poisoning. She took her time explaining and reassured the patient's wife she could care for her husband.

Roe wrote on a piece of paper. "When your husband wakes up, tell him he is no longer allowed to drink any alcohol." He handed her the paper. "Doctor's orders."

She stared at the paper. "None?"

"If he wants to live, he'll have to give up hard liquor."

She smiled and years faded from her face. "Thank you, Doctor."

Roe and Jules covered her husband with a blanket and left his wife sitting by his side, holding his hand. Jules had packed their medical supplies and handed him his bag. They stepped outside and surveyed the other patients with Dr. Payne.

"I've never heard of a prescription like the one you gave that woman," Dr. Payne said.

"The man's a drunkard," Roe said. "He needs a reason to remain sober before he cuts off his other leg."

"I just came from removing what was left of an eye from a man who got into a drunken brawl. The other fellow gouged out his eyeball. What a mess." Dr. Payne shook his head. "I'll support your order, but that's no guarantee he won't sneak a drink."

"A doctor can only do so much. The rest is up to the patient," Roe said. "Where do you want to begin?"

"I looked at a few before coming inside," Dr. Payne said. "Most are minor injuries. You took care of the worst one. I'll take care of this group over here. You can have those." He paused. "If that's all right, Doctor?"

Roe agreed, and they went to work. The most common injuries were cuts that needed cleaned and stitched. Some were burns or ulcers, and a few people had rashes or fevers.

During the war the injured were nameless men in torn and bloody uniforms. Here, he had to look in a patient's eyes. He saw the mixture of fear and trust. He asked for names and talked about mundane topics shared on porches or on strolls down shady lanes.

A little girl with tears in her eyes stared as he examined her hand. She had burned it on the stove. He gently cleansed the skin and applied a dressing to ease the pain and heal the wound. He wrote a prescription for an aloe lotion and handed it to her mother. "Have a pharmacist make this for her and apply it two to three times a day."

She shook his hand. "Thank you, Doctor."

He turned to the little girl." Don't touch anything hot."

She nodded, sharing a shy smile.

"You certainly have a way with the young ladies,"

Jules said as she sat beside him on the steps to the porch.

"A smile like that erases all the memories of the battlefield traumas." He looked around at the patients. "This is how I imagined the life of a doctor, not the endless stream of mangled bodies where the outcome of the patient was unknown once he left my table."

She hugged him. "You did a good thing today, Dr. Greystone."

He had been a broken doll, but Jules had given him back his dream of being a doctor. She had restored his interest in medicine, and she had awakened feelings he never thought possible. Romeo had loved Juliet, but he had lost her to another in the end. Did he dare think their story would have a happy ending? Clyde Cassell was out there, intent on destroying their future.

Ellen offered them plates filled with chicken, vegetables, and peach cobbler. "We have a wagon waiting to take you to the boat once you're done eating."

Dr. Payne joined them. "Looks like everyone is taken care of. I'll check on the amputee and try to keep him sober."

"I think his wife would appreciate it."

"Next time you're in Louisville, stop by my office. I'm not too old to learn, and you're a talented doctor. You learned a lot in the war."

"I still have plenty to learn, Dr. Payne. Medicine is always changing."

"We're in a great time of science and discovery."

Ryan dumped money from a tin cup and divided it between the two doctors. "This isn't much but those who could pay, gave."

Roe counted his.

"Isn't it enough?" Ryan asked.

"It's plenty. He gave half to Jules. "I need to pay my nurse."

"I thought she was your wife," Ryan said.

"I'm not that lucky," he said.

Jules was indispensable…to him. But she had to take her cousins home. She had to reconcile with her father. And she needed to punch Old Sourpuss in the nose.

Chapter Twenty-Six

Roe ate heartily while Jules played with her food. She should have been hungry, but her journey would be over soon. She would return home, her task accomplished. But it didn't bring the joy she had anticipated.

Roe was a doctor again. He had found his calling, his life-long dream of helping others, but did his future include her? Jules stole a glance at Roe seated beside her. He was so handsome. None of her suitors stirred her heart to beat in rapid excitement. She didn't dream of sharing a bed with the men who had proposed marriage or stolen kisses. She didn't want to return to her parlor and entertain men who bored her. She had told her parents she would never marry, but that was before she had met Roe. Now she couldn't imagine her life without him.

Like her sisters before her, she recognized this was the one man she wanted to spend the rest of her life with, but they were heading in different directions. She had to return home with her cousins and face Lara's gossip. Roe would remain on the *Jenny Lee* and see patients between the two cities. Dr. Payne had recognized his skill and would welcome him as a partner. What if once parted, they never saw each other again?

"I want to stay here with you," she said. "Theo can

take the children home. He wants to meet Chauncy Theodora. We could travel on the *Jenny Lee* and take care of patients on the river."

Roe's eyes widened. "You want to work as my nurse?"

Nurse? Jules stammered. A woman didn't propose marriage to a man, and she didn't know how to hint for a declaration of love. She had made a mess of sharing her feelings and her needs. "It's a bad idea. Forget it." She shoved a spoonful of food into her mouth.

"I'm flattered by your offer, but you have unfinished business. You did me a great favor giving me the gift of practicing medicine again, but you're a broken doll, Miss Beecher."

"Me?"

"Your father was mean to you. He made a mistake not waiting for you the night of the storm, and he hurt your feelings with harsh words."

"No, it was my fault. I promised to be on time."

"He's a grown man. He should have waited, especially if he had a cold."

"But I love Papa."

"Which is why it hurt when he criticized you in anger," Roe said. "You have to forgive him, Jules. You have to make amends."

She knew he was right. Ever since that night, a rift had ached in her heart. She needed to mend her relationship with her father. And that meant leaving Roe behind. "I'll make amends, and I'll come back."

Roe looked surprised. Didn't he want her to return? "You'd do that for me? Leave your family and friends and work on the *Jenny Lee*?"

No words of marriage. "I enjoy getting paid to

sing. I could make a living at it."

"You could sing, or wait tables, or be a nurse," Roe listed. "You could do anything you want, Jules. After you return home and face your fears."

Jules stood. "You'll miss me." She hoped.

He stood but said nothing. He pointed instead. The wagon was packed, and the children loaded among the trunks. Roe helped Jules board and joined her on the front seat as Ryan drove them to the landing where the *Jenny Lee* waited.

Chauncy greeted them as they boarded. "I see you found the children."

"We found trouble, too." Roe looked at the children, and Chauncy knew not to speak about Clyde in front of them.

"How is Theo doing?" Jules asked.

"Babs has been taking care of him. Theo protests all the fuss, but I think he's enjoying being pampered after all the years of looking after me."

"I need to look at his stitches," Roe said.

Chauncy raised a bushy eyebrow. "Are you sure you want people to know you're practicing medicine?"

"Didn't you know this young man is a doctor?" Ryan asked. "He helped my boy and other sick folks."

Chauncy grinned. "Welcome back, Dr. Greystone."

Roe shrugged. "I'd hate to waste my talent."

They said goodbye to Ryan, and Chauncy signaled for the crew to carry the trunks upstairs.

"Where are we putting the children?" Jules asked.

"You and the children will stay in Roe's cabin. Roe will board with Theo and me. We'll take turns sleeping and keeping watch."

Even though they were back on the *Jenny Lee*, they

weren't safe. Clyde was still a threat. She glanced around. Would she ever feel safe again?

"Come on, Jules," Caroline called as the children rushed up the stairs. She hurried after them. She wasn't going to let them out of her sight.

****

Roe signaled Chauncy to wait. "Clyde followed us to Laurel Holler. He killed a woman named Kallie."

Chauncy gripped the railing. "Another one?"

"Don't feel too bad. She poisoned the children's parents."

"Why would she do that?"

"Hate. It didn't end with the war. If anything, it's festering and growing. Look at what happened in Memphis earlier this year. She didn't like George Bauer's sympathies toward the Union. It was a petty reason, but the only one we could think of for her harming them."

Chauncy looked around. "I have the crew watching anyone who comes aboard, and I'll post guards on each deck near the staircase. We won't let Clyde near the *Jenny Lee*."

"He's wounded," Roe said. "And we think he drank some of Kallie's poisoned coffee. Hopefully he won't be able to cause any trouble."

"How is Miss Jules doing?"

Roe looked at the top deck. "She's wonderful."

Chauncy chewed on his cigar. "You kept your promise?"

"Yes, and it wasn't easy."

"At least you kept her safe."

Roe followed Chauncy up the stairs. "I blundered. When we found Kallie's body and saw Clyde at her home, we returned to Laurel Holler. I joined the sheriff to investigate Kallie's death and left Jules and the children at the local store. I thought they would be safe, but Clyde was hiding in the chicken coop. He almost had her." Roe paused on the top deck, searching for Jules. She was leaning against the railing with the children. "He cut her neck."

Chauncy gasped. "I didn't see a bandage."

"Nothing serious, but he could have ended her life. I know how Romeo felt when he believed Juliet had died. In that fleeting moment I knew how much I loved her. I haven't let my guard down again, but I'm exhausted. I'm trusting you and Theo will keep her safe while I sleep."

"We will."

Chauncy opened the door to his cabin, and Roe entered. He removed his belongings and his medical bag from the trunk. "I should check on Theo. Where is he?"

"He's in the pilot house. I'll send him down." Chauncy lifted the trunk. "You have everything you need?"

"The rest belongs to Jules."

"I'll put this next door."

Roe removed his coat and shirt and washed. Theo knocked and opened the door. "Captain said you wanted to see me."

"I want to look at your stitches." He signaled Theo to sit in the chair. He removed the bandage. "So how is the romance progressing between you and Babs?"

Theo blushed. "She's nice to me. She thinks I'm smart."

"You are smart, Theo."

"Only because the captain taught me to read and write."

"That's not the only reason. Look how you defended yourself against Clyde with a basket. And remember how you kept Chauncy alive during the war without any medical training. Other men couldn't have saved his life like you did."

"Do you think I'd make a good husband?"

The stitches were intact and healing. "Do you love her?"

He grinned. "I get all excited when I see her."

Roe folded a clean bandage. "Have you done anything you need to be ashamed of?"

He blushed. "I kissed her, but she said I could."

Why was he giving marital advice? He was as inexperienced as Theo, but as a doctor, he was expected to know about such things. "The best thing for you to do is talk. Find out as much as you can about each other. And Theo, your dreams need to match."

"Dreams?"

"Well, does she plan to live aboard a riverboat or do you plan to live on land?"

"Oh." Theo paused, his brow furrowed. "I thought she'd do what I decided."

Roe fastened the bandage on his neck. "If you love her, you'll want her to be happy. You and Babs should sit down and see how much you're willing to change for each other. Then decide if you can be that person and still be happy."

Theo put his cap on his head. "Thank you, Roe. I mean Dr. Greystone."

"You can call me Roe," he said. "After all, we're partners."

"That's right." He grinned as he opened the door. "Do you want dinner?"

"I ate before we boarded." Roe removed his boots. "Theo, keep a close eye on Miss Beecher while I sleep."

"The captain said Clyde is wounded."

"With nothing to lose," Roe said. "Be careful."

Theo saluted, an old habit, and closed the door.

Roe considered the words of advice he had given Theo. Jules had shared her willingness to compromise, but what was he willing to do to make Jules happy?

****

Chauncy handed Jules the key to Roe's cabin. "Everything is inside. You should get some sleep."

"I need to watch the children."

He turned toward the deck where Babs and Theo were playing with her cousins. They had given them chalk to draw on the deck boards. "I think the children are in good hands. We'll wear them out so they sleep tonight."

"Do you want me to sing after dinner?"

Chauncy patted her hand. "Are you up to it?"

"It'll be my final performance." A cold dread gripped her as she repeated the ominous words. She touched the scab on her neck. She'd almost forgotten Clyde wanted her dead. Had he succumbed to his injuries, or was he lurking in the shadows, waiting for an opportunity to strike?

Chauncy signaled to Babs, who joined them. "Help Miss Jules. I'll keep an eye on the children with Theo."

Jules shook her head even though she could barely keep her eyes open. "I won't impose on everyone. The children are my responsibility. I can't ask you to watch them."

"You didn't," Chauncy said. "We volunteered."

Babs opened the door to the cabin. "You must be exhausted, Miss Jules."

Babs was addressing her in the same manner as Chauncy and Theo.

Jules followed her inside and stared at the bed. She had slept in it with Roe. She glanced at the wall separating the rooms. He was so close and yet she couldn't reach him.

Babs helped her remove her travel clothes. "Did I hear you was going to sing tonight?"

"The captain said I could."

"Lot of people have been asking about Princess Jules." Babs handed her a nightgown.

Jules turned and dropped her bloomers.

"Oh!"

Jules looked at Babs. "What's wrong?"

"That's a nasty bruise."

Jules touched her tender hip. "That's where Clyde pinned me to the ground with his big boot."

Babs clutched the bed post. "The man who killed Rita and cut Theo?"

Jules nodded as she rubbed her tender backside. "He was hiding in a chicken coop and surprised me."

"How did you escape?"

Jules pulled the gown over her head and turned. "I don't know. He could have slit my throat any time." She touched the scab on her neck. "It was the oddest thing. He kept asking me questions." *This ain't the end of our talk.*

"You was lucky Dr. Greystone was there."

"Not so lucky for Roe. He wounded him, and

Clyde Cassell isn't a forgiving man."

"Theo won't let anything happen to either of you." Babs gathered her discarded clothes and placed them on a chair. "Theo admires you a great deal."

"He admires my sisters." Jules climbed into bed. "I haven't accomplished nearly as much as they have in their travels."

"He would disagree, and so do I," Babs said. "Do you think I'll ever earn Theo's admiration?"

Jules leaned on her elbow. "You already did, Babs. You helped when Theo was attacked, and you've taken care of him while he's recuperating."

"That's nothin'."

"It's everything. Have you told him how you feel about him?"

"No. He owns this riverboat, and I'm nothin'."

"Don't say that. Nobody is nothing. This war was fought for people who were told they were nothing so they could become something. We all have the potential for great things. We just have to be ready when the opportunity comes along to prove ourselves."

"I didn't panic or scream when I saw all that blood, and I wanted to," Babs said. "I thought Theo was goin' to die. That's when I knew I loved him."

"That's how it works. We know we love someone when we nearly lose them and can't imagine life without them." She pointed to the door. "Now go join Theo. Join the man you love."

Chapter Twenty-Seven

Jules woke to the smell of food drifting from the galley and the sound of guests in the dining hall. She stretched and climbed out of bed. It would take days in her own bed to feel fully rested, but she looked forward to singing tonight. She would have to choose a special song.

She found the children seated at the captain's table. Chauncy stood and offered her a chair. "You're not waiting tables. Captain's orders."

Jules looked at the work dress she wore but obeyed. She surveyed her cousins. "How do you like being on a riverboat?"

"We played games on the deck," Caroline said. "We threw bags into a bucket and hunted for treasure."

"I was a pirate!" George clapped his hands.

Chauncy laughed. "Theo and Babs kept them entertained. Poor Will is going to fall asleep in his plate if we don't get him to bed soon."

William's eyes kept fluttering, but each time they closed, his head would jerk, and he'd wake up.

Babs removed his plate. "I'll get you somethin' to eat, Miss Jules."

"Thank you, Babs, but you must be worn out." She stood. "I can get my own food."

"I'll clear my tables," Babs said, gathering the plates.

Jules went to the galley, nearly colliding with Lizzy as she came out through the door. She hugged her. "Floyd saved you and Dr. Greystone some of his food." She made a face. "I wish he'd let me cook."

"What is he serving?"

"Overcooked beef in a thick gravy over tasteless noodles."

"It can't be that bad."

"Shoe leather dipped in mud is tastier."

Jules laughed. Lizzy was exaggerating, but Floyd better guard his galley or he'd lose it to Lizzy soon.

Floyd was grumbling as he stirred his pot. "I ain't no fancy chef."

"It's me, Floyd."

He turned and smiled. "You I like." He waved his spoon. "That woman is going to drive me away."

"She only wants to help," Jules said. "Maybe she could make desserts."

He wrinkled his brow in thought. "Customers are always asking for cakes and pies."

"I need two plates." She grabbed a tray from the table as he loaded the plates with the beef and noodles mixture. "I need to pack my basket with some food for the children tomorrow before we reach Cincinnati. Do you have anything for them to eat?"

"I'll leave some sandwiches and fruit on the table, Miss Jules. You come down around noon, and it'll be ready."

Jules lifted her tray. "Thank you, Floyd."

Roe entered the salon as she moved toward the table. He was dressed for the evening and had shaved. He met her gaze and smiled. Gone was the moody man she had first encountered when interviewing for a waitress job. Quite a few other ladies preened as he passed, hoping to garner his attention. He ignored them, his gaze on her. Did he love her as much as she loved him? He took the tray from her, placed it on the table, and held her chair.

"Thank you, Dr. Greystone."

He raised an eyebrow. "Doctor?"

"That's what everyone is calling you," Jules said.

"I prefer you call me Roe."

The cargo is loaded, and I'll start early tomorrow for Cincinnati," Chauncy said. "You might be able to catch an evening train unless you want to spend the night on the *Jenny Lee*."

"Train!" George made a whistling noise and yanked on an imaginary chain.

William jerked awake and looked confused.

"An evening train sounds like a good idea. I think I'll be able to manage better if the children sleep through most of the journey." She forced a smile. "I wouldn't want to impose on your hospitality any longer than I already have."

Chauncy patted her hand. "Nonsense. We're honored to have you and your cousins as our guests."

Roe looked around. "We're going to have a full house for the games."

"And to hear you sing," Chauncy added.

"I hope I can remember the words to the songs I've chosen," Jules said. "I don't want to disappoint anyone."

"Can we stay up and listen to you sing?" Caroline asked.

"You can hear her from the bedroom," Roe said.

Jules looked at Roe. "I'm not *that* loud."

"Your voice carries," he said. "In a good way."

Jules turned to Chauncy. "Have you heard anything from my father?"

"I sent a telegram after you and Roe returned letting him know you have the children and will be returning home."

"Thank you, Captain."

Lizzy appeared at the table with Theo and Babs. "I have a gown for you to wear tonight. You can dress in my room while Theo and Babs put the children to bed."

Jules looked at Caroline. "I'd like to tuck them into bed first, then I'll join you."

Roe was waiting outside his room, ready to escort Jules and Babs. Theo remained by the door with another crew member. No matter how hard she tried to forget, the threat of Clyde Cassell lurked in the shadows. Roe barely spoke, his eyes alert to their surroundings. He blamed himself for Clyde's attack at the store and was determined not to fail again.

Lizzy was dressed when they entered the room beneath the stairs and stepped aside to show her a gown on the bed. "Isn't it lovely?"

"For me?" The pale blue silk matched her eyes. "This wasn't in the trunk."

"One of the passengers received it from a gentleman friend, but it didn't fit. She threatened to throw it into the river, but we persuaded her otherwise."

"It might fit Babs."

"I've already tried it on," Babs said. "My corset doesn't lace that tight."

Jules ran her fingers along the silky fabric. "I hope I'll be able to breathe when I sing."

Lizzy helped them dress and arrange their hair.

295

"Do you have something special planned for tonight?"

A sob escaped Jules. Now that Roe was a doctor, he had a career to occupy his time. She had a responsibility to take her cousins to Darrow Falls. This was their last night together.

Lizzy put her arm around her. "What's wrong?"

"I'm going to miss everyone." She hugged Lizzy, holding on a little longer to calm her tearful reaction.

"We'll miss you, but you'll always know where to find us."

"You're not leaving the *Jenny Lee*?"

"We have men aboard," Lizzy said.

"Have they proposed?"

"Not yet, but a woman has to take her future into her own hands and make plans," Lizzy said. "Men are terrible about imagining the possibilities."

"I hope all of you will be happy."

"What about you?" Babs asked. "Aren't you goin' to marry the doctor?"

"I offered to return and be his nurse, but he said nothing." She blinked away tears.

"You need to tell him how you feel," Lizzy said. "Men are dense when it comes to understanding women. We have to tell them in plain terms what we want and then they still have trouble delivering."

"Do you think he'd understand if I told him in a song?"

"A song might be the best way to share your feelings." Lizzy brushed a few curls around her palm to shape them. She pushed her toward the mirror. "You look beautiful."

Jules surveyed her image above the wash stand. She should be happy, but she couldn't vanquish an uneasy feeling. She forced a smile. "I'm ready."

Roe was waiting outside the door. He stared without saying anything, leaving her breathless.

"Don't you like the gown?"

"All eyes will be on you tonight." Roe offered his arm. Lizzy and Babs followed them to the dining hall. The room was full of guests, and crewmen were present, stationed along the walls and near the doors. Did they expect Clyde to make an appearance? She wasn't going to allow any fears of what might be ruin her last night on the *Jenny Lee*. She greeted everyone with a smile and moved from table to table as Roe took a position near the bar and stood guard.

She helped with the games, taking turns while the others waited on the tables. A group of men at one table were drunk and loud. "I wanna hear the princess sing."

Roe frowned and sent one of the crew to stand closer to the table. Jules stepped on the stage and signaled the piano player to begin. She wanted to keep the mood happy and sang several tunes by Stephen Foster, including *Come Where my Love Lies Dreaming* and *Will Thou Be Gone, Love?* The song began with Shakespeare's Juliet arguing with Romeo about a nightingale and lark.

"Wilt thou be gone, wilt thou be gone, love, gone, love, from me? Stay! 'tis the Nightingale that sings in yonder tree. Deem not 'tis the Lark, love, day is not yet near. Believe me, 'tis the Nightingale whose song hath pierced thine ear."

She gazed at Roe as she sang, signaling him to join her on stage.

"I can't sing."

"I've heard you. Besides, a man has to sing the part

of Romeo."

"My name is a secret," he whispered.

"Sing." His voice was deep and blended well with hers.

"I must be gone, love. I must be gone from thee. 'Tis not the nightingale that sings in yonder tree. 'Tis the Lark, 'tis the Lark, 'tis the Lark, 'tis the Lark, love, that sings in yonder tree."

He collected the coins tossed on the stage and wrapped them in a kerchief. "Why did you choose that song?"

"It seemed appropriate for two people named after Shakespeare's lovers."

He looked around at the crew standing guard as the guests collected their winnings and prepared to leave. He lowered his voice. "I am not comfortable expressing my feelings publicly."

She shrugged. "It's just a song." She headed for the walkway. "It's no different than my suitors reciting poetry."

"Is that what you want?" Roe paused on the step to the upper deck. "Clyde nearly killed you, Juliet, and it was my fault. I can't afford to lower my guard even for a kiss."

She ran up the stairs, pausing near the top. "Shakespeare's Romeo wouldn't allow anything to prevent him from making love to Juliet."

His voice carried up the steps. *"I am no pilot. Yet, wert thou as far as that vast shore washed with the farthest sea, I would adventure for such merchandise."*

It was from *Romeo and Juliet*. She smiled, recognizing the familiar words and gave her response.

"Thou know'st the mask of night is on my face, else

would a maiden blush bepaint my cheek for that which thou hast heard me speak tonight."

Roe ran up the stairs and took her in his arms. He pulled her close. "I will make you blush, sweet Juliet." Roe kissed her, long and deep until their breaths came in rapid response.

"There must be an empty room we could share," Jules whispered.

"Without a ring on your finger. Without your family's blessing?"

"I want you, Roe. I need you."

"You've slept in my arms, but I cannot promise sleep if we share a bed," Roe said. "My desire is too strong, and you are too willing."

"Would it be a sin to join when we know we won't be together after tomorrow?"

"What makes you think we won't be together?"

She pulled away. "Have you forgotten? I'm leaving for Ohio. I'm going home."

"And I plan to go with you."

"What?"

He looked hurt. "You don't want me to come with you?"

Jules hadn't considered Roe returning home with her. "But your work?"

"Theo and Chancy can run the boat. They have Babs and Lizzy to help them now."

"What about practicing medicine? I heard you talking to Dr. Payne."

"I have no patients. No one is going to miss me."

She threw her arms around his neck. "You would come?"

"I can't let you and the children travel alone. Clyde

knows you live in Darrow Falls."

Jules pulled away. He was only doing his duty to protect her.

"I almost prefer a confrontation with Clyde to meeting your father."

"Why do you fear Papa?"

"I have to ask his permission to marry you."

Marry? "You don't need his permission," Jules pouted. "I'm a grown woman."

"I will not steal you away no matter how much I am tempted," Roe said. "As the youngest of your sisters, I fear your father will not give you away as easily as the others."

"After nearly killing him, he will be glad to be rid of me."

"Our marriage is doomed until you forgive him."

"Why is that so important?"

"Someday I will do something to hurt you. Unintentionally," Roe said. "If you can't forgive your father for his error in behavior, how will you forgive me, a man you've only met?"

"I love you."

"You love your father. Much more than you realize or his harsh words wouldn't have hurt so much. You have to mend your relationship with him or ours is doomed."

"Is that why you haven't proposed?"

Roe nervously ran his fingers through his long hair. "What if your father doesn't approve of me?"

"But he's the one who brought us together," Jules said. "Didn't he name me Juliet?"

"I'll remind him of his choice when I ask permission to marry you."

"You may receive his blessing, but you'll have to convince me to say yes."

Roe stared, his face pale. "You don't want to marry me?"

"Do you love me?"

Roe hesitated as he glanced around the crowded deck.

Jules unlocked Roe's door. "When you can say the words, then I'll give you my answer."

He pulled her back, his arms caressing her bare shoulders. He kissed her, hard with a hint of anger. Then he raised his face to the sky. "I love you, Juliet Beecher. Will you marry me?"

Others on the deck stopped, turned, and waited.

"Yes," she whispered.

"I didn't hear you."

"Yes, I'll marry you Romeo Greystone."

Roe frowned. "You didn't have to say my name."

She laughed. *"How do I love thee? Let me count the ways. I love thee to the depth and breadth and height my soul can reach..."*

Roe silenced her with his lips.

Chapter Twenty-Eight

Jules had finally slept through the night without nightmares or waking at every sound. Theo and Babs had claimed the children after breakfast and were entertaining them on the deck while she packed. They would leave this evening for the trip home after arriving in Cincinnati. She had succeeded in finding her cousins, and Roe would become her husband. Roe was hers. He had pledged his undying love, and she had done the same. She had dreamed of her wedding and the night after. The memory made her blush.

Jules glanced around the tidy room and collected her empty basket. Poor Theo had neglected his duties as fairy. Floyd had promised to save some food in the kitchen. She paused on the deck. Theo was folding newspaper to make hats for the children. Babs was helping William fold his paper into triangles. They would make good parents. Thank goodness Clyde had failed to claim Theo's life.

Above, Roe was in the pilot house with Chauncy. A clear sky promised fair weather, and the *Jenny Lee* made good time as the paddlewheel churned the waters on its journey north and home. The basket swung on her arm. It wasn't going to fill itself. She hurried down the stairs.

Lizzy passed her on the steps. She carried a pitcher of water. "What's that for?"

"The captain. It's a warm day, and someone needs to look after him." Lizzy gave her sly smile.

When Chauncy and Theo visited Darrow Falls, it would be with their wives. "Don't keep him waiting, and tell Roe I'm packing the magic basket."

The salon had a few passengers huddled beneath blankets, trying to sleep after the late evening spent gambling. Breakfast had been cleared, and Floyd was mopping the floor, scrubbing at the stubborn tobacco stains. He waved when she showed him her basket.

Floyd had left the key in the galley door lock for her to enter. He had kept his promise. On the small table were sandwiches wrapped in paper with pears, peaches, carrot slices, and a chunk of cheese beside it. He had filled two jars with apple cider. It was a feast.

She carefully packed the basket, squeezing in a few cookies Floyd had baked for the children.

The door opened behind her. "You outdid yourself, Floyd. I can't thank you enough for the food." She heard the turn of a key and the door being locked. "Floyd?"

It wasn't the cook. Jules gripped the edge of the table to keep her knees from buckling. His beard was gone and his hair cut short, but it was Clyde Cassell.

She opened her mouth, but Clyde waved his Bowie knife in her face. "Scream, and I'll silence you forever."

Jules struggled to breathe as panic seized her. She closed her eyes to block the tears gathering on her lashes.

"Do you promise to be quiet?"

Jules shook her head in agreement.

Clyde pushed her into the chair. "Sit."

He sat opposite her, the basket between them. One

hand rested on the hilt of his Bowie knife, the point twisting on the wooden surface in front of him. His pallor was gray, nearly white. "You've lost a lot of blood."

"Thanks to your friend with the gun."

"Roe is a doctor. He can help."

"I need an undertaker not a healer." He coughed and raised the kerchief tied around his neck to his mouth. When he lowered the cloth, it was stained with blood.

"What do you want?"

Clyde removed his worn haversack and withdrew her hat, the one she had worn on the train. "Put it on."

Jules cautiously lifted the hat and stuck it on her head.

He squinted his eyes and studied her. "I saw you at the Mermaid's Mirth. You wore that slouch hat and men's clothing, but it's the same face." He stabbed his knife into the table, chipping away at the surface. "When I saw you on the train and that woman called you Miss Beecher, I remembered you were the one who shot Buck in the leg at the canal. I figured out you were the *man* who killed him at Mermaid's Mirth."

It was Cole and Jess who had fired the fateful shots at Mermaid's Mirth claiming Buck's life. Jules swallowed. She wouldn't put her sisters in danger with the truth. "Yes." She steeled her words as she recalled the details of the attack. "I shot at you from the kitchen."

"Who was the other fellow?"

She hesitated. She wouldn't put anyone else in danger.

He gouged a chunk of wood out of the table. "Tell

me!"

"My beau, Ed Herbruck." One of Lara's brothers. Clyde couldn't hurt Ed. "He was killed at Gettysburg. He's buried in the cemetery in Darrow Falls."

"You Beecher bitches have thwarted our plans too many times. Buck and I don't like losing."

Clyde talked as if Buck were alive. Had Clyde lost his last grasp on reality? Jules had no qualms about her future. She was going to die. She didn't fight the tears as they cascaded down her cheeks. At least she had told Roe she loved him. Her strength ebbed from her body. How did someone prepare for death?

"I followed you to the boat, the *Jenny Lee*. I remember Miss Jenny. Theo had her husband's coat. Spoils of war. Only he gave it back to her, the fool. She was at Manassas and sang a hymn for her dead husband. She had a perty voice, too."

He reached into his coat pocket and flipped a round object onto the table. Jules stared at the familiar coin. It was the five-dollar piece Blake had given her. She'd have a word with her brother-in-law about his definition of luck if she survived.

He used the point of his knife to tap on the coin. "Take it."

Her fingers trembled as she reached and slid the coin to her end of the table. "Why are you giving me the gold?"

"I ain't got no need for it where I'm headin'." His hand shook as he moved aside his coat. His shirt was stained red and yellow on his left side. "What does this tell you?"

"Gut shot." Her gaze met his. The whites of his eyes were yellow.

"A death sentence," he acknowledged, closing his coat. Clyde stabbed the table with the point of his knife. A chip of wood broke free as he dug a deeper hole in the surface. "The coin is payment for something I want."

She would rather die than let Clyde violate her. She looked at the door.

"It's locked," Clyde said, showing her the key before returning it to his coat pocket. Even in his weakened state, she would never be able to overpower him to unlock the door. Clyde was dying, but how long would it take for his last breath? A man could linger, especially one like Clyde, who had hate fueling his existence. "Let the doctor help you."

"He'd cut off my arms and legs before helping me!" Clyde stabbed the blade deeper, widening the hole. "Ain't you a nurse like your sister Miss Jenny?"

"Yes, but I can't save you."

"Only one thing will give me comfort." He stabbed his knife into the hole he had created in the table top and the blade stood upright. He pointed at her with a shaky hand. "I want to know how my brother died."

It was an odd request. He had died from a gut wound, too.

"You were there after I ran." Clyde coughed, covering his mouth with his kerchief. When he removed it, the kerchief was soaked, and blood stained his lip and chin.

Her sisters had said Clyde escaped through a window, leaving Buck behind. What did she tell him and what did she hold back?

"What did Buck say?" His eyes were filled with pain, and he clutched his side. "Tell me!"

She jumped and gripped the edges of the table to keep from bolting. Clyde was between her and the door with his knife between them, a temptation. Did he want her to try for it? Was he playing an awful game, taunting her to fight him, only to lose in the end? If she panicked, he would slice her into too many pieces to count.

She closed her eyes to recall the details of the story her sisters had whispered in the dark. While pretending to be asleep, she had listened to Colleen and Jessica discuss the shooting and death of Buck. She had never confessed to her eavesdropping. The words they had exchanged were too terrifying to repeat, but she spoke now. "You and Buck nearly killed Blake. You beat him until he was unconscious."

"That gold belonged to me and Buck. We followed Blake up from Memphis to Ohio where you wounded poor Buck."

She clutched the table edges, fighting to hold onto any courage she could muster. She had to keep him talking. Someone would miss her and come looking. She hoped. "Why didn't you give up?"

The Cassell brothers never give up. We weren't the best slave chasers for nothin'," he said. "Once Buck could walk, we followed Blake to Washington City."

"To The Mermaid's Mirth," Jules said. The place where Buck died.

"The manager said he'd gone to Antietam. Fool. Buck and I know a man don't have no advantage fightin' in a battle. One on one, that's a different story, especially if ya cheat."

"Like knocking Blake over the head when he returned."

"All he had to do was give up the gold."

"He had already spent it on a hotel in Cleveland."

Clyde grabbed the knife from its groove and pointed it at her face. "You and your man snuck in the back and shot at us."

"I believe you shot first." That's how Jess had told the story.

"Don't matter who shot first!" Clyde panted, straining to catch his breath. "Buck and me escaped to a side room. I jumped out the window. Buck was supposed to follow." His voice was soft, reverent. Beads of sweat trailed down his dirty face and dripped on the table, forming a muddy puddle. "He didn't. I got to know I didn't abandon my little brother."

"What?" The man had a conscience?

"I got to know before I die that Buck didn't curse my name."

He wanted peace after the murderous acts he had committed? Jules stood. "You shot Captain LaDonte, you cut Theo, and you killed three women. Four if I count Rita's sister. And those are only the ones I know about." Jules clenched her teeth and pounded on the table with her fist. "And you're worried whether you acted nobly toward Buck? How dare you value your brother's life more than their lives!"

He lunged forward and grabbed her wrist in a viselike grip that made her cry with pain. He waved the knife with the other. "I was his big brother. I was supposed to look after him. I did all the horrible deeds you said and more. I got to know when I git to hell, he won't turn his back on me."

"You want to go to hell?" Was the man insane? Of course, he was.

"Me and Buck worked in the coal mines when we were boys. Hell can't be worse than those black holes."

"Why did you kill those women if all you wanted was to know about Buck?"

"They got in my way." Clyde released his grip, swayed on his feet, and collapsed in his chair. He propped his head with his free hand. His breathing was labored, but Clyde wasn't ready to give up the ghost. Not until he had answers. "Buck was the only family I had. The only person who understood me or loved me."

Jules resumed her seat. She understood family. She needed her papa to love her. "I know how Buck died, but if you kill me, you'll never know."

He jabbed the knife into the table. "Tell me. And no lies."

Clyde didn't deserve the truth, but it wasn't in Jules to deceive someone, especially a dying man. "Buck had a gut shot, similar to yours," Jules said. "He knew he was going to die. Buck pretended to surrender so you could escape. He threw his knife at a policeman and wounded him before falling in the hallway."

"He didn't say nothin' about me?" Clyde sounded hurt.

Jules searched her memory for an answer. It had been so long ago, and she had tried to block any thoughts related to the Cassell brothers.

"Tell me what my brother said!"

Jules jumped, startled by his outburst. He wasn't dead, yet. "The last thing he said was '*Run, brother, run.*'" It was the truth. Buck's last words were for Clyde.

A slow smile creased Clyde's ugly face. Blood dribbled out of his mouth. "That ol' Buck. He knew how to go out in a blaze of glory." Clyde coughed and splattered blood on his coat. "I want one thing from ya."

"I don't owe you anything. I told you the truth."

"You killed my brother." Clyde gripped his knife. "You owe me."

Jules collapsed against the chair. "If you're going to kill me, be quick." She closed her eyes and whispered a prayer.

"I don't want you dead. You're one of the few women who stood up to Buck and me. I got to respect you for that."

Jules opened her eyes. "Then I can leave?"

"No. I want to hear you sing. You got a voice like an angel. It's the closest I'll ever git to heaven. I want a song from your lips to be the last sound I hear."

A song? He wanted her to sing after terrifying her? Was it another way to torture her? Would he cut her throat mid-note? She shook off her hysterics. "What do you want me to sing?"

"I remember a song people would sing when they were gettin' baptized in the river. I wanna hear it before I die."

"What's the song?"

"*Just as I am*."

"I know it." Jules recalled the words from singing it in church. "It's a song about remorse and asking God for forgiveness. I thought you wanted to join Buck in hell."

"I don't expect forgiveness for what I done. Buck and I were strong. We took what we wanted and nobody stopped us. You git away with enough, and you think everythin' belongs to ya. You keep takin' until somebody stops ya with a bullet or hangman's rope." He removed his floppy hat and placed it over the upright knife stuck in the table. "Sing."

Jules steadied her racing heartbeat. Clyde was dying, but would he outlast her song? Would he wait until the end to kill her?

"Sing!" he commanded.

She took a deep breath and sang, *"Just as I am, without one plea, but that Thy blood was shed for me, and that thou bid'st me come to Thee, O Lamb of God, I come. I come."*

Clyde let his head fall back, and he stared at the ceiling. "Buck, I'm comin', brother."

Chapter Twenty-Nine

Roe looked out over the wide expanse of the Ohio River. The trees along the shore were showing color, creating a rainbow corridor for their trip. The children on the deck below wore paper hats and followed Theo as if miniature soldiers on the march. Babs and Lizzy laughed as they participated in a mock battle. Where was Jules?

"Have you decided?" Chauncy asked as he poured a glass of water from the pitcher Lizzy had delivered.

Roe nodded. "I'd like to remain your partner. Who knows how much money I'll make as a doctor?"

"Are you sure you want to be a sawbones?"

"You were the one pushing me to resume my occupation. Besides, Dr. Beecher may need me." He reread the telegram Chauncy had received from Morgan Mackinnon before leaving Louisville at dawn.

"I didn't want to wake you," Chauncy said. "Especially with bad news. Do you want me to tell Miss Jules?"

"No." Roe tucked it into an inside pocket. "She can't do anything about it. I'll tell her on the train when we're close to her home."

"If he dies, she'll blame herself."

"I know. That's why I'm debating not to tell her at all."

Chauncy placed his hand on his shoulder. "You

have to prepare her for the worst."

"She wanted her father to be proud of her. If he understood what she's experienced these past few days, he'd be amazed by her courage and strength."

"You've changed your mind about her, too."

"Me?"

"Don't you remember? You thought others would eat her alive."

His first encounter was fresh in his memory. "She was so sweet and innocent. Still is," he amended. "She's the same even after everything she's experienced. I let the war change me. But I need to be true to who I was, who I am, and who I want to be."

"Things will work out, son. You and Miss Jules were meant to be together."

"You're more confident she'll still want to marry me than I am." Roe patted his pocket. "She may feel an obligation to stay with her family."

"Dr. Beecher has plenty of nurses to help him recover. I'm sure he'll be fine by the time you arrive." Chauncy handed him some money. "This belongs to Miss Jules."

He weighed the bag of coins in his hand. "She was good for business."

"You tell her she can sing on the *Jenny Lee* any time she wants."

"She won't hesitate to take the stage." Roe headed to his room to finish packing. He paused by the door when he heard the notes of a song. They drifted from the deck below. Was it Jules? He looked over the railing. The sound was stronger. Why was she singing? He walked toward Lizzy and Babs. "Where's Jules?"

"She headed for the galley to fill the basket for the

trip," Lizzy said.

"I hear her singing."

"Maybe the crew wanted an encore performance."

Lizzy was trying to reassure him. It didn't work. Roe hurried down the steps, listening as the hymn became louder. Something in her voice alarmed him. It was strong, clear, but sad. Too sad. He entered the dining hall where the crew and others were gathered outside the galley door. "What's going on?"

"I was mopping, and she went into my kitchen where I left food for her trip," Floyd said. "I left the key in the door, but it's been locked from the inside, and she won't open up."

Roe tried the handle. It was secure. "Get Theo. He has the spare keys." Roe pounded on the door. "Jules!"

She didn't respond to his cries but continued to sing. "Quiet!" he called as the noise escalated behind him. He leaned against the door. "Juliet! Talk to me, Juliet!"

"It's Clyde!" She shrieked but resumed singing. She was crying through the words.

Clyde was in there with her? Roe wrestled with the doorknob as if he could pull it free. He glanced toward the ceiling. What was keeping Theo?

The crowd parted, and Theo joined him. "What's happened?"

"The door is locked with Jules inside." He looked at Theo. "Clyde is in there with her."

Theo fumbled with the keys. "Are you sure?"

Roe pounded on the door. "Juliet!"

A man's laugh echoed from the locked room. Theo gripped his throat. "That's Clyde Cassell."

"Unlock the door!" Roe fought to snatch the keys

from Theo's clumsy fingers. Roe placed his hand against the surface. Jules was on the other side with a monster. He had promised to protect her and failed. He placed his ear against the door when the song grew faint. "Don't give up, Juliet. Don't give up, baby."

"I have it!" Theo inserted the key into the lock and turned it.

Roe rushed into the galley.

Jules sat at the far side of the table, an old hat covered her head, which rested on top of the magic basket. She didn't move. Was he too late? He caught a sob in his throat. "Juliet. Oh, Juliet, my love."

She raised her head, blinked away tears, and called his name in a hoarse voice. He rushed to her and knelt beside the chair. He examined her for injuries and found none. "I thought I was too late. I thought you were dead."

Her trembling arms clung to his neck, and she spoke between sobs. "I thought…he was going…to kill me. I was…so scared."

"Stay back!" Theo told the others gathered in the doorway. He approached Clyde cautiously. He lifted the hat and claimed the Bowie knife, pointing it toward Clyde. He jabbed at his chest. "I think I'll claim this. Spoils of war."

"Is he dead?" Jules whispered as she stared at Clyde. "Make sure he's dead."

Roe signaled for Floyd to enter. "Hold his arms." He pinned Clyde's arms behind the chair. Clyde's head fell back, and Roe felt for a pulse. He opened his coat and removed the dirty bandages covering a wound in his abdomen. "Give me the knife."

Roe held the shiny blade beneath Clyde's nose.

315

"He's dead." He returned it to Theo.

Roe removed Clyde's revolver from his holster. The cylinder was empty and the barrel bent. "The gun was for show. It's broken."

Theo packed the weapons in Clyde's haversack and stuffed the hat inside. He slung the bag over his shoulder. "You don't have to worry about the Cassell brothers no more."

Jules stood on shaky legs and reached for the basket, but Theo took it. "I'll carry it, Miss Jules."

Roe lifted her in his arms.

"Wait." She pointed at the table. "My lucky coin."

Had she gone insane? He retrieved the gold piece and placed it in her hand. "Lucky?"

She curled her fingers around it. "I'm alive. I'm luckier than the others."

Theo followed as Roe carried Jules outside to the walkway and headed for the stairs. The children were playing on the top deck with Babs and Lizzy. "Put me down. I don't want the children to see me looking like an invalid."

Roe placed her on her feet. She removed her floppy hat and crossed the deck as if nothing had happened. The children gathered around her, showing her yarn dolls they had made.

Roe took her elbow when she wavered. Roe turned to Theo. "Let Chauncy know about Clyde."

Theo handed Jules the container of food. "This basket has been on your family adventures, Miss Jules, but this one will be remembered by all of us."

"I'll have an exciting story to tell my sisters. Papa won't believe it."

Papa. "Come inside my room. There's something I

have to tell you."

She didn't question him. She trusted him. He had to tell her the truth. Roe led her to his cabin and closed the door. "You better sit down."

"What could be worse than Clyde Cassell nearly killing me?" She slumped onto the bed.

Roe sat beside her. "Morgan sent a telegram to Chauncy. It arrived before he left Louisville, but he waited until I was awake to show me. I debated whether to tell you, but I think you need to know the bad news."

She gasped. "What does it say?"

Roe unfolded the message.

"Dr. Sterling Beecher is recovering but suffered a heart attack. The family has gathered at his Darrow Falls home. Juliet needs to return home immediately."

"Heart attack!" Jules covered her face with her hands. "I killed him."

"No." Roe rubbed her back. "He's recovering, but I'd like to help out if I can convince him to allow me to see his patients until he recovers."

"We'll insist."

"If there's room for two doctors, I'd like to stay in Darrow Falls unless you want to leave home."

"You'd do that for me?"

"Marriage takes compromise, Jules. You were willing to leave your family and join me on the *Jenny Lee*. I'm willing to live in Darrow Falls if that is where our paths take us. Shakespeare may have brought us together, but no one is going to break us apart."

Chapter Thirty

No one was waiting at the Darrow Falls depot Monday morning when they arrived. They had been delayed to answer questions about Clyde's death when they arrived in Cincinnati and had taken a later train. They hadn't telegraphed their arrival time. A brisk breeze blew crisp colorful leaves across the tracks where they were caught in the corner of the building. Jules checked the children's clothing, tugging a knit cap to cover William's head. "Noah will have a buggy we can borrow." Jules pointed toward the blacksmith shop.

Roe turned toward the station master. "We'll collect our bags in a little while."

Jules hesitated at the intersection of Main and River streets and stared at the Wheeler Dry Goods Store. Matt would know how her father fared. "I need to talk to Matt Wheeler."

"Do you want us to go with you?"

She looked at the children. If it was bad news about Papa, she didn't want them to see her cry.

Roe smiled. "If you can face Clyde Cassell, you can face a small town boy like Matt Wheeler."

He thought she was going to confront Matt about his lies. That was better than her real fears.

"We'll wait for you at the blacksmith shop." He kissed her hand. "Try not to bruise your knuckles."

"I'm not going to punch anyone in the nose."

Jules entered the Wheeler store. Her eyes adjusted to the darker interior. Barrels containing dry goods were stacked to the right. Shelves to the left displayed bolts of material, threads, and straw bonnets. In front was a glass case displaying pocket watches, beaded reticules, and silverware. Matt Wheeler was behind the counter unpacking a crate and placing cups on a shelf. "Hello, Matt."

He turned. "Miss Jules." He looked relieved. "Your family said you traveled to Kentucky."

"I'm heading home now, but I'd like to know how Papa is doing."

He shook his head. "I don't know. I haven't been out there since he took ill," Matt said. "Your mother had me ride to Hudson to fetch the doctor. That was Tuesday."

"You're not helping on the farm?"

"Your sisters' husbands are doing all the work. Besides, I've been busy."

"Too busy to help?" Jules frowned. "I didn't say anything to my parents about the lies at the party because they needed your help on the farm."

"After you left the party, Lara told me what she said about you."

"Did someone say my name?" Lara entered from the back room. She was carrying a box.

Matt took it from her. "That's too heavy for you."

"I'm not helpless," she argued. A smile replaced her frown. "Juliet, I didn't know you had returned home."

Old Sourpuss was smiling. It was an unsettling rarity, but being called Juliet no longer bothered her. "We just arrived."

319

"We?" She stared out the window. "The children must be your cousins, but who is the man?"

"Dr. Romeo Greystone." Lara's face registered the name. "I found my Romeo."

"I was always teasing you about that," Lara admitted. "I didn't think it would come true."

"Neither did I," Jules said. "It's strange how life works out."

"Yes." Lara returned to Matt's side and removed suspenders from the box Matt had opened.

"Are you buying those for your brothers?"

"Oh, no," Lara said. "I'm helping unpack supplies."

Jules looked at Matt and back at Lara. "You work here?"

"Not exactly." Lara blushed as she looked at Matt. "I'm helping my husband."

Jules stared at the gold band on her finger. "You're married?"

"Saturday," Matt said. "I'm sorry you missed the wedding. Your sisters and their husbands attended."

She'd been gone a week. What was the rush? "I don't understand. You said those awful lies about Matt and me at the party."

Matt put his arm around Lara's waist. "She was upset. We had a fight, and I didn't know…"

"After you left, I burst into tears," Lara said. "I'm so sorry I struck you. I don't know why I did it. Matt was going to go after you, but it started to rain. The storm prevented anyone from leaving, and it forced me to talk to Matt."

"Everyone at the party found out, and when we crossed paths the next morning, I assumed you knew,"

Matt said.

"Found out what?"

"I'm expecting a baby," Lara announced.

Jules inhaled, afraid to breathe lest she betray her shock and dismay. Poor Matt.

"No, it's good news."

He'd read her expression in spite of her attempt to disguise her true feelings.

Matt smiled warmly at Lara. "I should have proposed sooner."

"When I suspected I might be in a family way, I was desperate not to let anyone know, especially my parents," Lara said. "I spread those lies so others wouldn't talk about me." She stepped forward, her arms open. "Please forgive me."

Jules hugged her. A week ago she might have been too childish to be sincere, but she spoke from the heart. "I hope you and Matt will be happy."

"We will." Lara's smile would be hard to become accustomed to.

Jules turned to the door but paused. "You haven't heard how Papa is?"

"I don't think he's any worse."

Jules needed to return home. She hurried across the street to the livery. Noah was hitching a horse to a buggy. He stopped when he saw her. "When you said you were visiting your cousins, you weren't being honest, Miss Jules. You scared us to death going off alone. And I felt like a party to your deception."

She looked at Roe. "I sent telegrams."

"Pieces of paper. They don't ease the worry of family, but it's good you're home. Everyone has been praying for your safe return."

"I'm sorry, but you can tell Tess she never has to worry about Clyde Cassell. He's joined his brother."

"That chaser is dead? Are you sure."

"Yes," Roe said. "I'm a doctor. I can certify the man is no longer among the living."

"Are you here to see Doctor Beecher?"

Jules put her hand on her heart. "Matt said he wasn't worse. Was he lying?"

"No, but he's looking for a doctor to take care of his patients until he feels better, Miss Jules."

"Then I'll be happy to offer my services," Roe said.

"Noah, are you telling me the truth about Papa?"

"Yes, but it's a good thing he didn't go to Kentucky like he planned. Tyler said if he had been traveling, he might not have made it."

She turned to Roe. "Let's hurry. I have to see him for myself."

"Of course." Roe helped them board. He paused at the station to load the bags and headed down the street.

"Could you hurry?"

Roe slapped the reins on the hindquarters of the borrowed horse. "I'm sure your father is fine. All he needs is bed rest." Roe studied her. "How did your confrontation go with Matt Wheeler?"

"He's married."

"Married?"

"To Old Sourpuss." She bit her lip to keep from laughing.

"Why would he marry her? You made her sound like a horrible person."

"She was, and for Matt's sake, I hope she doesn't return to her grouchy ways. Hopefully marriage will make her happy if something else doesn't. She's in a family way."

"She was rolling in the straw with Matt?"

Jules nodded toward the children in the back seat. They were wide-eyed and all ears. "She didn't want people to find out her secret so she fed them gossip about me instead."

"You were a distraction from the truth," Roe said. "I was looking forward to thrashing Matt to defend your honor."

"Doctors don't brawl," she said. "You have to protect your hands."

They reached the Beecher farm. Buggies were scattered in the yard, and horses were penned in the corral. If her father was recovering, why was everyone still at the house?

"Is this our home?" Caroline asked.

"Yes." Jules climbed down the steps of the buggy while Roe helped the children out. The front door flew open, and her sisters exploded out the door followed by their husbands. She was hugged by everyone.

"We were expecting you yesterday," Cory said.

Morgan shook Roe's hand. "Hey, it's Doc Greystone."

"Major."

"Morgan, now." He turned to Blake. "I served with the doctor."

Blake looked at Jules. "You returned home with a Reb?"

"The war is over, dear," Cole reminded her husband.

Jules introduce Blake and Cole, Tyler and Cory, Logan and Jem, and Zach and Cass. Jess hugged Roe and turned to Jules. "And you flew into a rage when I talked about Romeo Greystone."

"Romeo?" the others echoed.

"Don't look so smug, Jess. My resemblance to you almost ended my life. She shoved the old slouch hat into her hands. "Clyde Cassell saw me wearing this and thought I was responsible for Buck's death. He tried to kill me."

Jess paled. She touched the scab that had formed on Jules' neck. "Did he do this?"

"He did worse to the basket."

"The magic basket?" Jem looked at the basket Jules had taken the hat from. She snatched it to examine the repair. "What happened?"

"It saved Theo's life," Jules said.

"Theo? The telegram only mentioned Chauncy LaDonte."

"Theo would never leave the captain's side," Roe said. "They named their boat the *Jenny Lee.*"

Jem clutched the basket. "How sweet."

"They were returning the favor. After all, you named your daughter Chauncy Theodora," Jules reminded her.

"Who cares about a boat," Jess said. "What happened to Clyde?"

"He's dead, but not before killing three women and wounding Theo."

Jem's hand covered her heart. "Is he going to be all right?"

Jules looked at Roe. "He had an excellent doctor." She took his arm and led him inside.

Maureen was coming down the stairs when they entered. "What is all the commotion about? The children are finally asleep." She paused, her hand trembling on the bannister. "Juliet." She rushed down the final steps and pulled her into her arms. "My baby."

She remained in her embrace. "I'm sorry, Mama. I wanted you and Papa to be proud of me instead of ashamed. I couldn't do anything right. I was such a disappointment to you."

"Never." She pulled back to swipe at tears in her eyes. "When we received Captain LaDonte's telegrams, it eased our fears, but not completely."

Jules turned and ushered Caroline and her brothers forward. "Here are the children. I brought them home."

Maureen examined each of them. "Are you hungry?"

"I'll fix something," Cory volunteered. "Jules can sit with Papa."

"I don't know," Jules said. "Morgan said he had a heart attack. If he's angry with me, it could make matters worse."

"Nonsense. He's anxious to see you." Maureen patted her shoulder. "It will do his heart good to know you've returned safely."

Jules grabbed Roe's hand, but he hesitated. "Maybe I should wait."

"You're a doctor. You can tell me if he's truly all right."

She led him to the bedroom off the kitchen. The room was in shadows. Her father was asleep. She couldn't go closer and hovered near the door. She shoved Roe forward.

Roe leaned over Sterling's still form and felt his forehead. His eyes flew open. "Who are you?"

He stood upright. "Dr. Greystone."

Laura Freeman

"Another doctor? I've had my fill of doctors. I'm fine, but I won't be if I have to stay in this bed another hour." Sterling struggled to sit up.

Jules rushed forward. "But Papa, they said you had a heart attack."

Sterling pushed Roe aside. "Juliet?"

Tears blinded her as she hugged him. "Papa, I thought I could fetch the children by myself, but you were right. I was a foolish girl. It was pure dumb luck I accomplished anything. I ruined Mama's basket. Or I should say Clyde ruined it. He wanted to kill me after I recognized him on the train…"

Roe placed his hand on her shoulder. She had said too much. She took a deep breath in and out. "I delivered Caroline and her brothers safely home."

He pulled her into his arms. "I was most concerned about you, baby."

"My hide is tough, and you had a right to be angry with me."

"I was tired and ill, Juliet, and I was wrong to lash out at you." He stroked her cheek. "Can you forgive me?"

"Always. I love you, Papa." She hugged him again.

"I love you, baby." He turned to Roe. "I don't need another doctor, especially one as young as you."

Roe stepped forward. "I'm not here about your health, sir. I've come concerning Juliet."

"Juliet?" He examined her with a worried gaze. "Are you ill, child?"

"No, Papa. I'm in love." She joined Roe and grabbed his hand. "Meet the man I'm going to marry, Dr. Romeo Greystone."

"Romeo?" He looked at Jules. "I thought you hated

326

that story? You insisted everyone call you Jules."

"I was wrong," Jules said. "And I'm not afraid to admit it."

He looked worried. "Do you recall *Romeo and Juliet* did not have a happy ending?"

Jules gazed into Roe's eyes. "We're planning to write our own ending."

"We wish to be married, sir," Roe said. "With your blessing."

Sterling frowned as he surveyed them. "You were only to return home with the children. Not a husband."

The others had crowded into the room. Jem stepped forward and showed him the mended basket. "But Papa, a Beecher sister always brings home a husband when she goes on a journey with the magic basket."

www.ingramcontent.com/pod-product-compliance
Lightning Source LLC
Chambersburg PA
CBHW071525260626
47170CB00002B/512